FRACTALS

ALICIA ANTHONY

DRURY LANE
BOOKS

ALSO BY ALICIA ANTHONY

THE BLOOD SECRETS SERIES

INHERENT TRUTH (BLOOD SECRETS BOOK 1)
INHERENT LIES (BLOOD SECRETS BOOK 2)
INHERENT FATE (BLOOD SECRETS BOOK 3)

FRACTALS

ALICIA ANTHONY

ISBN: 978-1-7333624-8-1 (Print)

ISBN: 978-1-7333624-7-4 (Ebook)

Published by Drury Lane Books, Sedalia, OH USA.

Library of Congress Control Number: 2020924914

Keep up with Alicia online for up-to-the-minute news and reader extras:

www.AliciaAnthonyBooks.com

Cover Art by Emily Wittig Designs

For the students who wish to be invisible
and the teachers who see them.

Your stories matter.

PROLOGUE

ASHER

Before...

Asher Thompson spun a beer between his thumb and forefinger and surveyed the bar. A thick haze of smoke, now from e-cigs rather than the real deal, permeated the air, shrouding the patrons in a veil of fog.

He'd been here three hours and still wasn't sure why he'd come. This shit hole bar off an interstate exit to nowhere wasn't particularly convenient. Located outside rural Brookside, Ohio, yards from some nondescript truck stop, where dingy men drowned their sorrows in the bartender's cheapest escape. But why *this* place?

He tried to tell himself it was simple. Jo needed space and where else in this town could a teacher go at midnight on a Thursday night without fielding sideways looks from curious onlookers? Here, he was invisible.

He sighed and leaned against the hard wooden back of

the corner booth. He pictured Jo, his ex, as he'd left her, shoving clothes into an already overstuffed box, tears leaving thin makeup free rivers down her perfect complexion. She needed time to think, she'd said. But what she really wanted was a chance to clean her stuff out of the house without interference. Not that he'd try to stop her. He deserved to be left.

He shook the internal scolding away and fingered the bottle in front of him, the glass cold against his fingertips. The gauze over the knuckles of his right hand buckled and twisted as he spun the near empty beer between his thumb and index finger.

Stiffness crept into his fingers, stopping the gentle sway of the bottle against the scarred table top. He examined the bandage and flexed his hand, extending the fingers until pain sliced from his knuckles through each digit. He forced himself to take it–feel every punishing sting–until his eyes watered. He let go of a pent up breath and relaxed his fingers, allowing his hand to fall into a loose fist.

He was lucky he hadn't broken any bones. Like a drunk driver walking away from a fatal car crash, he hardly remembered the fight. But the fact that Jo's coworker had survived without permanent injury–hadn't even pressed charges–was a downright miracle.

That silver lining did nothing to soothe Jo's anger, though. He'd lost control. Exposed the Mr. Hyde side of himself, one he'd kept hidden from Jo for the two years they'd dated. But now she knew. And she hated him for it.

Asher took the last swig from his bottle of Bud Light and rubbed his forehead, the gauze scratchy against the skin of his face.

"Need some company tonight, sugar?" The pro's voice was syrup as she propositioned the man two tables over. But her eyes, laser focused on her prey, flicked up to Asher. The corner of her lip twisted, a smile maybe, as close as she could come to one.

Asher broke eye contact. He'd grown up around women like her. His jaw pulsed as he spun his beer again. He tried to ignore the driver slinging a coat over one shoulder, cashing out and following the siren out the door, braving the rain for what looked to be a well-worn piece of ass.

The plate glass window beside the front door glowed red behind the streaks of rain. The nearby truck stop marquee flickered, threatening to go dark at any moment. *Truck-n-Go. Jesus.* He shouldn't be here. Flashes of his former life, ghosts he'd worked for the last seven years to escape, whispered in his ear. He sat tall, stretched his back and sucked in a lungful of the faux smoke-laced air.

He raked his gaze around the bar one final time. The off-the-beaten-path truck stop pulled in the clientele experience had taught him to expect. A handful of long haul truck drivers, drowning their over-the-road loneliness by looking for some company, just like the last guy.

Rising anger flirted with the edges of Asher's consciousness, mingling with memory and tightening the muscles in his torso. He sucked in a breath for three counts and blew it out in an even stream, just as his shrink had taught him.

With the pro gone, there was only one other woman in the room—a past her prime waitress with a semi-toothless smile. Asher shook his head and laid some cash on the table. He needed to get out of this dump, find some nice respectable Applebee's to hole up in until Jo texted to let him know she was done. Maybe get a room at the Holiday Inn across from Millbrook and call it a day.

He checked the time on his phone—Applebee's was out of the question—and slid out of the booth, shrugging into his jacket as he walked. He'd only made it a few steps before the front door of the bar swung open with a too hard *thwack*. A flash of black left a trail of water, gliding from the entrance to the hunched over man at end of the bar.

Asher ignored her, weaving through the maze of tables toward the exit. He kept his head down, doing his best to over-look the familiar characteristics of the young woman tugging at the drunk's elbow. Petite form. Raven hair. The defiant angle of her jaw. *It wasn't possible.*

The girl spoke to the man in whispers.

Hateful comebacks spewed from the scruffy old man, the obvious regular who knew the bartender by name and had been drowning his sorrows in a bottle of Jack since Asher's arrival.

The furtive plea in the girl's voice wriggled its way into Asher's memory, sent a stab of hope-laced regret through his chest.

"Please, Dad, come home. I'm so sorry. We didn't mean for any of this to happen."

"You didn't mean to do it? Or for me to find out?" the man forced the words without taking his eyes off his drink.

Asher was too close to ignore her now. She was young. The age of his students. Dark hair clung to the pale ivory of her face and neck in thin, wet ropes.

"Can we just talk?" she pleaded again.

Asher's steps slowed.

Dressed in black from head to toe, her shirt–thin knit–clung to her curves, unbuttoned one button too far. Skinny jeans sucked tight against her calves and ass. Rain dripped from her clothes, her fingertips, the angle of her chin. *Pull it together.* Asher lowered his head, swallowing the unavoidable knot of recognition.

"Get out. I don't want to see you. *No one* wants to see you," Drunk Dad slurred.

"Hey," the bartender chimed in next, waving the girl away

like a gnat. "You heard him. Outta here. I ain't risking my license for you lot rats. Take your business somewhere else."

Asher wondered where that attitude had been ten minutes ago when the pro had been scoping out her next john.

The girl dragged her eyes away from the drunk long enough to see the man behind the bar. She wanted to tell him to go to hell, Asher could read it on her face, in the way her lips began to curve around the first syllable. But she was distracted, uncertain. She glanced over her shoulder, toward the door. Fear?

She laid a wet hand on the drunk's arm. "Please, Dad–"

The man jerked out of her grip. "Don't call me that. You're not my daughter anymore," he mumbled. He didn't even look as he swung a closed fist in her direction. His hand caught her in the mouth, sending her toppling backward onto the hardwood floor with a wet *thump*.

Asher rushed forward–instinct, more than purpose.

"Are you okay?" He'd said the same words to another girl once upon a time. *Emily*. He shoved at the ghost of a memory, reached for the flesh and blood crouched in wet clothes on the floor of a truck stop bar.

She stared at him. Met him with gray-blue eyes, a mix of hate and fear.

Asher pulled his hands back, palms up in defense. He whispered, "I just want to help."

When she reached for him, he knew. Maybe it was the way her fingers splayed against his forearm, wet warmth gripping his jacket–grasping for a lifeline. Maybe it was a chance to undo the wrongs that haunted his every waking moment.

No matter the reason, he knew she'd crawl under his skin, worm her way into his life. She'd threaten what was left of the façade he worked so hard to create, dredge up a past he fought hard to forget. But in that moment, with restless onlookers and an irate bartender spewing hate speak behind him, he didn't care. It was the right thing to do. The only thing to do.

He expected a protest when he wrapped an arm around her waist, ushered her outside, but it never came.

"What's your name?" he asked once the door swung closed behind them. They stood side-by-side under the narrow awning. Rain cascaded from the overhang, pelting them from inches away.

"What do you want it to be?" She pulled her hand away from her bloodied lip. Her young voice unnaturally rough and husky. He wasn't the only one faking his way through life.

He laughed, a one-syllable chuckle. "My name's Asher–Asher Thompson. That your dad in there?" He jutted his chin toward the entrance, working to keep his gaze on her face.

Her eyes shifted. A familiar wall sliding into position. She stayed silent. Gooseflesh rose along her exposed collarbone.

"You're drenched. I've got some towels in my Jeep." It was a statement. Nothing more. No intent. No malice. An innocent offer.

She nodded–two short bumps of her chin–and he led her across the lot to the passenger side, helping her in. The rain on his skin cooled him as he walked around the Jeep, forced reality in. *Emily's gone. This girl is not Emily.*

He pulled towels from the gym bag behind the driver's seat and passed them to the girl. If there was one silver lining from the fight, it was that he never made it to the gym that morning. He climbed behind the wheel and closed the door, cocooning them from the outside elements. Muffled drops of rain pattered against the metal roof, the only sound between them.

She towel-dried her hair, wrapping each rope strand in the white terry cloth and squeezing along the length before moving on to the next section.

"Carly," she said finally. "My name's Carly Dalton. And

yes, the jackass at the bar is my father." She checked her lip with the pads of her fingers, the bleeding had stopped.

"Nice to meet you, Carly." Asher hesitated, his hands planted on the bottom of the steering wheel. "How old are you?"

Her silence forced him to look. She studied him–wary, uncertain. "What does it matter to you?"

He watched her hands, pulling and squeezing the fabric of her shirt just as she had her hair. She fastened that third button. Asher couldn't help but notice her fingers, smooth and strong, but she chewed her nails–rough and too short. Her fingertips tinged in a metallic gray. She caught him looking, glanced down at her own fingers, and ran a thumb over the darkened tips.

"Charcoal," she said. Her voice suddenly reflected her youth. "I draw sometimes."

Asher remained silent. The urge to ask her what she was doing out here at night, dressed like that, threatened from the back of his throat. But he already knew why. And it was none of his business.

"I'm sixteen," she said, finally. "What about you?"

"Twenty-three," Asher reciprocated. "I'm a science teacher at Millbrook Academy."

A tiny smile crept to the corner of Carly's lips. "A teacher. Wow." A bubble of sarcasm huffed through her lips. "What are you doing out here so late on a school night?"

"Waiting." *What the hell kind of answer was that?* If she didn't already think he was a creep, she would now.

"Waiting for what?" She caught his gaze and held, fearless.

"Damsels in distress, I guess."

Carly shifted in her seat, glanced at the bandage on the back of Asher's hand. "That what happened to your hand?

Defending someone's honor?" She tossed the wet towel onto the floor of the back seat.

"Not exactly." Asher refused to say more. His reasons for the fight didn't matter anymore.

Silence filled the space between them. When he ventured another look, her eyes reflected the light from the Truck-n-Go marquee. "This place could use a knight in shining armor." She glanced toward the truck lot, her thunderstorm stare skimming once before coming back to him.

"Where do you go to school?" Asher never took his eyes off the curve of her jaw, the same soft angle Emily's had.

Carly shrugged, jutted her chin in defiance. "Well, I assure you, Mr. Thompson, it's not Millbrook Academy. I'm more of a public school kinda girl, if you know what I mean."

"Right," Asher responded.

Her eyes locked on his—teased, tempted. "So, you going to offer me a ride home, or what?"

ONE

CARLY

During...

Mr. Thompson once told me that when you look at tears under a microscope they have different qualities, varying patterns and designs depending on what kind of tears they are. Tears of grief, for example, are full of harsh right angles, shards of broken glass that have yet to vacate their frame. Tears of happiness, on the other hand, resemble the branches of a tree, extending up and outward as if reaching for the sky on a sunny day. I wondered what my tears would look like under Mr. Thompson's microscope.

Over the last seventeen years, I figured I'd cried enough to fill the chipped plastic bathtub in the dump we called home several times over. A lump surged in my throat, threatening, and I bit the inside of my jaw, staving emotion away, and picked at the corner of the sketch that lay in front of me, curling the paper's edge.

Today's tears would be different. I bet Mr. Thompson didn't have a slide for tears like mine. Would they resemble the violent cracks of broken glass or the climbing limbs of possibility? Both, maybe. Not that I'd succumbed to any, but in that moment I would've given anything to go back to the afternoon Mr. Thompson dug out those dusty slides. Ask him if it was possible to feel both grief and elation simultaneously. What would fractals of those tears look like?

"Carly?" Mr. Thompson's voice was too close. I turned my head toward the sound, sliding my open Biology textbook over my notebook, hiding the sketch I'd started in first period. *Doodles*, that's what my dad called them. I locked eyes with my teacher as he came up from behind. Of all the teachers I'd ever had, he was by far the coolest.

He knew I spent the majority of the school day penciling images on notebook paper rather than immersing myself in the most boring texts imaginable. I kept up with assignments enough to pass tests, but not enough to get out of after school detention. I wondered if he knew I skipped assignments on purpose. I refocused, felt the warmth of him watching me. I liked it when he watched.

The room slowly started to buzz. The low hum distracted me from the worried wrinkle that pinched the skin between Mr. Thompson's blue eyes. Around the room, every face turned my direction. A few leaned toward their neighbor to whisper some thinly veiled comment. Most wore expressions of curiosity, some of ridicule, one or two of boredom. But other than Mr. Thompson, only one showed anything close to concern.

I locked eyes with the blonde in the first row. Phoebe Anderson wasn't the most popular girl in our class, or the smartest, but she was perfect in all the ways that really mattered. And since my dad kicked my sister, Caroline, out of the house, Phoebe was all I had left.

I followed her gaze toward the classroom door. Through the glass I could make out two of them, standing there in their navy-blue suits, waiting for me to come out to the hall. I knew the look I'd see in their eyes. Pity. The one expression that made my skin crawl and my scalp prickle.

"They just want to talk to you." Mr. Thompson's voice was a confidential whisper. Quiet, but not quiet enough to keep the nosy juniors and seniors in my sixth period class from straining to hear. The warmth of his hand on my shoulder soothed the flicker of panic that sparked in my chest, squeezing, then releasing with every breath.

"Who is it, Mr. T?" A voice from the back of the room cut through the semi-silence. I caught the warning stare that Mr. Thompson shot at Bryce. Sitting two rows behind me, he was always irritating the kids around him. If it wasn't juvenile fake farts, or sexual innuendos, it was spitballs or paper wads targeted at the losers in the class. Namely, me. Mr. T was pretty good about keeping him reined in during class, but I knew when I came back–if I came back–Bryce would be ready with a new annoyance.

I nodded at Mr. Thompson and gathered my books, locking eyes with Phoebe as I navigated my way toward the front of the room. I pushed past her desk, my fingertips grazing across the smooth laminate, hesitating just long enough for her fingers to skim my flesh. She looped her pinkie around mine briefly before pulling away to the safety of her lap.

"I'll call you," Phoebe whispered as I shimmied past her desk. I couldn't tell her that I wasn't sure I'd be able to accept phone calls from wherever I landed this time.

Twenty-eight pairs of eyes drilled into the back of my skull as I walked toward the door. Time slowed, ticking on the ancient classroom clock. I wrapped my fingers around the door handle, turned one last time toward Mr. Thompson who stood just a few feet behind me.

His crisp nod, coupled with the familiar warmth from his eyes, infused me with a drop of courage. I nodded back, swinging the door open wide. I'd been fine until then. But walking through the door, leaving the safety of that room–of *him*–caused the lump in my throat to surge, growing twice the size. The suits stood, waiting. A short heavy-set man and a too-tall woman, the Laurel and Hardy of Children's Services, turned in unison to look at me. Maybe I'd have tears to analyze after all.

TWO

ASHER

The bell reverberated in Asher's ears as he watched Carly disappear through the classroom door. His stomach plummeted, churning the pizza pocket he'd scarfed for lunch. The only thing keeping it contained as he dismissed his sixth period biology class was the fact that Jo Harrison had been one of the agents who'd ushered Carly away.

Asher wasn't sure about much when it came to his ex fiancée, but the care Jo took with the cases she worked for the Department of Children's Services had never been in question. His relationship with Jo had ended the night he'd first met Carly Dalton. It took a while before he realized that Carly already knew Jo.

In fact, without Jo's help Asher never could have managed to get Carly into Millbrook. Jo was the one who'd helped him navigate his way around the red tape to secure the scholarship and make sure Carly had bussing. Jo's testimony to the school board had made that happen.

Asher had seen the look on Jo's face as she stood outside his classroom doorway, the grim set of her lips, eyes tired and sad.

Something bad had to have happened to warrant Carly's escort from school in the middle of the day. But she was with Jo. And right now that was the only peace of mind he had.

Students filed through the open doorway, already engaged in oblivious conversation. Someone pushed past him, jostling his shoulder. Asher's eyes tracked to the senior lineman who muttered an apology as he exited into the hall—a boy in a man's body, still coming to terms with his own girth.

"She'll be okay, you know." Phoebe Anderson's pale blue eyes looked up at him. "She's tough, Mr. T."

Asher cleared his throat, fighting an unexpected clench of emotion. "You're right, Phoebe. She is." He forced a smile at Carly's best friend.

"I could let you know if I hear from her."

It was a generous offer, especially from a Millbrook student. This time Asher could only nod, turning the corners of his mouth in what he hoped would pass as an appreciative smile. He followed Phoebe into the hallway, watched her white-blonde hair bounce as she disappeared into the throng of teenagers.

Bodies washed past. The predictable ebb and flow of high school students as they traveled, unconcerned, from one class period to the next. He pulled his phone from his pocket, sent Jo a text.

What's going on?

He hoped for a response but didn't expect one. It had been almost a year since Jo broke off their engagement and moved out of their house. She'd managed to forgive him enough to stay civil. Carly was on her caseload, that was the only thing binding them at this point, and he didn't deserve to ask for more. Lucky for him, fighting for the greater good of a minor had a tendency to bring people together, thank God.

From the beginning, Asher struggled with the red tape of

children's services–the due process of it all. In his years with Jo
he'd seen too many kids placed in crosshairs, returned to
guardians who'd been complicit in their abuse, simply because
blood was somehow thicker than the possibility of a safe, happy
home with strangers. It was a part of the system he'd never
understand. And he'd dated Jo long enough to know they didn't
remove students from school unless it was absolutely necessary.

The stress of her job and his, their differing opinions of how
to handle the turmoil of young lives being ripped apart, might
have played a part in their decision to separate. *Decision?* The
thought lodged the hard knot of a sarcastic laugh in his throat.
Who was he kidding? It was his own overactive imagination,
remnants of paranoia left over from childhood trauma, that
sealed his fate. His shrink would be proud of him for that realization.

Carly trickled through Jo's caseload a few months before
the breakup, a relocation case from another jurisdiction he'd
only heard about in passing. And when Asher pulled Carly off
the floor of the truck stop bar, he'd had no idea there was a
connection. In spite of his poor decisions that night, Carly gave
Jo a reason to speak to Asher again. She linked them, kept Jo in
his life, a feat for which Asher would always be grateful.

Getting Carly the scholarship to Millbrook Academy had
been the easy part. It didn't take a lot of convincing for the
majority of the board once they heard her story. A young girl
who'd lost her mom to cancer, lived with a dad spiraling into
addiction-riddled depression, and whose sister had just aged
out of any help the system could provide. All he could get out
of Carly was that she'd left, headed off to Columbus with a
boyfriend, while her younger sister fought alone.

But now that Carly was enrolled, people were talking. He
was aware how it looked. A young male teacher going to bat for
an underachieving female student, speaking up for her when

other staff members complained about her lack of effort. He even signed up to monitor after school detention so Carly wouldn't have to spend those hours in forced silence. He suspected she got enough silent treatment at home.

Asher slinked back into his classroom, shuffled papers on his desk as he waited for the next round of bodies to arrive. He glanced down at his silent phone, the screen still blank. The muscles in his arms jerked at the sound of the bell behind him. Two more periods before he could hunt down answers.

THREE

ASHER

Since the beginning of the school year, the teacher's lounge speculation simmered like a bubbling cauldron of suspicion. Whispers of disapproval–he spent too much time with Carly, cared too much, took an abnormally high interest in the smoky-eyed girl in his sixth period biology class. All of it boiled down to one overarching belief–they must be having an affair.

Three people knew it wasn't true–Carly, Jo, and himself– and regardless of what the gossip train at school would have him believe, those were the only three that mattered. Asher only ever wanted to help Carly, just like he'd wanted to help another lost girl all those years ago. Only this time, he swore he wouldn't fail.

He navigated the emptying hall toward the front office. Rubbed the tightened coil of muscle at the back of his neck as the snake of a memory crept up his spine. Even today, when he saw Carly from a distance, a ghost-stricken arrhythmia thumped in his chest. She'd been his student for almost seven months, and he still had to hold in the instinct to call her Emily.

He was aware that his own checkered past had drawn him

to Carly, the fact she bore a striking resemblance to a girl he should have saved eight years ago. His shrink had forced him to admit that much. But he'd only known Emily for a short time, had spent a grand total of less than twenty-four hours with her if truth be told. Carly was different. Over the past months, Asher had grown attached. Every shift in her mood, he noticed. Anytime she was absent, too quiet, uncharacteristically defiant, overly disheveled, or too made up caused him worry.

He couldn't be sure what happened in the trailer she walked home to every afternoon. Jo wouldn't say and Carly had never revealed any terrible secrets, at least not to him. But Asher knew the reputation of the neighborhood. Had seen her father in action in the truck stop bar. And he was too familiar with the dangers that lurked behind the veil of addiction. That, coupled with the expectations of strangers who were owed favors, was a lethal combination.

The knot in the pit of his stomach thickened as he knocked on Principal Baum's office door. Now in his second year at Millbrook, Asher could count on one hand the number of times he'd seen the inside of Baum's office. The air hung thick with the scent of old leather and musk, an odd combination for a principal's office. But then, Angus Baum was not your typical high school principal. The man was ancient, old school in every sense of the phrase, from his choice of aftershave and office décor, to his thinly veiled sexist views of the female teachers. Asher knew the only reason he'd been hired was because he possessed a Y chromosome.

"Have a seat Mr. Thompson." Baum cleared the rasp from his voice, a product of decades of cigars and bourbon, if Asher had to guess. "I thought you might stop by this afternoon." He nodded and motioned to the decidedly un-school-like pleather wingback in front of his desk.

"What happened today, Angus?" Baum was the only man

Asher had ever known named Angus. It seemed so unnatural that the entire staff called him by his last name unless speaking directly to the grizzled exterior of the man. And even then, the majority stuck with the more formal, Mr. Baum.

Baum's gray-green eyes lit on Asher, his hands collecting the wad of paperwork spread across his desk. He tapped the stack on end twice before depositing the pages in a wire basket on the other side of his computer. The sleek monitor was the only item in the office that indicated you hadn't stepped into an episode of *Mad Men*.

Asher pulled himself straighter in the uncomfortable chair, forcing an air of detachment he hoped would clear the hint of worry from his expression. He tried again. "Do you know why Carly Dalton was removed from my sixth period class this afternoon?"

The corner of Baum's lip turned up into a kind of smirk, as if he found some enjoyment from the trials of one of Millbrook's students. The principal leaned back in his chair, clasping his hands in front of him in a teepee, the perfect politician pose. "I've been asked to refrain from discussing the matter until the authorities know more."

Asher felt the heat of Baum's stare grating over him. It was this subtle act of intimidation that kept his staff from frequenting his office. Unfortunately for Baum, his practiced form of bullying didn't have the same effect on Asher.

"The authorities ... meaning children's services?" He'd seen Jo through the glass of the classroom door. But the man she'd come with was unfamiliar.

Baum unsteepled his hands, flattening them against the woodgrain top of his desk. "And PD ... homicide."

Angus Baum paused, releasing a sigh of resignation, while Asher's heart kicked into a higher gear, thumping against his chest wall with each possibility that flashed through his mind.

"Ah, who am I kidding? The busybody women in this place will have some barely recognizable version of the truth spread far and wide by dinnertime. Damn gossips."

The principal leaned forward, shaking his head in disapproval before addressing Asher again.

"The woman was Ms. Harrison, the student's case worker from the Department of Job and Family Services. I believe you two are acquainted." He shot a pointed glance at Asher before pausing to hunt through a desk drawer, unearthing a business card. "Detective Vic Moreno, Homicide." Baum read the card aloud.

The rock that had been pushing against Asher's sternum since sixth period expanded, sinking into his gut with a sickening churn. He looked away from Baum's unreadable stare.

"Is Carly in trouble?"

Baum cocked his head to one side and shrugged, taking a moment to return the card to its place in the drawer. "Can't say for sure. It's nice that you care so much about your students, Asher. But you know as well as I do that it was only a matter of time with that one."

The knot of agony in Asher's gut exploded. Hot spikes of anger radiated from the inside, out. He avoided Baum's stare, glaring out the window and into the parking lot beyond. Kids wove like ants to their cars, most of which cost triple the amount of his own used Jeep Grand Cherokee.

He pushed an even breath out through tight lips, working to remind himself that Baum didn't know Carly like he did. She was a good kid, smart and talented, albeit scarred and misdirected. She was a product of unfortunate circumstances, nothing more. She wasn't a criminal.

"Whose murder is the detective investigating?"

There was a pause, so long that Asher thought his principal

was dismissing him in that silent way he had, but when he looked up, Angus's eyes were boring into him again.

"The detective will want to talk to you. He'll be conducting interviews with each of Carly's teachers over the next day or so. Expect a call."

Asher felt the heat from his core traveling to his face.

"Carly's father, Stephen Dalton, was found dead this morning. Apparently, the circumstances are questionable. Carly's a person of interest."

The punch of words forced Asher back against the high-backed chair. A stunned silence filled the space between them as Asher worked to process the information.

"Sad, really." Sarcasm dripped as Angus continued. "It's always the quiet ones, though. You never know what's going on inside the minds of kids like that. As you know, I was against her enrollment from the beginning. Can't say I'm all that surprised. Can you?"

Asher fought irritation in favor of feigned composure. He needed to tread carefully.

"I could never suspect a Millbrook student of such a crime." He iced the conversation with the expected teacher line, "These kids are like family to me, Angus."

The principal nodded as if he understood. Old fart didn't have one emotion in that hardened soul of his. He certainly could never understand.

FOUR

CARLY

The air in the tiny interrogation room was thick—a mixture of body odor and stale coffee. I sniffed and rubbed at my nose, an effort to relieve the sense memory of time spent closed up in sleeper cabs with a similar scent.

Miss Harrison settled into the chair opposite me.

"Tissue?" she offered, misunderstanding my sniff, and pulled a wrinkled white square from her bag. "It hasn't been used, I promise."

She smiled as I reached for it. Holding it to my nose, I inhaled the perfume of Miss Harrison's purse. The light floral scent reminded me of my mother. The perfume just enough to mask the pungency of the air.

I glanced down at my oversized sweatshirt. The Ohio State block O was wearing away, the bottom left corner missing entirely. That was the side my mom used to prop her palette on when she painted. I shoved the used tissue in the front pocket and pulled the hem down low around my hips, eliminating the unflattering lump over my midriff. One of the strings for the hood was longer than the other, so I jerked them both tight, coaxing the ties into even gray snakes down my chest.

"Do you know why you're here, Carly?" Her voice was soft, soothing. Her cool hands reached for mine, covering them as we sat opposite each other at the small wooden table. Her thumbs stroked tiny arcs over my knuckles. The memory of my mother drawing the same soft crescents over my skin tickled a wave of longing loose, constricting my lungs into an involuntary sob. I choked down the suffocating knot in my throat.

I shook my head from side to side, partly to indicate I didn't know the reason for my visit, but mostly to shake away the unwelcome surge of emotion. I pulled my hands from hers and tucked them safely in the pocket of my sweatshirt. I squashed an imaginary bug with the toe of my Converse, mutilating it against the red and cream-colored tile squares that created a patchwork under my feet.

"Answer so we can hear you." I jumped a little, more from the unexpected jolt my chair received than from the command. I hadn't heard the detective enter the room, too lost in the battle against my own memories. Even so, for a man of his size he was incredibly stealthy.

"Tone it down a notch, Vic," Miss Harrison's voice was still the same smooth timbre, unrattled by the detective's demand.

I swiveled to get a better look at Detective Moreno. I'd seen him briefly in the hallway at school, but Miss Harrison had whisked me away to the car, shielding me from the clog of students filling the halls between periods, while Moreno had stayed to talk to Principal Baum.

The vibration of the bell that had signaled the end of sixth period still rattled through me. The realization that I might never hear the grating discord again sent a pulse of shock through my system.

"Face forward," Moreno snarled, again nudging the back of

my chair. I'd been able to stay calm until then. But the second physical jolt was enough to jostle a surprised gasp from my lungs. My heart rate stepped it up a notch.

"Sorry," I mumbled, not missing the scowl Miss Harrison was throwing the detective.

"It's okay, hon. Just relax." She asked again, "Do you know why you're here?"

I considered her question for a second time. "No," I lied.

The corners of her lips curled into what some might mistake for a smile. I knew it as pity. "It's your dad, honey. Your uncle found him this morning. I'll let Detective Moreno give you the details. But, Carly, he's gone. Your dad's dead."

Miss Harrison's voice was like caramel. I wanted to reach across the table, climb into her lap and wrap myself in its warmth. Let it flow down over me, cocoon me from the outside world. But voices like that, like Miss Harrison's, like my mom's, they always went away. Hot pricks of tears burned at the backs of my eyes. I wouldn't cry. Not now. Not for him.

"Mr. Carver is not my uncle," I said, focused on rectifying the misinformation.

"What's that?" the detective asked from behind me. I could feel his grip on the back of my chair. I scooted forward, away from the threat of his hands.

"The man we live with, Aaron Carver, he's not my uncle." A guarded look passed between Miss Harrison and the detective. "He's just a..." I swallowed the truth. "...friend of my father's."

Another secret glance passed between them. For people whose careers relied on skills of observation, they certainly weren't very good at hiding their own reactions.

"So, what happened?" I asked, staring at my stained fingers as I coughed through the pulse of emotion lodged at the back of my throat.

Miss Harrison's eyes sent a silent, *I told you so*, to Moreno and reached again for my hands, giving them a squeeze. "An overdose, Carly. Sometime last night. Heroin."

She wasn't even speaking in complete sentences. Maybe I was the first kid she'd ever had that lost a parent while on her caseload. An emotion akin to pity crept up from somewhere deep as I studied her eyes, darkened with a helplessness I'd only ever seen in the mirror.

"I'm sorry." Her voice was so soft I thought I might have imagined it. But there they were again, the rhythmic arcs of her tawny fingers over my knuckles, a stark contrast to the white paleness of my own. A tear that had been threatening to spill free tipped over the edge of my lower lid, skimming down my cheek. The heat of it made me angry. My dad didn't deserve my tears. But maybe this wasn't about him.

"How often did your father use heroin, Miss Dalton?" Moreno's tone had evened out. He tugged a chair from the corner of the room to the edge of the table. The scrape of metal on tile grated against my eardrums.

I shrugged. There was no point in lying about that, not now. "Daily, more than once probably. I didn't keep tabs."

"And Carver? You ever see him with drugs?"

It seemed to me like an asinine question. "My father was unemployed, Detective. Where do you think he got his hits?" I took a breath, dialed back the sarcasm. "Have you told Caroline? About Dad?" I could still hear my dad and sister arguing. Their voices, like two angry animals, vying for the last word. Maybe they'd found her. A balloon of hope expanded in my chest.

"We're working on getting in touch with her. Detective Moreno just needs to ask you a few more questions, okay?" Miss Harrison's hands were still latched onto mine, like talons on prey.

I nodded, forcing myself to look her in the eye, into the same scrutinizing pale green I'd seen the morning she'd first stepped into my life. I wanted to remember this. The emotion. The pain. I'd draw it when I had the chance. The care that emanated from her eyes into my own lonely gray-blue irises.

Moreno flopped open a folder on the minuscule desk in the interrogation room. He tugged at each pant leg as he lowered into the chair. He was a big man. Reminded me of a few of the truckers I'd met. A chill raised gooseflesh along my arms and legs as images of strangers' faces flashed through my mind. I could tell him. Right now. Tell him that for nearly a year and a half, my sister and I had spent most of our nights with strange men. That I already knew he wouldn't find Caroline at her apartment. That she was gone. Forgotten. But then I'd be the criminal. And Caroline wouldn't have a chance.

I turned my eyes back to my hands, pulling them from Miss Harrison's grip and tucking them into my lap. The detective watched me as I wrung my fingers. Silence grew in the room like a bubble, suffocating me.

"How long have you been living with Aaron Carver?" Moreno's voice was low, calm.

"Almost two years." It was the longest we'd been anywhere since Mom died.

"Did you get along with your father?"

I glanced at Miss Harrison. These were questions I'd answered for her—more than once. "I guess so. He drank a lot. The hard drugs were a more recent addition."

Miss Harrison lowered her head, chewed the corner of her lip before I continued.

"Mom died about eight years ago. Dad did whatever he could to keep from dealing with the pain. I got pretty good at avoiding him when he was drunk or high."

"And what about you? What did you do to deal with the pain?"

No one had ever asked me that question before. I stared into the inky pools of Detective Moreno's dark brown eyes. "I don't know. I draw, I guess."

Moreno nodded. "So was last night one of those nights that you had to avoid your father?"

"Every night is one of those nights," I wanted to say, but I didn't. Instead, I bobbed my head up and down, pinching the ends of my fingers, hoping to feel enough pain to shove the creeping vine of emotion away.

"I really need to see my sister." The words leaked out like a plea from a small child.

"I'll see if there's any news," Miss Harrison said, vacating her spot next to Detective Moreno and heading for the door. Her hand grazed my shoulder as she passed, and the lump surged in my throat, tears multiplying behind my eyes.

"I've got to say, Carly. You don't seem all that shocked by the news."

I lifted a shoulder and let it drop. What did he want me to say? "Am I supposed to be? Dad wasn't very good at doing anything in moderation, Detective. It was bound to catch up with him sooner or later."

Moreno nodded as if he understood. He tapped the click end of his pen on the pad in front of him. "Where were you last night?"

"Out," I pushed the word around the knot constricting my airway. "I left around ten. Spent the night with a friend. Phoebe Anderson."

Moreno scribbled the name in his book. "Before you left, though. Did you hear anything? Your dad wasn't arguing with anyone?"

I stared at the detective. "You said it was an overdose."

"We're just covering all the bases. I have to ask these questions."

Moreno squinted, narrowing his eyes at me. Waiting.

"You can ask the neighbors. There were people over. I don't know who. It's hard to hear anything over the music. I learned a long time ago that it's best if I stay out of the way." It might have been the most honest thing I'd said all afternoon.

"Walk me through the day, Carly. What happened when you got home from school yesterday?"

"I had detention, so I didn't get home until around 4:30. Caroline came for dinner. She hadn't done that in a while."

"Was Mr. Carver there?"

I shook my head. "Not right away. He got home later. Around eight, I think. Caroline was talking with Dad in the kitchen." I swallowed the almost lie. Talking wasn't the right word. "I was in my room getting ready to leave."

The sounds of my sister and father arguing roared in my ears. *"Let her go, Dad. It's time. Hasn't she been through enough?"* Caroline's words.

"You think I'm going to let you just take her?" my father growled back. The next words, aimed at me, dripped venom, *"Get in the van, Carlita."*

"To go to Phoebe's?" Moreno's voice interrupted the memory.

"Yes."

"When did your sister leave?"

I shrugged. "We left together. Around nine, I guess." True enough. "She dropped me off at Phoebe's." Lie. I could still smell the cigarette stench of Eli Carver's Econoline, feel the snake of my sister's arm around my waist as she pulled me closer on the seat. *"One more time, Carly,"* she'd whispered. *"Eli promised. Just one more time."*

I pulled myself up straight in the uncomfortable plastic

chair as Moreno prodded.

"And you went straight to Miss Anderson's? Stayed there all night?"

"Yes." Another lie. "I was tired. Had to get up for school."

"Miss Anderson can confirm this then? You were at her home, in bed, all night?" he asked again. Why didn't he believe me?

"Yes." *Liar.* Phoebe was used to covering for me, I just hoped I could get to her before Moreno did.

"What about this morning?" He pushed a photograph of a black duffle bag across the table. "We found this bad at the scene. A change of clothes inside. Is it yours?"

I met his gaze–nodded.

"So you stopped by." he tucked the picture away. "When? This morning?"

I dipped my chin one more time and he narrowed his eyes at me.

"Did you notice anything unusual? Anything out of place?"

If I hadn't been so close to getting caught in my string of lies I would have laughed at that question. Everything in Aaron's trailer was in a constant state of "out of place."

"No more so than usual, sir."

Moreno sat back, twirling a pen from one finger to another down his hand and back up again. I'd always wondered how people could do that without dropping the writing utensil. I'd spent hours practicing that very skill in the solitude of my own bedroom with no success. He stopped mid-twirl.

"What did you come back to the trailer for, Carly?"

A surge of adrenalin pushed through me, heating my face and threatening my cover. There was a lot I wanted to tell him. The pinpricks of conversation between Caroline and Eli seeped in.

Eli's soft, *"You don't have to do this."*

Caroline's rebuttal, *"She's my sister, Eli, I'm not leaving her alone. One last time. For her."*

I could tell Moreno what followed. Describe the stink of the sleeper cab. The hands of a stranger on my flesh. Returning to the van and handing over the night's cash to Eli, my sister already gone. I closed my eyes against the seep of memory. Eli's gaze as it traveled to the pavement next to a growling International. A stranger standing over my sister's crumpled body. The rumble of the Econoline engine as Eli coaxed it to life. My tear-thickened pleas screaming, *"You can't leave her, Eli."*

I cleared my throat and answered. "Paper. I had a paper due in biology. I had to come back for it."

Moreno scribbled in his notebook. I didn't mention the other reason, my reward for a night's work—a balloon of heroine I'd never use, and wouldn't dare take to school—now stuffed under a loose floorboard in the kitchen of Aaron's trailer.

"Where was your father when you came in?"

"Dad was asleep on the couch."

"Asleep," Moreno echoed. One of his heavy eyebrows twitched up, arching like a caterpillar over one eye.

"He was fine. Snoring." I tried to remember if that part was true.

Moreno sighed. Closed the folder. Tucked his pen into his jacket pocket. He slid his business card across the table toward me. "If you remember anything, call me whenever. Day or night."

I nodded. Mute. My chance to speak had passed.

"Sit tight for a minute. As soon as we locate your sister you'll be free to go."

I watched Detective Moreno climb out of the plastic chair and head toward the door. But some dark part of me already knew. They'd never find her.

FIVE

ASHER

Asher resisted the urge to drive straight from the parking lot of Millbrook Academy to the Brookside Police Station. Without talking to Jo, he had no idea if Carly had been taken there or somewhere else entirely. He'd learned a long time ago never to assume he knew what was going on with Jo's cases. Besides, he didn't know if the local PD would investigate a homicide or if they'd call in some other department. This town was no more than a blip on a map. It could go either way.

Out of options, and with a still silent phone beside him, he snaked his way out of the parking lot and toward his home at the edge of town. Asher was sitting on his deck with a can of Budweiser in one hand when the familiar trill of his phone pierced the low moan of the distant highway, obscured by acres of trees that lined the rear of his property.

"Asher," Jo's voice sent an involuntary spike of regret into his chest. Muscles clenched in protest. His name seemed better when she said it. He returned her greeting.

"I'm sorry about not returning your texts, but we've got a bit of a situation here." Her voice was low, the hum of conversation in the background meant she wasn't yet home. "I was hoping you might be able to help, just for a night or two."

Jo's words slid over him, smooth and warm. It had been all of three months since their last conversation. Over a year since she'd moved all her belongings out of the house they'd bought together. Asher turned to look up at the rear façade of the two-story. *Four bedrooms, large yard, perfect for a growing family,* that's what the realtor had said as they made their offer. He never dreamed he'd be living here alone.

"How's Carly holding up?" Asher fought to force the words out. It was the only thing he could think of to say.

"Remarkably well, considering. The detective, Moreno, is kind of a jerk, but I think he's settled down and is taking it relatively easy on her ... for now."

Asher released the bubble of air he hadn't realized had been trapped in his chest. "That's good," he managed, stifling the "How are you?" that sat poised on the tip of his tongue.

God, he wanted a cigarette right now. Something between his fingers to keep him occupied. A joint would be even better, but he'd given up that particular vice when he started teaching. If there was one thing a high school student could sniff out, it was weed. And he didn't need another incident scarring up his record.

"Asher, are you still there?"

"Yeah, sorry, Jo. I think I lost you for a minute." It was a lie, but a believable one. Reception had never been pristine out here, just north of the state park. "What is it you need from me?"

She sighed, lightly, but the speaker picked it up. "Look, you've already done more for Carly than anyone, and I hate to ask you this ..." She stopped talking. One silent second stretched into two.

"But ..." Asher pulled the one-syllable word out like taffy.

Jo sucked in a breath on the other end of the line. "You know what temporary care is like out here. It's no better than the hell she's been living in for the last two years. I can't just turn her over, watch her get sucked into the system. Not after what she's been through." Asher could hear the pricks of subdued panic in Jo's voice. The words tumbled over each other in a race to get out.

"Why would she need temporary care? She has a sister. Caroline's ... what? Nineteen, now?"

"That would work, if we could find her. She's not returning calls. Cops say it looks like she hasn't been in her apartment for at least a few days."

"Jesus, Jo." Asher scrubbed a hand down his face, tossed his nearly-full can of Bud into the trash can at the side of the house and headed inside.

"I'm sorry, Ash. I really am. I hate to put you in this spot." Her voice got quiet. Asher thought he almost detected a hint of regret. "We did all the paperwork to foster, that included emergency placements. I can't take custody unless I turn her case over to someone else. I'm not willing to do that. But she could stay with you...just until we work out something more permanent. It would keep her out of ..."

"Hell," Asher finished for her. "It'll keep her out of hell for a few more nights."

"Yes." Jo's voice was quiet, reflective.

"Promise me you'll find her a decent place within a week, Jo. The school board will have a coronary if they find out I've got a student living with me. Especially Carly. You should have heard Baum this afternoon. He's already tried and convicted her."

"I know, I know. You've got my word."

Silence spread between them. Words left unsaid. Apologies unspoken.

"You're a good man, Asher Thompson." Jo's voice was tentative. "Thank you."

Asher punched the end call button without saying good-bye. How the hell did he get himself into these messes? He was soft. That's how. His dad told him that time and time again. Maybe the bastard had been right. But soft was better than the hardened abuser his father had become with each passing year. God, how many years of therapy had it taken to uncover that revelation? Too many, that's for sure.

Asher took the stairs two at a time to the sparse master suite. Opening the medicine cabinet, he shoved a toothbrush in his mouth, staring back at the man in bathroom mirror. *"You overcompensate for your father's shortcomings,"* his shrink had said. When he finally got the nerve to tell Dr. Morrison about Carly, how he'd secured a spot for her at Millbrook, Morrison was less than impressed. *"Who are you doing this for?"*

The conversation replayed in Asher's mind. He couldn't answer then. But he could now. Helping Carly overcome her situation was penance for all the shit he'd witnessed his father dole out through the years. All the times he'd stood back and done nothing. Helping Carly was Asher's way to prove he wasn't a monster.

Asher rinsed the toothpaste foam from his mouth and trotted down the stairs. Shrugging into his jacket, he shook off unwelcome old memories and grabbed his keys from the hook beside the front door. Maybe he had helped Carly for the wrong reasons. But everything he'd done since leaving his old life behind had made a difference. Well, almost everything.

"You've got to learn to consider your own feelings," Dr. Morrison had said. *"One of these days the only one to get hurt will be you."* Asher cranked the engine of his Jeep, squealing out of the quiet cul-de-sac.

Thirty minutes later, he pulled into an empty space in

front of the short brick building that housed the Brookside, Ohio Police Department. Jo waited for him at the door, her portfolio tucked in the crook of her arm. Her dark brown hair pulled back off her shoulders. Professional.

"Have you told Carly?" Asher asked as he climbed the steps.

"No, we'll need to make sure she's comfortable going home with you. If not, we'll need a plan B."

Asher sighed. He picked up a whiff of Jo's perfume as he held the door. Light, beckoning florals. He closed his eyes against the memory of what could have been, breathed through the temptation, and followed her into the lobby of the station house.

SIX

CARLY

Mr. Thompson's voice filtered through the maze of cubicles. Detective Moreno had led me out of the interrogation room and offered me a seat near his desk, just inside the shoulder-high partition that separated his cube from the one next door. I'd been here just long enough to realize I wasn't cut out to work somewhere I'd be stuck inside a cardboard hut for eight hours a day. On the plus side, though, Moreno had returned my notebook.

I slid the side of my pencil along the lid of the eye I'd just drawn, straining to hear what Mr. Thompson, Miss Harrison, and Detective Moreno were discussing in the main aisle of the station house. Their voices were hushed, only every fourth word or so sneaking out and becoming audible from my perch three cubicles away. I gave up trying to piece it together and turned back to the drawing of Miss Harrison.

"Carly, could you come with me please?" Again, I hadn't heard him approach, and I jumped at his voice, breaking off a piece of graphite on the paper in front of me. "Bring your things," Moreno finished, disappearing behind the partition.

I shoved my drawing pad into my bag and did as he asked, following him into the same tiny interrogation room I'd been in less than an hour before. Mr. Thompson and Miss Harrison were already seated inside. She was talking to him quietly, her right hand balanced lightly on his khaki-clad knee. An unwarranted pulse of jealousy stirred in my gut, and I paused, giving it time to dissipate.

Mr. Thompson sat with his hands clasped, eyes cast toward the floor, nodding at whatever Miss Harrison had said.

"There she is." The social worker stood as I entered, a big smile plastered on her face. Too big, I thought, for a dead father and missing sister. But what did I know? My eyes drifted from Miss Harrison to Mr. Thompson. He wasn't smiling. In fact, he looked worried. Scared, almost.

"Carly, we ..." Miss Harrison only got a couple words out before Mr. Thompson stopped her, standing.

"Could you give us a few minutes alone?" His blue eyes flicked from Miss Harrison to Moreno. The pair seemed to hesitate, unsure whether or not they should leave.

"We'll be right outside if you need us." Miss Harrison followed Moreno out the door and I wondered whether her comment was directed at me or Mr. Thompson. She'd looked at him when she spoke.

"Have a seat, Carly." Mr. Thompson motioned to the empty chair next to him. "You probably already know that the police are having trouble getting in touch with Caroline, right?"

He was waiting for an answer. "Right," I said.

"Well, Jo ..." He glanced at me, second-guessing the use of her first name, it seemed. But I'd seen the way she looked at him. Heck, I'd seen them together a couple times before this. Tension, too much for a platonic relationship, sizzled between them. I wasn't oblivious. But I didn't like the reminder.

He cleared his throat and started again. "Miss Harrison

asked me if I might be willing to take responsibility for you ... just until they can find Caroline."

"I can take care of myself."

He sucked in a breath and looked away. "I know you can, Carly. But since you're not yet eighteen, the law says a guardian has to be appointed to watch out for you, at least temporarily."

He wasn't telling me anything I didn't already know. And there was no way I'd refuse his offer, but I kind of liked the way his forehead scrunched when he squirmed. "I'll be eighteen in a few months."

His eyebrow pitched and a smile tickled the corner of his mouth. "Ten months," he said, his eyes back on mine.

I shrugged. He remembered my birthday.

His smile inched a degree fuller. "Then you'll need a place to stay for a *few* months, won't you?"

The deep blue intensity of his eyes on me made my entire body hum. I fought the heat rising toward my cheeks, but it came anyway. I looked down, the strings on my ratty Converse sneakers puddled in untied disarray. *Thank God.* I bent to tie them.

He lowered onto the chair next to mine. "What do you say, Carly? Think you can put up with me until they find Caroline?"

The flush subsided with the mention of my sister. "Why not just put me in one of those halfway houses? You don't need to do this."

It was Mr. Thompson's turn to stay mute. His gaze shifted from me to the floor.

"Miss Harrison asked you, huh?"

He rubbed his hands down his thighs and stood. "Come on, Carly. Grab your things and let's get out of this place. I'm starving and I think we both could use a quiet evening. What do you say?"

⟨❧⟩

WE PULLED into Green Meadows Trailer Park about a quarter after eight after stopping for a bite to eat at Wendy's. I sucked a mouthful of Dr. Pepper from the straw of the take-out cup as I surveyed the trailer, relaxed a bit. The house looked empty, the windows dark. The only evidence of what happened was a ribbon of police tape wrapped around the iron handrail that led to the front door. The loose end flapped in the breeze.

"Do you want me to come in with you?" Mr. Thompson asked as he steered his Jeep onto the gravel pad behind Aaron Carver's decrepit old Mustang, still up on blocks under a metal awning. I glanced at Mr. Thompson, but my teacher wasn't looking at me. He scanned the tiny windows on either side of the front door, no doubt wondering what went on behind closed doors.

"Aaron's at work. I'll just take a minute to grab my things."

I popped open the passenger door and Mr. Thompson silenced the engine. His headlights illuminated the sandy exterior of the tin can Aaron called a home.

I jerked the ring of keys from my backpack as I climbed the stairs. I slid the key into the lock, hesitating when I heard him behind me.

"If it's okay with you, I'd really rather you waited out here," I said, turning to face Mr. Thompson. His eyes left the trailer and held mine. A sudden understanding passed between us as he looked at me. No. *Into* me.

A flicker of warmth started low in my belly, traveling up

through my core. I'd met a lot of men over the past year and a half, but Mr. Thompson was the only one with the ability to make me feel like a real person—a person worth wanting—with nothing more than a glance.

His lips tilted into a pseudo-smile, doing nothing to cover the worry etched across his brow. The pulse of heat bloomed in my chest, sending the threat of tears against the backs of my eyes. How long had it been since someone looked at me that way? Cared enough about me that it showed through a silent expression?

"Okay," he said. "I'll be right here if you need me." He stepped off the stoop and hung back, hands jammed into his jacket pockets.

My chest tightened and I swallowed the threatening tears. The door screeched on rusty hinges as I stepped into the darkened living room. The memory of my sister's words, spoken the night she'd first conned me into going out with her, raked over me, scratching and clawing like a caged animal. *We have to make our own way, Carly. Sometimes that means doing things that hurt. You just have to distance yourself. I promise, Car, it will all be worth it one day.*

I picked my way around the trash that littered the floor. The air was still thick with competing scents of cigarette smoke and marijuana. I only glanced at the broken-down couch once, refusing to allow myself to be dragged down by the reality of the last twenty-four hours.

I was rooting around in my dresser, cramming clothes in my backpack when my bedroom door gave a familiar squeak, swinging slowly inward. The piece of me that still believed in fairy tales wished for Mr. Thompson to be standing there. But this wasn't Disney, and reality—in the form of Aaron Carver—filled the doorway instead. His presence sucked the air from the room.

"Where d'you think you're going?" he asked, arms folded across his broad chest, shoulder resting against the door frame.

"Cops say I can't stay here. They're placing me with a guardian." I tossed the words over my shoulder, ignoring the recognizable scent of Aaron's own struggle with the bottle.

"What about me? They didn't think I could handle a girl like you?" He took a step inward, his fingers latching onto my elbow.

I jerked away, pulling a wad of underwear from the top drawer before shoving it into the front pocket of my bag and zipping it closed.

"Don't the county pay those foster parents?"

His words hit me like a wall. I hadn't figured that into the equation. Of course Mr. Thompson would get paid for keeping me at his place. "I guess," I admitted. "Maybe." I slung the bag over one shoulder and faced him. "Look, I gotta go."

"You and your sister have a debt to pay, remember? She cut out, so looks like it's up to you."

The tiny hairs along my arms stood at attention as Aaron filled the room. Imaginary ants began a slow march from the back of my neck and onto my scalp. I closed my eyes and breathed against the mounting panic. *This is no different than any other time.* I coached, calming the storm that raged in my chest.

Except, it was different. I pictured Mr. Thompson outside, waiting for me to return. I wondered how much he would hear if Aaron refused to let me leave without settling up first. I swallowed the knot in my throat, missing my sister more in that moment than I ever had. Aaron preferred Caroline, and she'd always done what she could to protect me from his unpredictable urges. A surge of terror clamped around my lungs as reality sank in. *What if she's gone ... for good?*

"My father's dead." The words bit into my tongue. "His

debts died with him." I straightened my stance, pulling myself up to my full five-foot-four inch height. I stared through him, judging the best way to flee.

There was no way around him. The calendar may have read March, but Aaron's wardrobe never changed, and today it prompted a sickening lurch in my gut. The thought of his skin touching mine, ribbed wife-beater being peeled off, ratty blue jeans unbuttoned ... I turned to the left, the bunk bed I'd once shared with Caroline blocking my exit. To the right, the dresser took up too much space, middle drawer hanging askew as it always did.

He reached a long arm around me and shoved at the lopsided dresser drawer, shutting it unevenly before closing the distance between us. He slid the bookbag off my shoulder. Tossed it to the bottom bunk. I glanced at it for a second or two, debating. I could leave it. Maybe borrow some clothes from Phoebe and come back tomorrow when Aaron was at work.

"C'mon, baby. A deal's a deal. I held up my end of the bargain. You and your daddy woulda been on the street if it wasn't for me. Least you could do is settle up before you go."

"Your deal was never with me." I tried to reason with him. But one look in his eyes told me it was pointless. Glassy, pinpoint pupils fixed in muddy brown irises. He was high again.

"No, but I gave you a place to stay. Last night ..."

A rough finger traced my jawline. He stepped closer and I retreated.

"And the night before that."

His final step cornered me against the far wall.

"Go to hell, Carver." I shoved his chest with both hands, but he stood like a brick wall. His arms caged me against the cool exterior wall. I ducked under his elbow, stumbling against the unseated dresser drawer. The corner of it bit into my thigh, knocking me off balance. Before I could get my feet under me, Aaron grabbed me from behind. Spinning me with rough, unyielding hands, he shoved me forward.

My head hit the bedpost with a crack before I crumpled to the floor. Stars danced as his knee slammed against my spine. I'd held in the scream until then. I writhed and kicked as he worked to turn me over, a trickle of blood from what had to be a gash on my forehead blinded my right eye. He gripped my wrists, pinned my arms to the worn carpet. He was stronger than I'd given him credit for.

"Shut up, you little bitch." He growled, stale breath against my face. One hand closed around my throat. The other freed my wrists in favor of hiking up my sweatshirt. I pushed against him, clawed, but every squirm was met with a tightened grip, the flow of oxygen reduced. Callouses on his palm scratched against the flesh of my midriff as he worked to free the button of my jeans. I kicked, but his weight on my thighs pressed me hard against the floor, immobile.

Aaron growled and jerked at the waist of my jeans. The button popped, ricocheting against something solid, the dresser maybe. His hand slid lower, pushing my jeans down over my hips. I pulled against him, screaming through the tightness in my throat. He shot a palm up to my face, covering my mouth with an oil-stained hand. I scratched at his face and arms, but he didn't stop. I bit the flesh that sealed my screams. The metallic taste of blood came just before his hand on my neck shifted.

The pain was immediate. And so was the panic. I gasped, but his two-handed grip around my throat only tightened. My lungs burned, ached for oxygen. Tears leaked from the corners of my eyes as he pushed against me, hardening against the skin of my thigh. A wave of nausea erupted in my stomach. Caroline's advice pounded like a pinball in my skull. *"Put yourself somewhere else, Carly. It's just your body. It's not the real you."* Aaron gave a final squeeze, pressing his thumbs against my windpipe until sparks at the edge of my vision turned everything white.

SEVEN

ASHER

The trailer was a dump. Asher leaned against the hood of his SUV, pulling in a breath through the cigarette he held between his thumb and forefinger. His headlights blazed luminescent beams onto the dingy metal siding of Carly's home. *Home.* When he'd driven her here from the bar last year, she'd made him drop her off at the roadside entrance to the trailer park. Now he knew why.

Jo had to have seen the condition of the place on one of her visits. Yet another reason he could never be a social worker. Too much red tape to cut through before any action could be taken. The fact that this is where Carly had been living since landing in Brookside almost made him physically sick.

Thump, like the slam of a dresser drawer. Maybe she was wrapping things up. It had started to drizzle since she'd gone in, but he refused to get in the Jeep. His gut churned with thoughts of what may have happened to Carly in this used up tin can of a home. He'd experienced enough in his own life to know that poor didn't equal bad, but the littered bottles and handful of used needles collecting near the side of the porch stairs gave him reason to suspect the worst.

His mind cleared with the next *thump*. Louder, and punctuated by a short-lived staccato scream. He dropped the cigarette on the ground and launched in a sprint toward the door. Asher twisted the handle. Once, twice, three times. Locked. He reared back, as far as the makeshift front stoop would allow, and rammed the door with full force. It popped inward, emptying him into a darkened living room.

He hesitated, listening while his eyes adjusted to the darkness. A musty scent accosted his nostrils, flanked by the pungency of body odor and drugs.

An angry voice and small bumps against the wall to his left, pulled him out of the momentary haze. His heart jackhammered against his sternum as he ran to the hallway. Everything had gone quiet—too quiet.

"I shoulda done this a long time ago." A man's voice wafted from the nearest bedroom door. Asher flattened his palm against the flimsy woodgrain and shoved. The soles of two Converse sneakers winked up at him and then went still.

A hulk of a man straddled Carly. One hand wrapped around the soft flesh of her neck, the other disappeared between her thighs. Asher didn't think. He lunged. Threaded his arms under the stranger's shoulders, and yanked backward. A thick palm stayed planted around Carly's neck for a split second, long enough to pull her head upward. Asher fortified his grip on the man's torso, dragging him farther from the girl, forcing him to release his choke hold. Carly's head hit the dirty carpet with a sickening *thunk*.

"Get the fuck off her." Asher jerked the man into the confines of the hallway and landed a kick to his side. The attacker groaned, rolling onto all fours, tucking what was left of a hard-on into his jeans. Asher turned his attention to the bedroom. Carly lay still–too still. "Jesus," Asher breathed.

"Who the hell are you?"

Asher turned as the man pulled himself off the floor, zipping his pants.

"You the guardian?"

Asher ignored him. Focused on the pale girl sprawled on the floor in front of him, the side of her face bloodied, hair in tangles, body exposed. The girl he was responsible for. "Carly," he said. He pulled a blanket from the nearby bed to cover her midsection. Anger boiled inside like lava. He held her shoulders and shook lightly, whispering her name. The gasp from her lungs was the sweetest sound he'd ever heard. Her eyes fluttered, opening on him just as the force of a fist found the side of his head.

He spun toward his attacker, holding the dresser for balance as he lunged. Asher felt the warm ooze on his cheek, the heat of it blending with the ribbon of rage that seeped from a long-sealed core.

Images of the night that changed him forever pulsed through his brain. The man in front of him no longer a stranger. His surprised face now morphed into that of Asher's father. With each punch, Asher rode a wave of redemption. He landed one blow after another, feeling nothing, deliverance against a barrage of memories he'd fought so hard to forget. Every pent-up emotion, every ounce of hatred poured out of him.

"Mr. Thompson, stop! Please, stop!" The voice started small, but grew louder, closer. He didn't stop, though. Couldn't. Not until the form on the floor in front of him was still, huddled in a fetal position, begging for mercy. Just the way his father should have been.

Cool hands found his face. Light blue-gray eyes focused on him. Pleading, pulling him back to reality.

"It's over," Her lips were moving, but he couldn't pair them with a voice. It was too far away. The red edges of rage dissolved as she pulled him closer. He closed his eyes against the storm in her eyes. His chest heaved. Lungs burned. It had been so long since he'd felt this ... this ... *What was it?*

Release. He closed his eyes and breathed.

"MR. THOMPSON, say something. Are you okay?"

He was sitting now. On a wooden chair in the tiny kitchen of the trailer home. *How did he get here?* Perspiration trickled from his brow. He wiped it away, studying bloodied knuckles. He couldn't remember. Asher squinted against the cool sensation of a wash cloth against his cheek bone. He sucked in a breath.

Her face, concern laced with fear, contorted as she kneeled in front of him. "Carly," Asher whispered. The sound of his own voice cleared some of the haze as reality launched a slow climb through him. He scanned the empty place on the floor where he last remembered the man.

"It's okay." Her voice soothed him. Made him want things he knew were wrong. "Aaron left–crawled off to lick his wounds. He's gone for a while."

She smiled at him. A genuine smile that lit up her face. Had he ever seen her smile before? Really smile? He couldn't remember. Remnants of bloodstains on her forehead and cheek, the imprint of finger-shaped bruises on her neck, beckoned for his attention in the low light of the kitchen. He traced one of the purple welts with the tip of his finger. The heat of her skin vibrated through him. He drew another ragged breath.

"You saved my life." Her eyes were closed when she said it. But when she met his gaze a moment later they were wet, glistening with some emotion he couldn't place. Need? Want? Trust? A combination of all three?

"We should go," he managed through the remnants of fog in his brain. His voice was deeper than he intended. A rough-edged version of himself. He cleared his throat. "Did you get your things?"

She nodded, slinging a pack onto her shoulder. Watched as he rose from the kitchen stool. Mirrored his movements. As they picked their way through the living room to the front door, she slid her hand down his arm, tangling her fingers in his. He didn't stop her.

"Are you okay to drive?" she asked, slipping inside the passenger door he held open for her.

He looked away, pulled in a lungful of the damp night air. Raindrops pelted his skin, just as they had the night he'd met Carly Dalton. His body buzzed. And for the first time in a long time he felt alive. Asher wanted to soak it all in, this feeling of invincibility that coursed through his veins.

He looked back at the woman–*girl*, he reminded himself–in the front seat. "It's not far," he said, smiling at her. A stab of longing wound through his gut when she smiled back, settling into the pit of his stomach as a knot of fear. Not for himself, but for her. For the first time, the façade she put up day after day at Millbrook was absent. He'd seen the real Carly. And they had more in common than he'd ever imagined.

EIGHT

CARLY

Mr. Thompson's house wasn't what I expected. The lines of the two-story Colonial reminded me of the home I'd grown up in. Every shingle and sheet of siding screamed family from the back of the quiet cul-de-sac. A strange choice, I thought, for my twenty-something bachelor teacher. But then I remembered Miss Harrison. As we pulled up the driveway, I half-expected Jo Harrison to walk out the front door with a toddler balanced on her hip. This wasn't *his* home, it was *theirs*.

"Nice house," I said. It felt like the right thing to say.

He thanked me and killed the engine. The newer development on the north side of town was about as far as you could get from Green Meadows Trailer Park and still stay in Brookside. For that, I was thankful.

I ran my fingertips up and down my neck, testing the ridges of puffed skin, proof of what was sure to turn into a rock star bruise. The skin just below my jawbone stung, and it was becoming more and more painful to swallow. Even talking was a chore if I wanted any volume. I shivered through the memory of Aaron's hands on me. *Jackass. I should have let Mr. Thompson finish the job.* The thought came unbidden, but it was honest.

I suppose it should have scared me, watching my teacher pummel the man that had made my life a living hell over the last couple years. But it didn't. It drew me to him. I'd seen the darkness in his eyes–the break from reality. I'd seen a similar expression in my own eyes reflected too often in the side view mirror of a sleeper cab.

The girl who climbed into those eighteen wheelers was not the same girl that sat in Mr. Thompson's biology class, doodling in her notebook. Not the same girl that stood here now, clothes spilling out of a barely zipped bookbag, in front of a house I'd only dared imagine.

And I knew the Mr. Thompson who saved me tonight was not the same one who stood in front of his class in a neatly pressed shirt and tie, trying to get teenagers to care about cellular respiration. No. Tonight he'd become a man he'd rather forget, a version of himself spawned by god-knows-what. But I'd seen the monster. And no one could ever take that away from me. A smile tickled the corner of my lip as he held the front door open and invited me in.

THE GUEST ROOM was on the opposite end of the hall from Mr. Thompson's. I had my own bathroom with a tub twice the size of the one in Aaron's trailer. Staying here was going to be like staying at the vacation resorts Mom and Dad used to take us to before Mom got sick. I slowed at the memory, sorting my meager stash of clothes into small piles before depositing them into empty dresser drawers.

The drawers closed smoothly, not even a hitch. I swallowed

and hazarded a look at the reflection in the mirror. My hair was tangled, coiled into mats fit for a rat, and sticking up at odd angles along the crown of my head. I smoothed the strands with my fingers. Mascara had run from my eyes, pooling in dark circles in the depression under my lower lid. Dried blood formed an abstract outline from a small cut near my hairline, running southward to my right eye. I headed to the bathroom for a rag and some warm water to wash the remnants away. I ignored the angry bruises on my neck. I'd deal with them tomorrow.

When I was done, I padded from the upstairs bedroom down to the kitchen, a spacious eat-in that opened up into a family room, complete with stone fireplace. No trash littered the floor. A blanket was neatly folded along the back of the living room couch. Even magazines were stacked in neat piles on the coffee table. I'd forgotten what it was like to live this way.

A sliding glass door opened from the kitchen onto what I assumed was a deck of some sort, although in the dark it was hard to tell. I snatched my Wendy's cup off the counter and headed outside. The wooden decking was cold and damp against my bare feet, but I didn't care. It felt good, a reminder that all of this was real.

I leaned against the far railing and looked over. It wasn't much of a drop to the ground below, ten feet, tops. But the yard sloped downward toward a tree line. Even though the house was part of a development, none of the other homes were visible from the deck. A dog barked in the distance. The only evidence we weren't alone.

"You get settled in okay?" His voice startled me. I spun around to find Mr. Thompson leaning against the side of the house. A beer sat within reach on the two-person bistro table next to him, and the pinpoint red glow of a cigarette hung from his fingertips.

"I didn't know you smoked," I said, my insides vibrated with an unexpected wave of nervousness.

He looked down at what was left of the cigarette and took one last drag before stubbing it out on the glass top of the table and flicking it over the edge of the deck.

"I don't," he said. Smoke curled from his mouth as he exhaled. "I quit a few years ago, but sometimes when I get..." He stopped talking and stepped into the light. What I saw sucked the air from my lungs. He'd changed clothes. Out of his regular button down and khakis and into a pair of dark wash jeans and a t-shirt. The t-shirt hugged the muscles in his chest, a trait only barely visible under the cover of his daily uniform. I swallowed and looked away, trying to shake the new image of him.

"Sorry," he added. "I wasn't really thinking. If it bothers you, I won't."

"It's not good for you," I started before I realized he wasn't talking about cigarettes anymore. Light from the kitchen glinted off the red and silver can as he tipped it back and forth in his hand. "No, it's okay. It's your house. Most people can handle their alcohol a whole lot better than my dad could."

Mr. Thompson chucked the can into a nearby trash can. I could tell by the damp *thunk* it made when it hit that it was nowhere near empty.

"Do you want to talk about what happened tonight?"

I shook my head, occupying my lips with the straw from the to-go cup. I turned away, looking out over the trees. We stood in silence, the events of the evening stringing between us, tethering us together like boats in a storm.

"Mr. Thompson," I started, after the silence became too much.

"Asher," he answered, prompting me to turn toward him. "If you're going to live here, unless we're at school, just call me Asher."

"Asher." I tested it out on my tongue. Pretended I'd never used it in my own imaginary scenarios. It sounded even better out loud. Heat flared in my cheeks and I was glad for the shroud of darkness. "Thank you for what you did back there, at Aaron's." I turned away again. It was easier if I didn't have to face him.

"Anyone would have done the same thing, Carly."

"No. No, they wouldn't...they haven't." I let the silence pass between us. The implication that it had happened before hung over us like a heavy cloud. I waited until I heard him suck in a sigh before turning to face him. He ran the palm of his hand through his short-cropped hair to the back of his neck and around to his jaw, scratching at stubble from what had turned into a very long day.

"Why didn't you tell someone what was going on?" His voice was nothing more than a whisper. Like saying the words aloud made them too painful to process. "Did Jo know?"

"Miss Harrison? Of course not. No one knows," I managed before the first tear tipped belligerently over the rim of my left eye. "It wasn't just me. It happened to Caroline, too. But we had a place to stay. Food to eat." The words spilled from me. Gushing out into the night.

"You're saying what happened tonight, this happened often?" I could hear the note of rage disguised by disbelief in Asher's voice. "Carly, look at me."

"You don't know what it's like to live on the street, or in shelters. They're the worst. At least at Aaron's we knew what to expect."

When I turned, he was standing directly in front of me. My heart fluttered. *Was I really ready to do this?* He put his hands on my shoulders, and the words flowed. "I never fought him like that before."

"Jesus, Carly," Asher said under his breath. "You're seventeen. Didn't anyone try to stop him? Your dad? Did he know?"

"Caroline used to ..." I shook my head, words clotted at the back of my throat. I paused, letting the tears fall. "I'm sorry you got pulled into all this. You're the last person I want to hurt."

Asher pulled me to his chest and smoothed my hair. The heat of his breath on the top of my head untangled the knot in my gut as he spoke. "You didn't hurt me, Carly. But you've got to report Aaron. You've got to tell the police what he did to you–to Caroline."

"I can't," I said, shoving him away. He released me immediately, sending a hot spike of regret through my chest. My arms chilled where the warmth of his hands had been. "Not until I find Caroline. Aaron's one of many. I can't risk turning him in until I know my sister is safe."

"How many?" Asher asked.

I brought my eyes up to meet his, a silent plea for understanding.

"Fine." Asher raised his palms in defeat. "For now."

He waited for me to nod in agreement.

"How can I help?"

I stepped toward him. My hand drifted toward the bruise that colored his cheekbone.

"Carly," his voice dipped low. A warning. But he didn't pull away.

"Don't tell Miss Harrison what happened tonight." I tilted up on my toes and pressed my body against his. "Don't tell anyone." I closed my eyes as the worlds inside me collided. "Please help me find my sister."

NINE

ASHER

Asher pulled out of Carly's embrace. Could almost taste the Dr. Pepper hanging on her lips. His head throbbed, and in the second it took for him to back away from Carly, he'd felt it. The hastened beat of his heart, the hum in his core, the pull that accompanied the instinctual reaction to kiss the lips within inches of his.

"This can't happen." He picked her hands up off of his chest. Circled her wrists with his fingers, gripping only tight enough to keep her from touching him. But her eyes devoured him, sent a stab of longing he didn't fully understand into his core. How long had it been since he'd been with a woman? He shook his head against the silent thought. It didn't matter. "You can't stay here like this."

She wriggled free of his grasp, offering a quiet apology that sucked the air from his lungs. Rejection stamped across her face. Asher stood rooted to the deck, watching as Carly disappeared into the house. *What the hell just happened?* He pulled in an unsteady breath and closed his eyes. A cold breeze washed over him. *You almost kissed a student.*

What had he been thinking? He scrubbed a hand over his jaw. What if she told someone? Other students—or worse, Jo. Panic lurched in his chest, churned like the ignition of a freight train. He braced himself against the deck railing, looking out into the silent night. A frigid blast of winter air swung around the corner of the house, pressing against him and cooling the heat in his core.

Somehow, he knew she wouldn't tell. Besides, she was not a kid. Was a matter of months shy of legal. *Ten,* he reminded the devil on his shoulder. Technically, in the state of Ohio, sixteen was the age of consent. He'd lose his job, but no court would prosecute him. Except the only one that mattered. *Jesus.* He scrubbed a hand down his face.

The court of public opinion was far harsher than any legal entity that existed in the world today. A pain stabbed through his cheek and into his temple, alerting him to the clench of his jaw. He relaxed and rubbed the achy muscle. They'd both been traumatized. Neither one thinking clearly. She was lonely, stuck in a cycle of abuse that reinforced only one way to get attention. He'd been in therapy long enough to recognize the signs, even if he couldn't always identify them in himself. Asher sighed. He needed painkillers and sleep. Everything would be clearer in the morning.

CARLY'S ROOM was dark by the time Asher locked up and climbed the stairs. He pushed her door open a crack, a slice of light skimming across the floor and onto the bed. She looked peaceful, eyes closed, lips parted in sleep, her raven hair splayed on the pillow behind her. So unlike the girl hovering on the brink of death in Aaron's trailer.

Asher pulled the door closed. His mind was still processing

what had happened. It seemed as though he'd lived three life-times in the time it had taken for him to pick Carly up from the precinct and get her back here.

In the hours since leaving the trailer, his body was slowly starting to paint a clearer picture of the animal he'd become. He'd gone from nursing a headache from a simple right hook, to the full-blown body aches of a man who used every ounce of energy to pummel another human being nearly to death.

He turned on the sink in his bathroom and ran his knuckles under the cooling stream of water. Swollen and red, the skin along the joint in his middle finger oozed blood. He washed his hands for the fourth time since he'd been home, scrubbing at already sore flesh, as if he could wash the events of the evening away.

Satisfied that the remaining blood was his own, he flicked off the light and dried his hands. Forcing himself not to look at the reflection in the mirror, he coerced his legs into carrying him the twelve steps to his bed. His mind spun in the darkness. So many possibilities. Would Aaron come looking for him? Hell bent on settling the score? That scenario seemed pretty damned likely. Aaron Carver didn't strike him as the type to give up easily.

What about Carly's sister, Caroline? Did Aaron have something to do with her disappearance? Figuring that out would be first on Carly's agenda, he knew. But she'd refused to tell the police anything about what she and Caroline had been through—the "deal" they'd made to keep a roof over their heads.

Asher breathed through the churn in his gut. He didn't know the details, but he'd seen enough tonight. He'd known from the moment he'd met Carly she wasn't like the kids he taught at Millbrook. Artistic, withdrawn, he'd seen his own past in her. And now, those similarities were giving way to monstrous reality.

He squeezed his eyes shut in the dark, as if doing so would keep the images from coming. Images of a girl he barely knew. A kiss he'd shared a lifetime ago. Now meshed with the heat of Carly's breath on his lips. Carly was about to kiss *him*. Not the other way around. *You stopped her*, he reminded himself, whispering the words into the darkness. But damn it, he'd felt the pull—struggled to keep his body from reacting to the flood of memories, past mixed with present. Soft lips, sweet tongue. Those thunderstorm eyes. *Emily*.

He relaxed, sinking into the memory as it morphed. Mysterious clouds gave way to the Caribbean sea-green of Jo's eyes. He could see the bronzed skin of her shoulders, feel her flesh under his fingertips. He invited the memory.

They'd bought this house together—for their future, before their world imploded. Jo still cared about him, that was clear. But she'd never let herself be with him. He knew that now.

He pictured her next to him, recalled the melodic tones of her laughter as they lay naked together in bed. His palm on the growing swell of her belly. His stomach clenched as he fisted the empty pillow next to him. Gone. Thanks to him, all of it was gone.

TEN

CARLY

The weight of the duvet on my body woke me. At least, that's what I told myself. I shoved at the assaulting blanket, damp with sweat, and threw my legs over the side of the bed. I looked around the room, early morning light streamed in through curtainless windows.

"You're safe," I said under my breath. "They can't hurt you. Not here."

I pushed up from the mattress, struggled to control the too fast breaths that puffed from my mouth. Snippets of the argument between my father and sister filtered through my memory.

My dad's inebriated baritone, *"Haven't you done enough damage?"*

My sister's retort, *"She's not your property to do with what you want. She deserves a chance."*

I shuffled to the bathroom, both voices interrupted by the weight of Aaron on top of me, hands around my neck, suffocating.

I stared at my reflection in the mirror, splashed water onto my skin. Barely noticeable freckles sprinkled over the bridge of my nose. Dark hair hung in limp waves over my shoulders. Eyes the color of the clouds on a dreary day. I was so different from Caroline and her shiny blonde curls and piercing blue eyes. Caroline was the spitting image of our mother. I, unfortunately, took after Dad.

I scrubbed a washcloth over my face, patting the area around last night's scuffs gently. At first Caroline trained me to feel flattered. *"You can do this, Carly. They want you. You just have to pretend to want them back."*

Men did pay for *me*, asked for *me*, wanted *me*. But the longer I stayed, immersed in the inescapable trap of drugs and money, the more I understood the truth. They didn't pay for *me*. They paid for sex. And they didn't much care where it came from, as long as I did what they wanted. And until last night, I'd never been rejected.

As if I needed to add to the drone of self-loathing, the light of morning brought a new perspective. I owed Mr. Thompson an apology. Last night was stupid. I couldn't even say why I'd done it. Maybe I wanted to be close to him. I certainly wasn't the only girl at Millbrook harboring fantasies about Asher Thompson. But I was the only one to ever act on them...at least, as far as I knew.

He'd been so close. Was so understanding. It just happened, as if I couldn't control what I was about to do. I sucked in a deep breath. He'd never look at me the same way again, not with what happened at Aaron's coupled with our moment on the deck. What if he'd already called Miss Harrison to arrange for a new guardian? I shrugged at the face in the mirror and stood tall.

"He has every right to hate you." I said the words to my reflection as I mixed a palette of concealer and dabbed it over my bruised skin. *You did this.*

I brushed away the tear skiing down the cheek of the girl staring back at me. The familiar tickle of regret surged in my core. The heat of resentment bubbling and gurgling its way to the surface. Even if he had reported what happened, Mr. Thompson deserved an apology. He deserved to know that whatever happened from here on out wasn't his fault.

I pulled on a pair of jeans and a sweatshirt and padded downstairs. The plush carpet on the steps tickled the bottoms of my bare feet until it gave way to the cool hardwood of the first floor landing.

Mr. Thompson stood at the breakfast bar in the kitchen, gaze lowered as he scrolled through his phone. Dressed in his normal khakis and a blue button-down shirt, hair neatly combed, I could almost believe the last twenty-four hours had been a figment of my imagination. His sleeves were rolled up to just under his elbow, and the top two buttons of his shirt remained open, in their pre-tie position. He glanced up, shoving the cell in his back pocket, the deep purple bruise along his cheekbone proof that what happened last night was real.

"Morning," he said, pouring a cup of coffee and offering it to me. I took it, although I never could choke down black coffee. He must have noticed me staring into the inky liquid, because he followed it up with, "There's sugar in the third canister from the left." He nodded toward a trio of matching silver containers lining the wall near the stove.

"Thanks," I murmured, barely able to face him. In the light of day, my bonehead pass at my biology teacher seemed excruciatingly idiotic. I pulled a chair up to the breakfast bar and hunched over my coffee cup. Taking baby sips, my thoughts ping-ponged between self-ridicule over making such a fool of myself and wishing for some creamer.

"I don't have any creamer, but there's some milk in the

fridge. We can pick up whatever you like from the store on the way home from school today if you want."

There he went again, with the mind reading crap. Of course, I knew he couldn't read my mind, but he was one of the most observant men I'd ever known. More so than my dad had ever been, even when Mom was alive.

I mumbled another, "Thank you," and swiveled toward the refrigerator, and him.

I tried to ignore him as I reached for the milk. He stood with his back against the counter, lips pursed on the edge of his mug, watching me. *He's waiting*, I thought. *Waiting for you to apologize.* That, or he was trying to decide how to tell me he'd booted me out. At this point, either was possible.

"Did your bruises really go away that fast?" he asked, taking a step toward me. I replaced the milk and closed the refrigerator door with an unintentional *smack*.

The chuckle escaped before I could censor myself. Just one more reminder of how different our lives were. I guess he wasn't used to having to cover a face full of bruises on a regular basis.

"It's makeup," I tossed over my shoulder, returning to my stool. The room filled with awkward silence. "I could show you, if you like."

"Well, considering looking like the winner of a prize fight isn't exactly part of the Millbrook faculty dress code ..." The sarcasm left his voice as he added, "I'd appreciate your help, Carly."

I fought against the flutter that started low in my belly when he said my name. I'd have to get myself under control if I was going to stay here. And after a night spent–safe–in his spare bedroom, snuggled in the luxury of a pillow-top mattress, the last thing I wanted was to be forced out.

Ten minutes later, Mr. Thompson sat on the toilet seat in

the guest bathroom while I mixed concealer and eyeshadow to combat the angry red swath of flesh across his cheek.

"It won't cover the scuffs, but it will tone down the bruise. You're still going to need a story for anyone who asks what happened." How surreal to be giving my teacher advice on how to cover up the after-effects of an all-out brawl?

"What's your story?"

Our eyes met. I bit at the corner of my lip, refocusing on the makeshift palette in front of me.

"Trip and fall is always a winner. Just make sure it's believable. Like, you could tell them you slipped down the stairs of your deck last night. It rained, so the wood would be slippery. Totally believable."

"Okay, deck klutz, it is." He smiled up at me, blue eyes twinkling. Relief wove itself like a ribbon through my insides. He didn't press me about my own story. I finished the spackling job in silence. When I finished I stepped aside, nodding toward the mirror so he could check it out.

I watched the eyes in his reflection widen. "That's amazing, Carly, really. It doesn't even look like makeup."

His compliment tickled my lips into a reluctant grin. "I was going for au naturale," I said, feigning a French accent.

The light in Mr. Thompson's eyes darkened. "How many times have you had to do this?"

"On someone else?" I hedged. He tilted his head, a silent, *You know what I mean.*

I shrugged. Truth was, I'd lost count a long time ago. Nights spent on the lot were rough and home was rougher. A better question was, how many times did I *not* have to do this.

"You don't have to answer that. I'm sorry. It's just ..." He turned to face me. "You could have told me what was going on at home. I could have helped get you out of there."

"And go where? Foster care? No, thanks." I gathered the

brushes and bottles of makeup scattered over the sink top and shoved them into the gallon size plastic baggie I'd brought them in. Mr. Thompson seemed to take the cue and backed toward the door.

"We should call the precinct today and see if there's any word on your sister."

I nodded, fighting the rush of emotion that threatened to obliterate my own makeup job. Why was he being so nice? After he had to pull Aaron off of me? After the way I behaved on the deck? I didn't deserve nice.

ELEVEN

ASHER

Asher had learned through experience that there were two places in the world where gossip thrived like a living, breathing animal, feeding on desire and fear in equal parts. One of those places was a teacher's lounge at lunchtime. It was precisely why he steered clear of the glorified break room where his colleagues scarfed down Lean Cuisines and whole wheat sandwiches at a rate that made him believe the sport should be considered for the next Olympic Games. How the women in that room could dish the dirt on that day's unfortunate bastard and shovel in grub at the same time was a skill he had yet to master. Thankfully.

His hand paused on the doorknob of the lounge longer than it should have. He gauged the drone of voices on the other side of the door. Low pitched whispers followed by laughter. Carly had done an amazing job trying to make his face look somewhat human this morning, but he'd noticed the looks. Heard the whispers. If he was going to make it through the rest of the day, he either needed to brave the belly of the beast for a Red Bull or find that AP English teacher who was rumored to keep a flask in her bottom desk drawer.

A snort from inside the room as the group erupted in a fit of laughter gave him the distraction he needed.

"Afternoon, ladies." He'd learned to be the first to break the silence. It was the only way to avoid the awkward hush that always accompanied his unexpected appearances.

He ignored the mumbles of cordiality and walked straight to the vending machine, hoping the chilly response had nothing to do with the possibility that he'd been the topic of their lunchtime conversation.

He slid a dollar bill into the machine and waited the obligatory five seconds for the machine's brain to kick into gear and release the can. He breathed a silent sigh of relief as the Red Bull tumbled from its perch on the top row and into the bin at the bottom.

He heard the whispers behind him first. "Um, Asher?" Lindsay Grant, the PE teacher and resident queen of storytelling, caught his attention. "I heard you had an accident last night. I hope everything is okay."

Asher felt his insides clench as he turned to face her. He forced a chuckle. "Yea, just missed a step, that's all. I'm fine, though. Thanks for asking."

He tried not to notice the squint of suspicion. The glance at his bruised right hand. With a quick salute, he exited exactly how he'd entered. Closing the door behind him, he paused for a moment, waiting for the volume on the other side to increase to a post-rumor level.

He'd witnessed it in his former life, been privy to the male version of the rumor mill before he'd ever considered going into teaching. Although decidedly less vindictive, the gossip he'd encountered while on the road with his father was just as brutal.

Going into education had been Asher's way of dealing with the memories that plagued him—a roadmap by which to prove that he was nothing like the man who'd raised him. He'd spent too many summers curled in the sleeper cab of his father's semi-truck. There, he'd discovered books, escaped into fictional worlds or researched species that seemed, to him, more evolved than the men who surrounded him on the road.

Asher sat by as his companions leered at young women in truck stops, shot up or snorted between runs, and welcomed visitors who served only one purpose. Back then, he'd done whatever it took to put distance between himself and the monster he called, "Dad."

Now Asher had new memories to join the old. Reels that married two worlds he'd fought for so long to keep separate. Images punched at him, Carly being used, abused. He'd got to her in time last night, but what would have happened if he hadn't? He knew the answer to that question, and it wasn't an outcome he was willing to repeat.

His phone vibrated from his back pocket and he pulled it out to find a text from Jo.

How'd it go last night?

Asher stopped in the middle of the hall, ignoring the rush of students as they flowed by on either side of him.

He typed back a quick response.

Fine. Any luck finding Caroline?

Asher watched the three pulsing dots for a minute. His cue that Jo was typing something. Each passing moment watching the dots unknotted a spool of hope in his chest. But when the message finally came it was a short and impersonal.

No.

Asher shook his head and walked on, cracking open the can of Red Bull as he swung the door to his classroom open, the faces of the students within chasing away his lingering demons. The bell echoed from the speaker above his head, slicing into the dull throb in his skull and signaling the end of his lunch and the beginning of his fifth period physics class.

TWELVE
CARLY

"What happened to you?" Phoebe grabbed me by the shoulders and shook me back and forth when we finally saw each other during lunch. "Why didn't you call me last night? Who were those people yesterday? Why did they take you out of here? Are you okay?"

"Slow down, Phoebe. Last night just got kind of crazy. But everything's all right. I'm fine."

Phoebe's blue eyes scoured me from head to toe. I couldn't help but look away.

"You're lying." She crossed her arms over her chest and stared me down.

I held my food tray with both hands in front of me. Nothing on it looked even remotely appetizing–rectangular pizza pocked with pepperoni bits, a layer of cheese in all its plasticky glory glistening up at me. The square nook next to it harbored a pile of corn. Pizza and corn. Who thought up that combination?

"One of them was Miss Harrison," I started. Phoebe already knew about Jo Harrison's monthly visits to Aaron's trailer. It was a topic of conversation, a running joke between them every time Carly was forced to spend a weekend cleaning the place up for the state's scheduled visits. They'd heard case-workers like Jo Harrison were overworked and underpaid, but *scheduled* visits ... really? Phoebe shrugged a shoulder and tilted her head from side to side, as if to say, *Get on with it.*

"The other was a cop, Detective Moreno." My scalp prickled when I said his name. The hair on my arms and legs rose as if in protest. "They came to tell me my dad died."

It sounded so benign when I said it, as if he'd passed away peacefully in his sleep. But nothing my dad had done since Mom died had been peaceful.

"Oh, my God, Carly." Phoebe's voice was a rush of air. Her eyes wide–a deer in the headlights. "That explains the detective who came to talk to my dad this morning."

My chest tightened with her words. The prickles along my scalp turned vicious, driving into my skin like knives. The room swirled. Faces around me jumbled. Voices engaged in lunch-room conversation morphed into the din of indecipherable screams. I stared at the food in front of me. *Calm down, Carly. Get a grip.*

But with each logical bit of advice my brain spewed, another equally illogical thought retaliated. *Everyone's going to know what you are. It's just a matter of time.* A wave of heat washed over me, followed by cool clamminess. *Dad's gone. Caroline's gone. No one wants you. You are alone, Carly Dalton ... alone.* The word screamed in my skull.

"Carly? Are you okay?" I could hear Phoebe's words, but my body was frozen. My mouth sewn shut with the thread of panic.

I WOKE on the floor of the cafeteria, a sea of faces looking down on me. My head pounded and my right elbow felt as if it had been ripped out of its socket.

"She's waking up." The words rippled through the crowd, still out of focus as it parted, making way for Miss Franklin, the school nurse. I squinted through uncooperative eyes, scanning the crowd for Phoebe, blinking against each loss of focus.

"I'm here," her voice came from above me, somewhere near my head. A hand I assumed was hers stroked my hair. Her touch soothed me.

"What happened here?" Miss Franklin's voice was gruff. And I couldn't help the instinct to shut my eyes again. "Carlita, right?" she asked the crowd. Only Phoebe corrected her.

"She prefers Carly." It was the first time I'd ever detected a hint of fear in Phoebe's voice.

I fought to open my eyes again, but they wouldn't comply. Images I couldn't control drifted in and out of my brain with the wave-like rise and fall of the cafeteria din. I could disappear—close my eyes and never wake up. It was an enticing option. One worth considering. Who would miss me now?

<hr>

I REGAINED consciousness in a darkened room. The only light was the flicker of a television mounted high on the opposite wall. A machine beeped a soothing rhythm in the background, muted only by quiet voices from the far side of the room.

A stab of fear shot through me, my eyes flicking open as I struggled to sit, my head constricted by something against my face. I swiped at the tether. Heard the panicked squeak erupt from my own lungs.

"Whoa, whoa, whoa, just hang on there hot shot." Mr.

Thompson appeared at the side of my bed, readjusting the plastic tubing strung across my cheeks. "It's just oxygen, Carly." His eyes were calm, searching. "How do you feel?"

"Like I've been trampled by a herd of elephants," I admitted through the gravel in my throat. Mr. Thompson pushed a button on the side of the bed, and a motor hummed, pushing my body toward a semi-seated position.

He smiled, but it didn't reach his eyes. Miss Harrison stepped from the shadows to join him at the side of my bed. A blade of disappointment sliced through me.

"Where's Phoebe?" I asked, mostly to keep from wondering what Mr. Thompson had told Miss Harrison while I was dead to the world.

"She ran down for some dinner. She'll be back soon," Miss Harrison answered. The cool of her fingertips traced my arm, ending on my hand before she wrapped her fingers around mine, giving them a squeeze. "Detective Moreno has some questions, Carly. Do you think you're up for it?"

"Maybe we could give her a few minutes, Jo. She just woke up." There was an edge in Asher's voice that I wasn't used to. Jo removed her hand from mine, her feminine form replaced by Detective Moreno's wall of masculinity.

"The sooner we get to the bottom of what happened to Carly, the sooner we can figure all this out and go home." The detective shifted his focus from Asher to me. "Start putting our manpower where it belongs—on finding your sister."

I nodded, swallowing the knot that swelled in my throat. Moreno dismissed Mr. Thompson and Miss Harrison, pulling a chair close to the bed. Miss Harrison, hurried away, but Mr. Thompson lingered, watching me, waiting for my silent nod to let him know I'd be okay answering the detective's questions on my own.

"Tell me what happened after you left the precinct yesterday, Carly."

I remained silent. What did he already know? What options did I have? Protecting Caroline meant protecting Aaron, Eli, and the mastermind behind it all, Reed Sutherland. Just the thought of his name unleashed a pounding pulse to the side of my head.

The memory of my "initiation" flooded back. Caroline's promises. Her gentle urging. Reed's cold, hateful stare. *No.* I wouldn't go there. Not today. Not with Moreno here. I closed the gate, keeping the worst of the memory at bay. But the fact remained, if anyone knew where Caroline was, it was Reed Sutherland.

I squinted against the dull ache that throbbed in my skull. Lies would only be hard to keep track of later.

"Mr. Thompson drove me to the trailer park to pick up some clothes," I started. "The house was dark when we pulled in. I didn't think anyone was there."

"Was Carver inside?" Moreno asked as I fought the choke of tears in my throat.

I nodded. Moreno scribbled. I wanted to grab the pen from his hand, break it in two.

"The bruises on your neck." Moreno looked up from his notebook. "How'd you get those?"

"Aaron wouldn't let me leave," I started. My chest tightened, the threat of exposure a hard knot against my sternum. *You know Mr. Thompson already told him. He just needs to hear it from you.* Whether or not that was true, the thought unlatched the lock in my throat. Aaron's threats, his attack, poured out. With every sentence I spoke, the knot loosened.

Detective Moreno's black eyes stayed on mine, growing softer with each detail that he scribbled in his notebook. "When did Mr. Thompson enter the house?"

I shrugged. "I'm not sure. I blacked out. When I came to, they were fighting."

Moreno nodded. His large hand drifted to the edge of the bed, hovered there, threatening to cover mine. I pulled my hand out of reach. "Carver ever do anything like this before, Carly?"

I wanted to nod. Wanted to tell Moreno that last night was no different than any other, except last night I fought back. Aaron was the reason I hated leaving the lot. His expectations when we returned were somehow worse than what we did in the cabs of complete strangers. Maybe it was because my dad was nearby, on the other side of a paper-thin wall. Maybe it was because he did nothing, even though he had to hear. But in spite of the memories flooding my brain, the words wouldn't come. Not without Caroline.

I swallowed the urge. "No, sir."

I felt him stare at me for a beat. "I know you're scared, Carly, but please understand. The more I know—whether it happened last night, last month, or last year—the more I can help."

A tendril of panic snaked its way down my spine. "I understand."

He pulled a business card from his pocket, identical to the one he'd given me yesterday, and slid it onto the nearby table. "We'll have more questions as the case develops. For now, I'll let you get some sleep."

I sucked in a deep breath and watched Moreno's broad back disappear into the hall. His words continued on a loop through the back of my brain. *The more I know, the more I can help.* I'd given him enough ammunition to go after Aaron, but for him, that wasn't enough.

I closed my eyes and pulled the covers up to my chin, sinking into the foamy discomfort of the hospital pillow. Giving Moreno a blow by blow of where I spent most of my nights would only hurt me. It had been my choice, after all. I wasn't kidnapped. Hadn't been forced at gunpoint. Aaron, Reed, and Eli had offered a way out. Caroline took it and I followed.

The first silent tears—relief maybe—pooled onto the pillow next to my head and I brushed them away. I'd chosen this life, however asinine that sounded. And I couldn't risk the fallout of total truth. Not until I knew where Caroline was.

THIRTEEN

ASHER

I f Jo wasn't standing in a hospital filled with people, she'd be screaming at him right now. Rightfully so, Asher figured. Her eyes hadn't blazed at him like this since the night she left him. But he had some questions that deserved answers, too.

"What the hell happened, Asher?" She poked her finger into his chest. "I've got a juvenile ward of the state with finger-shaped bruises around her neck and a gash on her temple that should have seen stitches. The man responsible for her safety appears to have been in a bar fight, and said juvenile is now hospitalized after having a massive panic attack in front of a cafeteria full of her peers. I've got people to answer to, Asher. I need to know what happened."

Jo's words stoked the coals of anger in Asher's core. He could tell her she should have checked in on her more, that she was just as responsible for Carly's situation as he was ... maybe more so. But he didn't. Instead he forced a tight, "It's not that simple, Jo."

"Tell me what happened, Ash."

He sucked in a breath and blew it out in a steady stream,

attempting to put a damper on the fire that raged inside. "I took a girl into hell to pick up a backpack's worth of clothes last night, Jo. You were supposed to be checking up on her. You were the one that was supposed to make sure she was safe over the last eighteen months, so you can keep the lecture to yourself."

Asher watched Jo's jaw go slack, her eyes dampen. *Damn it.* He turned away, ran a hand through his hair and lowered himself to the two-person couch in the waiting room.

"Carly was attacked at Aaron's?" Jo sat next to him, her knees grazed the side of his thigh. She took hold of his chin and twisted his head to the side, exposing marred flesh. It had been nearly twelve hours since Carly's makeup job, and the flesh-tone concealer had long since worn away.

Jo's eyes softened. She released his chin and took a deep breath, sliding against the seat back next to him. "I knew Aaron Carver was bad news. From the moment I met him, I knew. But there was nothing I could do. Legally, my hands were tied. Carly never implicated him in any illegal activity. I'd been more concerned about her father hurting her than Carver."

Asher remained silent. This wasn't his story to tell. And he'd be damned if he broke what little trust he'd gained with Carly over the past twenty-four hours.

"Just tell me this, Asher, did Carver do that to you?"

Asher wrung his hands, sliding the pad of his thumb over the scabs coloring his right knuckles. A life he thought he'd escaped had snaked back in, proving to Jo that she'd been right to leave. He hesitated for a breath before nodding his head, confirming her suspicions.

"What did you do to him?" He could hear the fear in her voice–fear he'd put there. He hated himself for it. Regret laced with the fire of indignation as he considered her question. That's what really mattered to her, wasn't it? It didn't matter that the bastard had his hands wrapped around Carly's neck and his dick out of his pants. "He's fine," Asher answered through the clench in his jaw.

"And what about Carly when you were cowboying it up, huh? She didn't need to witness that kind of violence, Asher. You of all people should know that." Anger seethed from Jo's voice. "Where was she?"

Asher sucked in a breath, his own frustration building. He stood, stretching the tension from his back.

"Jesus Christ, Asher. Tell me those aren't your thumbprints on Carly's neck."

Asher spun to face Jo. "You know I had nothing to do with that." The words hissed out of him. The accusation from a woman he'd once loved was too much. "Do you really think that I ..." He left the question unfinished. Obviously, she did, or she wouldn't have asked.

He moved as far away from Jo as he could, walking toward the window on the other side of the waiting area. The sun was setting, its last rays of light glistening off the cars in the hospital parking lot.

"I'm sorry." He heard Jo approach, felt the warmth of her palm on his shoulder. "I know you would never intentionally hurt her. It's just ..."

Asher removed Jo's hand from his shoulder. "It's fine, Jo. I deserved that."

"Maybe you should call Dr. Morrison, set up an appointment or two?"

Asher nodded, the lump in his throat choking him. He'd already called the shrink on his lunch break. It had been a few months since his last session, but Jo was right. Something about this situation with Carly had shifted him out of neutral. The worst part was, he wasn't convinced it was a bad thing.

"Jo?" He turned to face her, ready to ask the question that

had plagued him since her call yesterday afternoon. "Why me? Sending Carly to live with me ... there have to be more qualified homes than the guy with repressed anger management issues."

"You're a victim of childhood trauma, Ash." Jo's voice was soft as she stepped into him. Her hands skimmed down over his shoulders before stopping to loosen the tie at his neck. He could feel the heat of her through his clothes. "Carly needed someone familiar, someone she could trust. You were the best choice."

Asher caught Jo's hands in his own as she dropped them from his chest. She shook her head, just once, but she didn't step away. He'd apologized a thousand times for what he'd done, for becoming a jealous lunatic after they lost the baby. Jo dealt with the loss differently. She dove into her job, working longer hours, trying for a promotion to head caseworker. If it hadn't been for his interference, she probably would have gotten it.

Instead, he'd waited for her one night in the parking lot of the Department for Child and Family Services. He'd planned a romantic dinner at their favorite restaurant. But she'd called to cancel. Told him she had to work late. So when she exited the building, laughing, matching some strange man's gait stride for stride, he'd lost control.

Asher remembered getting out of his car, slamming the driver's side door and heading toward Jo and her friend. He remembered throwing the first punch. But he had no memory of beating the man so badly he could barely see. Jo's panicked voice had been what pulled him out of it that night, just like Carly's had at Aaron's.

Jo left him immediately, moving out of the home they were supposed to raise a family and grow old in. Now he was left with a hulk of a house that felt emptier each day and a mortgage he could barely afford. He'd considered getting a dog, but he didn't deserve the unconditional love.

Somehow, Jo managed to talk her coworker out of filing charges. To this day Asher believed there could have been something going on between them, but he never saw them together afterward. Even when he ran into Jo around town—at the store or the movie theatre—she was always alone.

"Carly is a good kid. She deserves better." Asher used the words to buffer the memories creeping into his brain. He'd only come unhinged like that one time before. His own father had been the focus of his fury that night. The man who drugged and forced himself on Emily, the girl Asher had treated to dinner earlier that same evening.

Asher braced against the memory of Emily's eyes on his as he watched her climb out of his dad's truck. Seven years ago felt like yesterday. He could still feel the buzz of anger that had coursed through his system. Hear the voice of the officer that interrogated him. See the crime scene photograph of Emily's body, pale and broken, less than thirty yards from his dad's rig, Asher's phone number still scrawled in Sharpie across her palm.

"Carly deserves someone who cares about her, believes in her. That's you, Asher." Jo's voice brought him back to the present, sent a ribbon of calm though him. "I never should have accused you. I'm sorry."

Asher shook his head, running his thumbs over the silky skin across the back of Jo's hands. That was one piece of the puzzle Jo was wrong about, though. He wasn't above blame. When he'd seen Aaron Carver's hands around Carly's neck, white hot rage flashed through his brain. There was no care, no empathy—just pure, unadulterated, rage. Every ounce of hatred he'd had for his father had come rushing back. And that kind of anger was dangerous.

"CARLY WAS VERY COOPERATIVE." Detective Moreno's shadow preceded his arrival. Jo and Asher turned toward the open entry door. "But I still think she's holding back."

The knot inside Asher's gut tightened.

"Deputies picked up Carver about thirty minutes ago. He admitted to the assault." Moreno shrugged. "Wise decision considering the amount of drugs we found in his car."

Moreno sighed and lowered into a waiting room chair.

"Carly needs to understand that we aren't the enemy. I don't think this attack was out of character for Carver. But right now, last night is all I have. The more information I can get about the history of this situation, the better off it is for everybody."

Moreno narrowed his stare at Asher. "She trusts you. What she tells you might be our only way in. Do you understand where I'm going with this, Mr. Thompson?"

Asher nodded, but Moreno was already speaking again, his eyes boring into Asher. "Carver's worked over pretty good. There's a chance he'll file charges." Moreno was silent for a beat, the heat of his scrutiny forced Asher to step back. "But bruises don't lie. If Carly's story has even a hint of truth, I wouldn't worry about it. You did what anyone would have done under the same circumstances."

Asher crossed his arms, pulling away from Moreno's coal black stare. He accepted the comment for the acquittal it was, ignoring the creeping tendrils of guilt that always followed his episodes of blind rage.

"D.A. will be filing charges first thing in the morning. We've got enough to hold him on the drug charges and attempted rape of a minor." Moreno let the statement hang in the air. "Maybe getting Carver off the street will help convince Carly that we're on her side."

Asher thought he detected a hint of emotion in Moreno's final words. Just like Asher, the detective was hiding ghosts of his own under a gruff, bad cop, exterior. Even so, Asher doubted he'd be able to coerce Carly into talking. In her mind, there was too much at stake.

"She's worried about her sister," Asher said. He could've added, "That's why she won't talk." But he didn't. Let Moreno interpret it his own way.

Moreno met Asher's stare. "We're doing everything we can," he said.

Asher nodded and shook hands with the detective, watching him retreat down the hall. Asher and Jo were halfway back to Carly's room before he realized she was holding his hand, fingers laced through his in familiar comfort.

FOURTEEN

CARLY

My best friend's body heated an oval of mattress next to me later that evening, both of us tucked under the cloud-like duvet in Mr. Thompson's guest bedroom. I studied the ceiling while words poured from chapped lips, filling Phoebe in on the events of the last twenty-four hours. Well, some of them anyway. I'd never intended to involve Phoebe, but Caroline had been missing for almost forty-eight hours. I knew what I had to do, and I needed help to get it done.

Phoebe's brows clenched together. Her eyes darkened, signaling suspicion.

"What is this?" she asked as I reached into the nightstand, handing over a spiral-bound notebook stuffed with loose-leaf charcoal drawings.

"Just some sketches. The cops were fascinated with the ones I had on me when they pulled me from school. They'll be back with more questions and I can't handle them going through everything, you know?" I tested my skills of persuasion. "Moreno won't let this go. He'll be back for more. I thought you could put these with the others. They're safer with you."

Phoebe took the notebook, fingering the rough-edged pages that stuck out at odd angles. "Why not tell the cops everything? It's their job to help, Carly. But they need all the facts. They need to know what Caroline was into."

Sweet, good, innocent, Phoebe. Stuffing away some incriminating drawings was one thing. Acting as my built-in cover when I was late for school or corroborating a lie when even the makeup wouldn't cover the bruises was par for our relationship. And until tonight I'd managed to keep the reasons behind it all a secret, shield her from the life I led after dark.

"As long as Caroline's still out there, I can't give up on her. He'll kill her. Maybe she's already dead, but until I know for sure, I can't tell them the rest. And you can't either."

We sat huddled on the bed, Phoebe's blue eyes scoured mine, waiting. I had to give her something.

"I knew Dad was dead, Phoebe." The silence in the room thickened, pressing in on my ears. "Before school, I saw him. He just lay there, eyes open. He looked right at me, through me."

"Jesus, Car."

Phoebe's whisper clotted in my throat and I had to force the rest of the confession. "I didn't do anything. Didn't call an ambulance, the cops, nothing. I just left him there. Turned my back and walked away. What do you think the cops will make of that?"

Phoebe shifted closer to me on the bed. She reached for me, brushing a tear from my cheek before sandwiching my right hand between her palms. She pulled her hands toward her face in prayer position. Her breath skimmed the tips of my fingers.

"He never rescued you, Car. All those days you came to school with bruises. They'll think he got what he deserved."

A choked sob escaped the tightness in my chest as she pulled my hand closer to her lips. Phoebe had beautiful hands. Long, pale digits with manicured nails, usually painted some shade of sunny pastel. Today's choice was a happy coral hue. My hand looked out of place between hers. Knobby knuckles, a product of too much cracking and popping if my mom had been right, topped off by well-chewed cuticles. It was a less-than-ladylike look, but in the circles I ran in, no one seemed to care.

Phoebe's crystalline eyes found mine and I forced myself to hold her gaze, prove my honesty.

"I get you're afraid to tell them about Caroline. But you could have told me, Car." Phoebe's eyes pooled with hurt. "You said she was trying to clean herself up, to get you out of that house, but you said yourself, she was a user. Addicts relapse. That fight with your dad could have been the tipping point."

I picked at the corner of the duvet. "She would never abandon me." A bead of defiance dripped from my voice. I sucked in a breath and blew it out, shutting down the instinctive reaction.

"I didn't mean it like that. And I know by keeping quiet you think you're doing the right thing, keeping Caroline safe. But what about you? Maybe it's time to ask for help."

I stayed silent, quelling the urge to scream, "I am asking for help. I'm asking you." Truth seeped through my veins, urging me to let it out. Phoebe had always had that effect on me, since the day she approached me in the girls' bathroom at Millbrook.

I'd told Phoebe about Aaron. But there was no need for her to know that Caroline's story—drugs, prostitution—was just as much my own, minus the addiction. Even I wasn't sure how I'd escaped that particular addendum to the unwritten contract Reed Sutherland had drawn up with his buddies to keep business running smoothly.

"You have to tell the cops about what she was doing at the lot. If you're right and she's out there, it's the only way to find her."

I sighed through the disappointment. I didn't expect Phoebe to understand, but I hoped she'd try. The image of Caroline climbing into the cab of her last trick and never returning surged into memory. I squinted my eyes to chase it away.

Phoebe studied our hands, still sandwiched together, and arced her thumb along the edge of my own, sending an uncomfortable tingle up my spine.

"We're friends, Carly—best friends. Why didn't you tell me what Caroline was doing before now?" She looked at me. "My dad could have—"

I clenched my jaw against the words about to exit her cherry red lips. I sat up straight in the bed, pulling my hand from hers and shoving at the pillows behind me, inching myself higher against the headboard.

"That. The words you're getting ready to say, that's why I never told you. The last thing I needed was for my best friend to go running to her daddy." The words sliced at my tongue as I spit them out. Phoebe couldn't control that her dad was a prosecutor for the district attorney's office any more than I could control the fact that mine had been a drunken loser. But Phoebe only stared—blue eyes widened, but unscathed. Proof that having a dad with clout didn't exempt her from being as calloused as me. Phoebe just hid it better under her father's veil of money.

"I'll help you, Carly. You know I will." She picked up the sketchbook from its position on the mattress, flipping through a few pages. She paused on a drawing I'd made several months back, not long after we'd met. It was a close-up of Phoebe, sitting against a tree at the back of her dad's property.

I could almost feel the wash of the warm breeze on my skin. It had been one of the few times I'd actually felt like the teenager my birth certificate proved I was. A bottle of wine stolen from her dad's fridge had helped loosen me up. But I'd captured Phoebe's open-mouthed laugh perfectly.

A slight smile tugged at my best friend's lips as she scanned the drawing, eyes drifting over the image of herself. But she brushed it away as quickly as that summer breeze had faded. She snapped the notebook shut and shoved it deep into her backpack, hazarding a glance toward the bedroom door, cracked ever so slightly. Music from downstairs drifted our way–Mr. Thompson's attempt at giving us privacy, I assumed.

"Promise me one thing, Carly."

My chest tightened. I didn't do well with promises. Chances were she'd ask for something I was incapable of giving.

"Keep yourself out of it. Let the cops do their job."

My jaw clenched, sending a shooting pain into my temple. Phoebe didn't understand. I was crazy to think she ever would. But keeping the drawings was enough. I could take care of the rest on my own. Besides, I had a better chance of finding my own sister than the Brookside Police Department did, with or without my admission. Reed and Eli seemed to have some sixth sense when it came to cops. I'd seen it in action. The last thing I needed was Caroline caught in the crossfire.

"Promise?" Phoebe urged.

I couldn't look at her now. Those pale blonde curls, the eyes that saw only black and white, never any shades of gray.

She reached forward, tucking a lock of hair behind my ear. Her fingers trailed along my jaw, lingering a moment too long. "I know this is hard for you. But we can't have any more secrets between us, Carly." Her voice was a whisper. Leaning in, she pressed her lips lightly against my own.

Heat surged into my cheeks. Instinct forced me back, increasing the space between us. Her eyes were glossy, face flushed.

"We all have secrets, Carly. Some of us just hide it better than others."

This revelation complicated matters. But I understood where it came from. The need to be close to someone who understood–saw you for who you really are–was a powerful drug. Even if it only lasted a moment.

I'd felt it with Mr. Thompson–almost. There was something to be said for the warmth of skin beneath your fingers, the pressure of a kiss, the taste of desire.

Phoebe leaned forward again, her lips soft and warm against mine, her breath sweet. A ribbon of warmth unspooled in my gut with the memory of Mr. Thompson's menthol-laced breath on my lips. I'd grown accustomed to the stale aftertaste of the truckers–the bitterness of old coffee and unfiltered cigarettes–and I'd been shocked by the refreshing mintiness of a man who rarely lit up. I closed my eyes and relinquished myself to Phoebe's kiss. If there was one thing I knew how to do, it was fake it. This was an act I could follow.

By the time we separated and my eyes met hers, I could tell she bought the flush in my cheeks as reciprocation. If that's what I had to do to get her to keep my secrets, then so be it. I'd done worse.

She smiled, lifted herself from the side of the bed and gathered the duvet higher around my waist, like a mother tucking in a sick child.

"Take care of yourself, Car. Get some rest. I'll call you tomorrow."

I returned her smile, watching as she slung her backpack over one shoulder and then the other. Phoebe reminded me of Caroline in all the ways that mattered. Soft. Pretty. Happy. She could have any guy she wanted—now I knew why none of them ever stood a chance.

She switched off the overhead light and pulled the bedroom door closed. I shimmied under the warmth of the comforter, a smile still pulling on the corners of my lips.

"Car?" Phoebe cracked the door open, shoving her head inside. "You scared the shit out of me today, you know?"

I nodded, shrouded by the darkness of the room. "I know."

"Don't ever do that to me again."

"Never." I promised, chewing the inside of my lip while she hung, silent, in the doorway. I stayed still. Not until my lungs started burning did I realize I was holding my breath. I closed my eyes, made a conscious effort to stay quiet as I pulled a thread of air in and pushed it out.

I focused on the ceiling in Mr. Thompson's guest room, nothing but smooth, unmarked plaster, grayed by the moonlight that cut a ribbon over the foot of the bed. When Aaron visited my room at the trailer park, I'd count the stains on the ceiling. Over and over again, thirteen small, dark circles of filth.

My lungs would scorch from the instinctual clench of air—waiting for the inevitable rattle of the door handle. Now, in the silence of Mr. Thompson's house, I waited for a reprieve—a reprieve from Phoebe's expectations, her demands. The skin along my scalp prickled. I closed my eyes against the crescendo of panic launching a slow but steady march through my chest.

The solid *click* of the bedroom door came just in time. Phoebe's trotting footsteps descending the stairs, murmurs of Mr. Thompson's voice as he walked her out—firm reminders of where I was. No flimsy locks. No hollow-core doors. No monsters waiting for me on the other side.

FIFTEEN

ASHER

The knocking started before 8:00 a.m. Asher pulled himself from sleep. Snagging a pair of jeans from the chair next to his bed, he slid into them and headed for the stairs. A glance at Carly's closed bedroom door sloughed the remaining fuzziness away. He trotted downstairs to the entryway and yanked open the door.

"It's early." Asher mumbled, checking his watch and clearing his throat. Moreno stood like a brick wall on the other side of the threshold. "Carly's still asleep."

"My apologies for the early hour," Moreno said, without sincerity.

Asher could feel the detective's gaze latch on him, sliding over the reddened scuff and purpling bruise shining like a beacon from Asher's cheekbone. *Shit.* Asher turned, veiling the injury as best he could in the darkened entryway.

"I wondered how you got away without Carver leaving more of a mark. Good makeup job yesterday."

Asher gave up the façade. He scrubbed a hand down the

back of his neck, rubbing at the coils of tension that twisted inside.

"There've been some developments. Wanted to catch you before Carly woke up. I know how teenagers like their sleep. Got one of my own at home." Moreno chuckled. "May I?"

Asher hated the idea of talking about Carly behind her back. The thought of her coming downstairs, finding them locked in conversation, made his stomach turn. A knot of warning squeezed in his gut as he swung the door open wide, stepping aside to let Detective Moreno through.

Asher glanced up the landing toward Carly's door. Still closed tight. He followed Moreno down the hall, stopping in the laundry room to snatch a clean t-shirt off a pile of clothes that hadn't yet made its way upstairs. He shrugged into the cotton, taking one more breath before joining Moreno in the kitchen. All he could do now was hope Carly was a deep sleeper. Somehow, he doubted it.

"Can I offer you some coffee?"

Moreno accepted, and Asher busied himself with the coffee maker. Whatever the detective had to say would require full caffeination, he was sure.

"Mr. Thompson? May I call you Asher?"

Asher nodded, squaring up with the detective over the breakfast bar. He thrummed his fingers against the granite countertop. "I assume this isn't a social visit, Detective. So, what is it you unearthed?" It took energy he didn't yet have to keep the bitterness from his voice. Spawned by long line of experiences with officers over the course of his own life. They all had motives. Moreno had put up a good act last night, but he was no different.

The detective shifted on his seat. The stool groaned in protest under his weight.

"What can you tell me about Carly's artwork?" Asher's brow furrowed before he could stop the reaction.

"Not a lot. She's good. Has never had any formal training. I don't know much about art, but she's probably one of the most talented kids I've ever met."

Moreno lifted an eyebrow, nodding. "Can't say I disagree there. She's got our sketch artist beat, that's for sure."

Moreno pulled an envelope from the inside pocket of his jacket. "We were called to the Anderson house late last night. Seems Mr. Anderson found a sketchbook of Carly's among some of his daughter's things." He paused, watching. The heat of his stare dragging over Asher's face.

"Phoebe Anderson is Carly's best friend." Asher worked to make the comment sound benign. "They spend a lot of time together. It's not odd for her to have some of Carly's things." That was good for Carly. Made her sound like less of a loner.

"We know Carly drew when she was with you in after school detention. Even found some sketches in her biology notebook when we picked her up from Millbrook. Thought maybe you could shed some light on this one in particular."

Moreno unfolded a copy of one of Carly's charcoal drawings. He smoothed it on the counter between them. "Seen this before?"

Moreno's stare spiked a rush of adrenaline through Asher's core. The rush morphed into a full-blown tsunami as he pulled the edge of the paper closer. In shades of gray, a girl stood, legs shoulder width apart, arms hanging down at her sides. She looked into a darkened room. Barely visible, in the background, the image of a man sprawled low on a broken down couch, what looked like a trickle of blood trailing from his arm.

Asher's heart raced, thumping an erratic rhythm as his eyes found the syringe. Dangling, almost as a limp afterthought, from the girl's right hand. He forced a breath, focused on controlling the percussive beat in his chest, all while Moreno watched.

Asher cleared his throat, coughing lightly into his fisted hand. The knot that seemed to have taken up permanent residence in his throat since Carly came to his home tightened around his vocal cords. He scanned the full image one more time. Checking to be sure his eyes hadn't betrayed him. But he knew what he saw, and he knew it was exactly what the detective had seen, too.

"What do you see?"

"A girl." Asher stalled, pushing the photocopy across the counter and scrubbing a hand through the hair on the back of his head.

"Anyone you recognize?" Asher heard the accusation in Moreno's voice, but there was no way he'd be the one to point fingers. Not about this. Not when the drawing could be nothing more than the wishful thinking of a lonely, abused teenager. He dragged his eyes once more along the lines of graphite. Dark hair hung limp across thin shoulders. A too big sweatshirt draped over a slight frame, drooping well past her waist. The detail was too perfect. Jesus, even the frayed hem was there on the page for all to see.

"I'm going to need to talk to Carly about this." Moreno was matter-of-fact.

"You think she did it. You think Carly killed her father." It wasn't a question. Asher knew the answer. Moreno had a confession in his hands.

The detective's heavy brows scrunched together as he tucked the drawing back into the pocket inside his blazer. "This is all I have, Asher. An abusive father holing his family up with a creep like Carver would be motive for just about any young girl. Unless I get more information out of Carly, what else am I supposed to believe?"

A creak from the stairway sent a spike of worry down Asher's spine. A protective instinct he didn't know he possessed kicked in, erupting from his gut and spilling over into his chest. The dangling syringe imprinted like a scar on his subconscious. Carly needed a lawyer. And not some pimple-faced court appointed attorney fresh out of law school.

The adrenaline coursing through his veins amplified Carly's footsteps on the stairs. He leaned across the countertop, jaw clenched. "You should believe the truth, Detective. She's the victim here."

"I'd like to believe that," Moreno answered, pulling away from Asher as Carly slipped into the kitchen from the hall.

"Believe what?" Her voice, young, innocent, her whole life ahead of her. Just the sound of it cooled the heat that coursed through Asher's veins. He'd be damned if he'd send her in to talk to Moreno alone. For once in his life, he was in control. As her guardian, this was his call. But how would it look? In the court of public opinion, Carly was a victim—the girl who'd lost it all. The girl whose sister was missing. But once she lawyered up, the public would become judge and jury. They'd turn on her like a rabid dog.

"I'd like to believe we'll find your sister, Carly." Kudos to Moreno for reading the situation. The clench in Asher's jaw relaxed.

Carly turned an empty coffee mug in circles between her palms. She searched them both—watched them.

"Is there news?" The words were tentative, landing like a soft pillow. Asher motioned for Moreno to follow him toward the door.

"None yet, I'm sorry."

Asher stared at the detective. For once, he believed Moreno truly was. The men walked in silence through the hall and into the foyer.

"I understand your need to protect her, Asher. Believe me, I do. My instinct tells me this girl's been through more circles of hell than most of us can count, and somehow she's come out the other side. But abuse twists the mind and we don't know what she's capable of." Moreno stood there for a moment. Giving Asher time to absorb his words. "I'll give you a couple days while we process the rest of the drawings. Talk to her. Let me know what you find out. We *are* on the same side here, but I can't sit on this much longer." His eyes burned into Asher's.

"Understood." Asher nodded, opening the door. The chill of early spring air lifted the hairs on his arms. "I'll be in touch, Detective. In the meantime, Caroline Dalton is missing. Find Carly's sister."

SIXTEEN

CARLY

"He knows something, doesn't he?" I asked as soon as Mr. Thompson was far enough up the hallway to hear me.

Asher paused, but didn't answer. Instead he walked toward the coffee maker, filling the empty cup that still sat on the counter. I watched from the barstool, staring into the caramel colored liquid in my own cup. A razor's edge of fear sliced into my chest, possible scenarios flashing through my mind. I clenched my jaw against the onslaught of images. *Had they found Caroline? Was she dead? Did they know who did it?*

"Whatever it is, I can take it." Even as the words slipped out, I was unsure of their truthfulness.

"Carly."

I knew that tone of voice. It was the same tone the hospice nurse had used to tell me my mother was dead. I choked on my next sip of coffee, the knot in my throat too thick to avoid.

"You okay?" Mr. Thompson asked, moving to the edge of the breakfast bar.

I nodded, recovering. I flattened my palm and angled it in

the air toward him, just in case the idea of patting me on the back like a small child crossed his mind.

"Is it Caroline?" I managed to choke out.

Asher shook his head, taking another sip of the inky black liquid in his mug. "No. Still no word about your sister." His eyes found mine, penetrating me. I forced myself to hold his gaze. There was more. "Moreno has some of your drawings."

"I know." I shrugged. "They took my stuff when they hauled me out of your class the other day."

I ignored the tickle of panic that started low in my gut, igniting a slow rolling boil of my insides.

Asher pulled the stool next to me out from under the bar, settled onto it with his knees facing me, his coffee mug nestled between his palms. He took a deep breath. "They have *other* drawings, Carly."

Asher let the silence stretch, allowed it to do the talking for him. The churn in my gut clawed at my insides, working its way into my chest. The hair on my arms lifted, and the ants along my scalp returned. I pulled in a measured breath, an attempt to control the rising attack. *How could Moreno have them? They were safe, with Phoebe.*

"Did they show you?" It was a whisper. All I could manage under the circumstances. My voice was small and uncertain, and it polluted the air between us, weak and worried. I hated myself for it. *Get control of yourself, Carly. You are better than this.* The anxiety attacks hadn't started until after Caroline moved out, leaving me alone in Aaron's trailer, forced to confront the life we'd earned without her. With my sister, I'd been strong. Without her, defenseless.

I hazarded a look at Asher. His lips were set in a hard line, the vibrant blue eyes I'd used as a distraction on so many occasions now clouded with a hint of pity. The anxiety in my stomach shifted, morphing into hot spikes of anger.

"Don't look at me like that."

"Like what?" Asher's brows scrunched together in confusion.

"Like I'm some kind of pity case." I shoved back from the bar. The stool behind me toppled before the coiled muscles in my arm launched my half-empty mug across my teacher's spotless kitchen. The mug shattered against the corner of the upper cabinets, raining debris to the floor. Those drawings were mine, the one thing I could control. No one had a right to them. Anger erupted from within, spewing volcanic ash on anyone that got too close.

"Carly, stop." Asher reached for my arms, but I jerked away.

"Don't touch me," I screamed. I grabbed whatever I could– frames, vases, lamps. I hurled loose items through the air, toward walls, onto ceramic tile, hardwood floor, anything that would provide the satisfying crash of destruction that my soul so desperately needed.

Rage flashed. Misdirected bits of hatred for things beyond my control–at Asher for looking at me like an abused animal, at Phoebe for not doing the one thing I'd asked of her even after I'd given her a piece of myself, at my father for looking the other way, at my mother for leaving me when I needed her most, at Caroline for landing in a heap beside a stranger's rig, for fucking herself up enough to turn one last trick, and maybe worst of all, for turning me into a prostitute.

My chest heaved with exertion by the time I'd gone through the list. The heat of tears stung my cheeks as a decorative clay bowl crashed against the stone fireplace, shards of it dribbling in chunks to the hearth below.

The room fell quiet. The only sound, sniffs of uncontrollable tears. I sucked in a lungful of air as reality returned. I skimmed the mess I'd made in my teacher's once immaculate kitchen and living room. Lamps shattered. Magazines scattered. Glass broken. Frames bent, photographs askew. The ceramic bits of a coffee mug showered over the tile of the kitchen floor.

"I'm so sorry," I managed before the sobs came. Hot, snot-filled hiccups that wracked my whole body. My knees gave way and I cowered on the floor, head in my hands. The pain of just one emotion tore at my insides–guilt.

SEVENTEEN

ASHER

"I'm so sorry." The words tumbled out of Carly between sobs, over and over again like a skipping CD.

Asher stood, rooted in his position by the bar. The storm had passed, but the damage still needed to be assessed. He stepped toward the hunched figure on the floor, dark hair draped her face like a curtain. He swallowed against the memory that invaded his mind.

"It's okay," he whispered. He managed to avoid the shards of glass, but hard chunks of ceramic bit into the bottoms of his bare feet as he crouched next to Carly.

"Why are you doing this?" Her voice, wet and thick with tears, pulled at him. He reached to tuck a strand of hair behind her ear. Why couldn't he have done this seven years ago? His chest clenched against the guilt that accompanied lost opportunity.

"I'm just trying to help, Carly." He had to say her name. It was the only way to distance himself from the past creeping up on him.

"I don't deserve your help." The words sliced, severed the

part of him that had somehow managed to move on, the part that edged his life toward normalcy. There'd never been a normal in his life. He knew that now. If only he'd known it then.

"I'm not doing any of this to help *you*." He wasn't sure where those words came from. But they struck the silence of the room like lightning, injecting the space between them with an honesty he'd hidden even from himself.

Her breath hitched. Her legs folded under and she shook her hair back with a twist of her head, the storm in her eyes finding his.

"I'm not perfect, Carly. No one is."

"Then why?"

"You remind me of someone I used to know. Someone I cared about. Someone I should have helped when I had the chance."

"I'm not your charity case." Hate seeped back into Carly's voice, daggers dulled by curiosity.

"Then maybe I can be yours." Asher let the words hang. He focused on Carly's eyes, fighting for a foothold with a girl that he never should have let into his life, let alone into his home. But she hadn't run away yet, and neither would he.

"This *someone*," she stretched the word out, gave it weight. "Is that why you lost your shit at Aaron's?"

Asher sighed and readjusted to a more comfortable position on the floor. "My shrink would probably say so."

He noticed the slight tip of the corner of her lip.

"Who was she?"

Asher picked at remnants of Carly's destruction, pushing the debris into a neat pile with the tip of his index finger. "Her name was Emily."

"Just Emily?" Carly prompted for more.

"My dad was a long-haul trucker. I spent most of my

summers on the road with him. Emily waited tables at one of the truck stops along my dad's route. So, yeah, just Emily." Asher could see her name tag like it was yesterday, her name typed in crooked, upper-case letters, adhered to a slim black panel of plastic by a slice of white tape.

The clouds in Carly's eyes shifted.

"I was seventeen—my last summer before college—when I finally got the nerve to ask her out. I ordered some awful platter from the diner just to have an excuse to talk to her. I should have noticed the signs, her looking over her shoulder the whole time we talked. Checking to make sure no one was watching as I scribbled my number on her wrist. But none of that raised an alarm, not until after..."

Asher paused. Memories flooded back, choking him with a fresh knot of guilt.

"After what?" Carly asked.

Asher shook his head. "Nope. Your turn. I give you a little, you give me a little, fair enough?"

It took Carly so long to answer that Asher was afraid she'd say no. Turn him away and tell him to go to hell. It certainly wouldn't have been out of character for a girl in her position. But he'd watched Carly long enough to see through the rough exterior.

He'd paid attention in class, watched her draw. She was an observer, a listener. And other people's stories provided her sustenance. Asher figured everything she saw and heard earned a place in her store of thoughts. How else would she be able to cope with the abuse and neglect she'd been through? His own personal experience had taught him that becoming someone else was the best solution, the only way to leave your past behind. But, by God, it required research. And right now, he had a story she could use.

Carly finally nodded in agreement. "What is it you want to know?"

"Moreno showed me a drawing of a girl." Carly's expression remained blank. "She was holding a syringe. There was a man lying on a couch in the background."

Carly swallowed—the first sign of recognition.

"The girl in the drawing ... is it you?"

"What happens if I say no?"

"Then I believe you. We move on."

"And if I say yes?"

Asher paused. He didn't have an answer for that. Would he report her to Moreno? Turn her in? Let her face the repercussions of desperate actions amidst all the other horrors? He knew he wouldn't—couldn't—hand her over to the system.

"Then we figure out what to do about that ... together."

EIGHTEEN

CARLY

I couldn't remember ever being looked at the way Mr. Thompson–*Asher,* I corrected–was looking at me now, his blue eyes wide, honest. His jaw set in perfect confidence that whatever the problem was, we could fix it–together. I resisted the urge to scoot closer to him, to feel the warmth of him, prove to myself that he was really still there. I busied my hands in my hair instead, working it into a messy bun before admitting, "It's just a drawing."

Asher's entire body relaxed. He didn't even try to hide the audible sigh of relief.

"I knew it would look bad if the cops found it. That's why I gave it to Phoebe. So much for the bond of friendship, huh?"

"I'm sure she has a good explanation, Carly." Asher reached for an escaped chunk of hair that slipped down the side of my face.

I closed my eyes. Heat rose into my cheeks as his fingertips brushed my skin, tucking the strands behind my ear.

"Don't blame her until you know the whole story."

My eyelids snapped open. "You know why she did it, don't

you? What did Moreno tell you?" I shot the questions at him rapid-fire, locking in on his gaze.

"I know you feel betrayed, Carly, but I swear to you, Moreno didn't tell me any more than what I've already told you." His eyes shone a clear honesty I wasn't used to. The sudden burn of tears singed the skin under my eyes. I jammed my fists against my eye sockets, fighting the onslaught of emotion.

"It's not like I never thought about it, though."

A crease worked its way between his brows, a moment of confusion washed away by sad understanding.

"Killing him," I added for clarity. I cleared my throat and readjusted my position on the floor, extending my legs and pushing myself backward so I could lean up against the couch. Asher's mouth hung open a bit, paused in mid-search for the right words. I didn't give him a chance. He didn't want to hear the truth, anyway. No one did. "Your turn now. What happened to Emily?" I brushed the pebbles of ceramic from my jeans, alleviating the pressure on the divots in my knees, wishing I could slough off the shards of betrayal as easily.

Asher's face changed, like storm clouds rolling in, churning up the atmosphere. In that moment he shifted, folding his arms across his chest. The open willingness of a stoic supporter transformed into the solid brick wall of painful defeat. "You're not the only one with a father who'd have been better off dead."

The ache of guilt tightened in my chest, but I couldn't keep the words from slipping out. "Did your dad hurt her?"

Asher shrugged his shoulders and shook his head once, as if shaking off the cape of truth wrapped around him. "She got tangled up with the wrong people. Was probably a runaway. I never did find out for sure."

There was a long pause. The tick of the mantle clock fired in the silence. Mr. Thompson sighed and leaned against the sofa. The closeness of his body warmed me from the inside and I couldn't help but wonder what it would've been like to be the object of his affection.

"I knew something was wrong when I went out to meet her later that night–after the diner. She never showed. Some guys I'd seen hanging around the lot jumped me from behind. Beat me up pretty good, stole my cash. But I recognized one of them, knew it wasn't a random robbery. I managed to make it back to my dad's truck before she was gone."

A sliver of panic threaded through my lungs. I licked my lips and swallowed the growing knot. He did understand. I slid my hand toward Asher's, laced my pinkie around his, the cool of the floor seeping into my palm. He looked down, but didn't pull away.

"I heard them first. I knew the sound–was used to the struggle. My dad liked it that way. Paid extra, in fact. The rougher the better. He never cared if they got hurt."

"He raped her?" The words drifted with a shiver down my spine.

Asher lifted his shoulders again, like the movement was easier than words. I understood that. He pulled my hand toward his lips. His jaw ticked and he changed his mind, sandwiching my hand between his, eyes focused on my fingers. "Not sure you could call it rape. Dad always paid in either drugs or money, sometimes both. But she saw me watching when she climbed out of his cab."

A flash of memory sliced through my skull, morphing into a collective everyman. Rough hands, rancid breath, the drooping cloth ceiling of a semi built before I was born swaying with his motion. The rhythmic pressure of him, the grunts of a stranger's pleasure. Buried moments in time bubbled to the surface. Anger slid in alongside sadness, obscuring the memory of pain.

"Emily ran. I should have followed. Instead, I went after my dad."

"Like you went after Carver?"

Asher nodded, holding my gaze, seeing me. "They found Emily the next morning, in the woods beyond the truck stop parking lot. She'd slit her wrists, bled out in the brush. My number was still scrawled across the inside of her arm. Didn't take the police long to find me."

"Why are you telling me this?" I jerked my hand away from Asher, reality coming too close. "What does any of this have to do with me?"

Asher turned his eyes on me, clouds gone, clarity restored. "You asked me why I was doing this, why I was helping you. I'm trying to help you understand." He shook his head. "You remind me of her in so many ways, Carly. The way you have of pushing people away, closing yourself off from the rest of the world. I may not know the details of what's happened to you, but I do know that dark look in your eyes."

Asher cradled my face in his hand, brushed away the rogue tear with the pad of his thumb. I wanted to scream at him. Yell for him to go away. But the nugget of need inside me overcame the urge.

"There were moments when I saw the real Emily. I know I did. But it was rare. Just like it is with you. I didn't understand it then. But I do, now. What she was going through, her reason for ending it, had nothing to do with me. But I should've done more to stop it. I knew what was going on in that cab and I let it happen. I was too much of a coward to face my own father. Instead, I waited for her to come slinking out with shame plastered all over her face. I fucking stood back and watched—no, worse—I *judged* her. And she knew it. I won't make that mistake again."

What if it's too late for me, too? I wanted to say the words, put them out into the open, but I couldn't do it. They felt jumbled in my throat like a stopper clogging a drain. I shook through the clench in my chest. "Well, I'm fine. Really. I'm no whore, Mr. Thompson." I watched as the effects of my word choice reverberated through my teacher. His jaw ticked, muscles rigid.

"Neither was Emily."

A flutter started low in my belly. I wondered what it would be like to have a man who defended me like that, who refused to let my name be tarnished. I brushed my fingers along Asher's arm. "I'm sorry. I didn't mean ..."

"She was a victim, Carly." His voice was tight. "They took advantage of her–used her."

"But she agreed to do it."

Asher swiveled toward me. His eyes blazed into mine–hurt, fear, and something else I couldn't quite put my finger on.

"Doesn't that make her just as guilty?" I asked.

"She didn't have anyone to trust, no one to protect her, to help her say no." A pause thickened the air. Asher's voice got quiet, barely a whisper. "Carly, Aaron wasn't the only one, was he?"

I shook my head and looked away, trying not to let the truth shine through. "I'm just a girl with a sad story. Nothing more."

"You're so much more."

The flutter in my belly took over, launching into a frenzy that sent a wave of heat through me. The dead part of me sprang to life. Asher was the only man I'd ever been attracted to. Everyone else was a transaction. *Was this what it was supposed to feel like?* I suddenly understood the addiction–the insatiable need to be in someone else's arms.

I leaned forward. Hot puffs of breath mingled in the air between us. If he didn't feel the connection, he was damned good at faking it. "I want to be more..." I whispered, "... to you."

"Carly ..." His hands gripped my biceps, pushing me away. "We can't ... I can't ... I'm ..."

He didn't need to finish. I saw what I needed to see in the rapid rise and fall of his chest–the emotion in his eyes. Need. Redemption.

"I know." I traced the collar of his shirt with my index finger. "It's against the rules, but don't you ever think about it?"

"Jesus, Carly." Asher rose from the floor in one swift movement, brushing the debris from his jeans. "I don't know what you think this is, and I will do whatever I can to help you, but I'm your *teacher*." His stare burned into me as if that word meant something.

I almost told him then that he wouldn't be the first member of his profession that had neglected the rules in favor of carnal desire. As if on cue, a bead of doubt dripped through my chest. But maybe that situation had been more about power and less about attraction. He'd never looked at me the way Asher did. The thought infused me with the confidence I needed to finish what I started.

"This is about Miss Harrison, isn't it?" I looked back at Asher as he crouched to pick up a smashed frame from the floor near the fireplace. He rearranged the pieces of glass on top of a photograph, one of him and Jo.

"I'm sorry if I gave you the wrong impression, Carly. If you want to think of me as a friend, that's fine. But that's as far as it can go. Do you understand?"

I nodded, pinching my bottom lip between my teeth, the sudden urge to tell Asher everything threatened to spill free. But that wasn't part of the plan. I knew how he'd react if I tried to kiss him, and as much as it hurt to be rejected, if throwing myself at my teacher was what I had to do to get the house to myself, then so be it.

NINETEEN

ASHER

Asher knocked on Jo Harrison's door that night with more force than he intended. When she answered a moment later, the words spilled out. "You've got to find a new placement, Jo. I don't know how much longer I can keep her at my place."

Jo's expression exploded with worry. "Is she okay? Where is she?"

"She's at the house. Asleep. Safe," Asher said, forcing calm into his voice. "The problem is me." He extended his hand toward Jo, holding the cracked frame, complete with a photo from their gender reveal party.

"What is this?" Jo hesitated, eyes searching, lifting the frame from Asher's outstretched hand.

"I thought you might want it. Carly had a moment this morning. This was one of the casualties."

Jo met his gaze and Asher felt the air shift between them, heavy with shared sorrow, unyielding remorse for words left unspoken, a life unlived.

"Come in, Ash." Jo stepped away from the door, gesturing for him to follow. "Tell me what happened."

The apartment was smaller than he expected. The bare walls gave the space a minimalist appearance that bordered on unlived in. But the scent he remembered–honey and jasmine–surrounded him, warming him from the inside. A pang of guilt jabbed into his gut as he trailed Jo into the kitchen.

"Moreno showed up this morning," Asher started. "Thinks Carly could be involved in her dad's death. One of her drawings is pretty incriminating."

Jo nodded, understanding. Either Moreno had already shared this with Jo, or she was putting on a good show. She picked up an already poured glass of wine from the kitchen island and pulled a beer from the fridge, offering it to Asher. He took it from her, the cold of the bottle icy against the heat of his hand.

"And what do you think?"

"She claims the drawing is just that. I want to believe her."

"But you're not sure," Jo said what he'd been too chicken shit to admit out loud.

"After Moreno left, she had a melt down. I can't even tell you what triggered it." Asher shook his head and ran a hand over the back of his neck. "Me asking too many questions, I guess."

He went on to explain the aftermath, shards of glass and broken artifacts from his life with Jo sprinkled across his kitchen and living room floor. He didn't blame Carly. He was well aware that he was the problem. He was the adult. Whatever she felt for him was his responsibility. And somehow, she'd read his weakness.

He already regretted spilling Emily's story to Carly. He should have been establishing boundaries in the wake of her outburst, not breaking them.

"How'd you get her to calm down?"

"I didn't try to stop her. Sometimes it helps to be able to let it out."

Jo led him into the living room. If the morning had been bad, the afternoon had been worse. He and Carly had cleaned the mess together, the burn of her gaze following him wherever he went. Sometimes, when he'd catch her looking at him out the corner of his eye, he could swear it was Emily staring back.

A familiar warmth, almost forgotten since the breakup with Jo, started in his fingertips and spread into his chest. Dr. Morrison had warned him about doling out pieces of his life without ever allowing anyone to see the full picture. But the words got stuck.

"You know her, Ash. You're with her every day. What do you think is going on with her?" Jo lowered to the living room sofa, tugging Asher down next to her.

"I think she's confused. Scared. She's desperate to connect with someone and only knows one way to do it."

Jo sucked in a wobbly breath. Understanding dawned across her face before she fixed her gaze on the wine glass in front of her. "She made a pass at you?"

"Nothing happened, Jo," Asher shifted closer. Read the uncertainty in Jo's expression.

"Does she know you're here?" Jo's index finger absently rounded the rim of her wine glass.

"No. She was asleep upstairs when I left. I think the meds they prescribed at the hospital knocked her out."

"Maybe I should turn the case over. Maybe I'm part of the problem."

"You're not the problem." Asher reached to brush Jo's hair over her shoulder to reveal her face. He let his hand linger. "She's got more to deal with than dead parents and a terrible home life."

"How do you know?" Jo pulled back from his touch. "If she has a crush on you, I can't be helping."

Asher watched as the woman he loved tried to make sense of the world around her. "What happened with Carver at the trailer park wasn't a one-time thing. She's been abused, Jo. Sexually."

"Did she tell you that?" Jo stood and stepped away, eyes wide.

"Not in so many words." Asher shook his head, focusing on the bottle hanging from his fingertips rather than the woman he'd tried to make a life with. "She didn't need to."

Jo paced a few steps. "I suspected. From the very beginning. But there was no proof, Ash, nothing. You know how this job works. My hands were tied."

Asher studied Jo. Her forehead scrunched. She was trying not to let the guilt take control. "I told her about Emily."

"What the hell, Asher? What were you thinking?" Jo's expression morphed from pained to livid in the space of a microsecond.

"She needed to hear it. She needed to know why I agreed to help her. That she's not alone. I couldn't lie to her, Jo. She's been lied to enough."

Jo's glare subsided.

"Right now she thinks the world is out to get her. I needed to prove to her that it's not. That *I'm* not."

Jo sighed, returning to the couch. She reached for her wine and sipped, replacing the glass on the table before speaking again. "This isn't just about Emily is it? It's about your father, too."

Needles of hard truth flirted with Asher's lips, but he held back. "Abuse like that messes with your head, Jo."

Jo put both hands on either side of Asher's face, pulling his gaze up to meet hers. "I'm sorry," she whispered.

Asher shook his head. She had nothing to apologize for.

"I'm sorry I never asked more questions. Never gave you a chance to explain. My entire career is built on second chances. It's what I do. I find resources to help people evict whatever demons lurk inside." Jo paused. "But I never helped you fight yours."

"This isn't about me," Asher said. A bubble of regret expanded in his chest. The memory of the night he found Jo on the floor of the master bath, her tears mixing with a smeared puddle of blood that pooled beneath her. What he wouldn't do to go back to that night. Hold her closer as the doctors confirmed what they already knew. Change how he'd reacted when she'd pulled away, thrown herself into her job. If he'd had it to do over he never would have let the jealousy seep in.

Jo leaned closer, watching Asher's response as her lips met his. Asher melted into the warm familiarity. The kernel of need in his gut broke open as he reciprocated, losing himself in the way her lips fit his, the airy moan that escaped her mouth between kisses. God, he'd missed her.

Jo pulled away slowly, skimming the scuff on his cheek with her index finger as she released him. She reached for another swig of wine, leaving Asher to wonder how much she'd had before he arrived.

"It's always been about you, Ash. I was selfish. I could have found somebody else to take Carly, but I knew that for her, you'd say yes. I chose you," she whispered.

Asher cupped the side of Jo's face as he traced the curve of her bottom lip. "Why?" he whispered. "Is this is some kind of test to see if I've changed? If so, I'm failing miserably."

Jo swung her head slowly from side to side. Tears glistened from the corners of her eyes when she looked up at him. "I missed you, Ash. But I didn't realize how Carly's situation would affect you."

The nugget of hope Asher had carried since the night Jo walked out solidified in his chest.

"I never meant to hurt you."

"You never hurt me, Jo. I could've said no. But Carly's alone. She deserves a chance to break free."

"Do you think she can? Break free? Or do you think she'll end up like Emily?" Jo picked at the edge of the cushion between them.

Asher tilted her chin and looked Jo in the eyes, losing another piece of himself in the pools of green that stared back at him. He could lean in, kiss her again. The tilt of her chin and slack in her mouth willed him closer, stoked the fire of need in his gut. But that wasn't why he'd come. He dropped his hand.

"Emily was desperate, Jo. Desperate people do desperate things. Carly's sister is missing. Her father is dead. Moreno has incriminating sketches. And Aaron Carver's bound to exact revenge at some point. Carly is nothing right now if not desperate."

"What can we do?"

Asher shrugged. "I don't know, but asking for a new placement doesn't mean I'm walking away, Jo. I'm in this until we find out who's responsible for hurting Carly. But if I want to make it out the other side, I have to pull back."

"I know. I understand." Jo's expression told him that she did. "I'll do whatever I can to find her a safe place, Ash."

Asher nodded and stood, grabbing his jacket off the back of a chair as he passed through the kitchen. "I should get back."

"Carly is my responsibility, Asher," Jo said, following him to the door.

Asher turned, gaze locking on Jo's eyes. Eyes that once held hope for a future, now laced with guilt and pain. "She's ours. It'll take both of us to get her out of this, Jo."

"It was my job to keep her safe. I missed the signs. I'm the one who failed her."

Asher started to speak, but Jo's finger against his lips stopped him.

"Don't let her under your skin, Ash. Don't let her undo everything you've worked so hard for." Jo tipped up onto her toes, her wine-sweetened lips pressed against his, heating him as she pulled him close, soft curves molding against him.

Asher's body responded and he leaned into the contact. His hands found her face, urging her closer, thumbs skimming her delicate jawline. He needed this. The warmth of her body against his enveloped him, chasing away the demons that lurked in the shadows.

TWENTY

CARLY

I heard Asher push open the door to my bedroom. Made sure my breathing was even, my eyes closed in the moonlight that stretched across the white duvet. I waited until he'd been gone ten minutes to sling the covers back and get to work.

The cul-de-sac where Asher lived backed up to the state park. A little research and a healthy dose of satellite imagery was all it took to figure out the best way to get to the truck stop where I'd last seen my sister.

It wasn't hard to coerce Asher out of the house. He'd been on edge since my outburst, looking for a way to put space between us. I'd watched the way he gathered the broken pictures of Miss Harrison, as if a part of himself had been smashed into shards right along with those photographs. And if I had to guess where he was now, it would be with her.

I shook the hot threat of rejection from creeping up the back of my throat. I'd never been with a man who hadn't paid for the pleasure and I couldn't help but wonder how it changed the experience. I shrugged through the what-ifs and stuffed the phone I'd bought for the occasion into my backpack

Moreno's discovery of that drawing gave me a deadline. Asher was protecting me for now, but he wouldn't stay on my side forever, especially if I kept stirring up the memory of ghosts he'd rather forget. I wondered how deep the similarities ran. Emily was abused and broken, that part was clear. Maybe that's all the resemblance Asher needed.

As for Phoebe, I'd given up trying to figure out why she'd betrayed me. It didn't matter now. Moreno had my drawings, and he would come after answers. I needed to be prepared when he did.

A TWENTY-MINUTE SLOG through the damp under-growth of the wooded park emptied me out exactly where I hoped it would—about thirty feet from where Eli's van had been parked less than a week ago. Thirty feet from where my life changed forever.

The truck stop marquee flickered as I crept toward the commercial lot. The T was dark. The R beside it blinked at regular intervals, changing ruck-n-Go to uck-n-Go every second or two. My mind replaced the R with a letter of its own. Seemed appropriate.

The chain link fence along the edge of the lot had been cut years ago, probably by some trucker who needed to take a piss and didn't feel like walking all the way to the main building on the other side of the expanse of asphalt. I squeezed through, blocking out the clawing fingers of memory.

I hid in the shadows along the fence and slid out of my backpack, pulling Caroline's old stilettos from the bag and filling the void with my own ratty Converse. I'd already down-loaded and sent a message through the same CB app Eli used. And by the time I checked my phone at the edge of the lot, it had blown up. Four missed messages, all wanting commercial company. But only one was from the man I was after—Snake-Master103.

I texted him back.

50-70-90, SNAKEMASTER103. INTERESTED?

I held my breath. My fingers trembled as I punched the send button. My chest clenched and I forced a breath. The last thing I needed was a mental breakdown at the side of a truck stop parking lot.

ALWAYS, the response came.

I typed the expected question. WHAT COLOR IS YOUR HOUSE?

The lingo came easily. I'd watched Eli do it often enough, usually when he thought I was passed out or high. I was pretty good at faking both. But I'd seen the texts, heard strangers' voices pose the same question over the CB radios in some of the trucks I visited. I hit send and slid the phone into the front pocket of my bag. I already knew what truck I was looking for. The app pinged a reply as I re-zipped, tucking the backpack under a shrub on the other side of the fence. I'd need to be able to grab it quickly on my way out.

One scan of the lot and I saw it. The same truck I'd seen Wednesday night. My breath hitched in my chest as the memory of that night flooded back. My sister's fight with my father. Dad's insistence I was his. Caroline's promise, *"One last time."* Eli's words as he tried to talk Caroline into staying. Caroline's refusal. Memories blurred with my own tricks followed by the walk back to a sisterless van.

Now that I was here—in this place—I could open the gate, let the worst of it through. My sister's body heaped on the ground outside the International. Her legs collapsed at odd angles under the weight of her body. Her blonde hair splayed out over the blacktop, halogen light playing along the length of it as it obscured her face.

That's all I saw before Eli pulled me in, closing the door of the van and starting the engine. I could almost feel the phantom grip of his fingers on my shoulder as he held me down on the floor. Could still hear him curse under his breath as the one person he was never supposed to call appeared beside us. His shadow a swagger as it passed through the amber glare of the Econoline's aged headlamps.

The shadow spoke to the driver of the rig. Kneeled near my sister. Stabbed something into her before the two men lifted her into the cab of the truck. I think I screamed. But I don't remember.

"You didn't see anything, Carly," Eli's voice rang in my ears. *"Caroline was never here. You understand me?"* The van rocked over uneven pavement as we left the lot. Eli's eyes focused on mine through the rear-view mirror. *"You saw nothing."*

I shook the onslaught of memory away. *Focus,* I told myself, my breath puffing a cloud of vapor in the chilly night. I worked my way along the outskirts of the lot toward the line of trucks, wondering if Emily's handlers had played a role in her suicide. Had they chased her into the woods after Asher walked away? Taunted her? Teased her? Watched her bleed out, just like Eli watched Caroline? Just as I'd watched her?

Asher was right. We had more in common than most teachers had with their students. It was easier to think of Emily as I headed toward the semi-lit section of parking lot. I'd known girls like her. Girls who died alone, thinking no one cared. If only she'd known the impact she'd made on Asher. Maybe she would've tried harder, fought to break free, like Caroline had fought with my father.

An involuntary sob clawed its way out of my throat, forcing me to double over mid-stride. *Breathe,* I coached myself, refusing to be drawn into the sinkhole of despair that plagued every moment since Caroline landed in a heap on the ground next to a growling International. *There's nothing you could have done for her then,* I reminded myself. But I was here now—and I wouldn't leave without figuring out what happened to my sister—or die trying.

TWENTY-ONE
ASHER

It was almost midnight by the time Asher finally made it home. Carly'd left a note for him on the table. He picked it up, studied the scrawl he knew too well.

Mr. T~

I'm sorry about tonight. Realized I have some apologies to make, so I've gone to Phoebe's for the night. I'll be back tomorrow morning. Don't worry.

~C

A pang of guilt stabbed into his gut. This was supposed to be the place Carly could feel safe, wanted. And somehow he'd managed to push her away. He ran a hand through his hair. At least Phoebe lived in a good neighborhood, away from Aaron and any retaliation he might inflict. The memory of Carly on the floor in that trailer thickened like smoke around him. Her eyes as she pulled him off of Aaron–scared and unsure.

Jo was right, subjecting Carly to behavior like that would cause more harm than good. But what should he have done? Called the cops? Waited for them to arrive? Watched as Aaron finished what he started? He'd been that guy once, and he'd be damned if he became that person again.

Asher shook the thoughts away, shrugging out of the fog that sent pinpricks of rage into his core. He focused on the groceries he'd picked up on his way to Jo's, tucking away one item after the next in the kitchen before moving into the living room and pulling out five newly purchased frames from the final Walmart bag.

He fingered the images scavenged from Carly's outburst, snapshots that now lay limp and forgotten on the mantle where they'd once been framed. Asher peeled the plastic from the whitewash frames and replaced the picture of the happy model couple with one of the engagement photos he'd had taken with Jo. Both of them smiling, unaware of what would happen in the coming months to tear them apart.

He moved down the line, one photo to the next, ending with the last photo he'd taken of her. He wasn't even sure if Jo knew he'd taken this one. She was out back, on the deck, eyes closed, waning summer sunlight filtering through the trees, giving her an ethereal appearance as she swayed to the beat of music Asher could now only hear in his mind. He'd framed this one after the breakup. And it was undoubtedly his favorite.

He thumbed the edge of the frame, allowing his mind to replay the kiss he'd shared with Jo just hours before. He wanted to enjoy it. To take it for the olive branch he hoped it was, but truth remained, and he had doubts. Jo didn't know who he was, not truly. She knew he was broken, but he'd never shared the most horrific parts of his past with her. A past that would surely scare her, lead her to believe she'd made the right decision by leaving him eighteen months ago.

Jo was looking for a partner—a husband, a father to future babies. And Asher wasn't sure he could live up to the expectations. Maybe those fears were what made him snap in the parking lot a year and a half ago. Or maybe he was just born this way–destined to be a monster in his own right. After all, if his own father was any indication, Asher was most definitely not decent fatherhood material.

Asher stepped back to study the photographs. Happy moments, the darkness inside him hidden by the love of a woman he didn't deserve. Images from a life that tonight had felt just within reach.

TWENTY-TWO

CARLY

I checked my surroundings, glanced toward Eli's usual parking spot–empty. Unusual for a Saturday night, but considering the heat Aaron had been under from the cops, it didn't surprise me. His father's arrest wouldn't keep Eli away forever, though. Reed would never allow that to happen.

Reed had other girls, other lots, but the money here was too good. More than likely they were holed up at Reed's, planning their next trip out. The thought curled my fingers into a fist until my own fingernails dug into my palm. I opened my hand and sucked in a deep breath, tamping down the fire of anger inside my gut.

I unbuttoned two more buttons on my blouse, the black lace of my bra peeking out through the gap. Skirting the well-lit, video monitored sections of the lot in favor of the darker edges, I headed toward my target.

"Hey, sugar, what you doin' here?" I jumped away from the voice, my hand instinctively covering my semi-exposed chest. I hadn't even seen the woman approach.

In the shadows I couldn't make out her face, but the

whites of her eyes glistened at me when she slithered from her post along the fence, reaching thin fingers toward my shoulder.

"This ain't no place for a young girl," she said through gritted teeth as I jerked away.

"I won't be here long," I said, my voice stronger than I expected it to be. "Just a regular on the schedule tonight, then the lot's all yours." I'd never had to worry about turf wars when Eli brought us, but I'd borne witness to some of the brawls that erupted between the regular lot lizards.

She snuffed at me, the drag of a coke addict snorting their last line. Her, "Make it quick, sugar," disintegrated into the shadows as I hurried toward the last stranger who'd seen my sister alive. Caroline's old heels slipped on my damp feet, the pavement sucking at them, trying to slow me down, warning me not to go.

When I reached the semi, I slowed. My heart pounded in my chest. *Why are you doing this?* spun through my brain. The truck was exactly as I remembered—an old sun-faded International—square, missing the fluid edges of the newer models. I ran my hand down the driver's side door. The paint was dry, rough, leaving a film of dust on my fingertips. My breath sucked from my lungs. Caroline's fingertips trailed down the same door. The thought of her standing there, waiting for the driver to invite her in, cocking her head in that seductive way she had.

I'd never figured that part out. I was too chicken-shit to seduce the drivers that invited me in. It was a business transaction, after all. Nothing more. I could never pull off the act that lured in the regulars—earned higher tips—pretending it meant more than it did. But Caroline had always been the best actress around.

I clicked my stubby nails across the thin semi door. For as

hulking as they were, I always wondered why they didn't have more substantial doors. It popped open right away.

"Thought you'd never get here, darlin'." He had dark hair and a sinewy build. His eyes were the eyes of the sleep deprived and drugged. Sunken back into his face, they appeared almost black in the darkness. He wore a stained white t-shirt, the fading logo of some bar I'd never heard of emblazoned on his chest. He reached a hand out to help me into the cab.

I stood rooted to the blacktop. Asher's face swam in my mind, his disappointment if he knew where I was. *I can't do this*, I thought. But then Caroline's words, the same ones whispered to me the first night I'd come to the lot filtered through my brain. *"You can do this, Carly. Don't think about the guy or what's happening, just remember your why. It's for us, Carly. This is our way out. The only way."*

I smiled at the man inside the truck. This one was for Caroline, no one else. I reached for his hand. It was sweaty, and I almost lost my grip as I pushed myself from the ground up the steps and into the cab. He grabbed my hips and held me in front of him, pinning me between his body and the steering wheel. He removed his left hand long enough to pull the door closed.

My skirt rode up my thighs, helped by his fingers as they skimmed my leg from mid-thigh to waist. I squirmed out of his grip and into the passenger seat.

"Ain't you a cute little thing," he said, leaning toward me. "How old are you, darlin'?"

"How old do you want me to be?" I replied. It was a canned answer to a question I was used to being asked.

The trucker grinned.

I scanned the interior as I took care of business. There was no sign of a struggle, nothing broken, at least not that I could see in the darkness of the cab. But it had been a few days.

"50, 70, 90," I repeated the text I'd sent earlier. "What kind of company are you lookin' for tonight, sugar?" I affected the southern slur, complete with cutesy nickname, that seemed to be the going dialect for the girls in this business. My sister had trained me well.

"What'll you do for a hundred dollar bill?" he asked, pulling a crisp bill from the back pocket of his jeans. I snatched it from him and tucked it in the waistband of my skirt. I'd been hoping for the lesser of three evils.

"*It never takes longer than fifteen minutes.*" Caroline's words again filtered through my memory. "*Think about the possibilities, Carly. Once we pay off Dad's debts, we'll make $100 every fifteen minutes. There are lawyers who don't make that much.*"

The excitement in her eyes had been palpable. But I was different than Caroline. Didn't have the ingenuity she had. The money meant nothing to me. For me, it was always about her.

"*You two stick together,*" Mom had said to me in the hour before she went to sleep and never woke up. "*You're sister's a dreamer, Car. But dreams can only take you so far. You're my practical one. She's going to need you to keep her grounded. Promise me you'll stick together, no matter what.*"

I'd made that promise. So, I'd done it. Schooled by Reed, I followed my sister into the cab of my first john. And she was right. It never lasted long. The more I did it, the easier it became. All I had to do was remind myself of our reasons: food, rent, security, and once our Dad's debt was paid, a future. But no matter how often she reminded me, I knew the only reason I was really turning tricks was to keep us together.

Even now, as I readied myself to follow the driver into the sleeper, there was only one reason I was here. Tonight was about justice, about getting back what I'd lost. The world owed me that much. The world owed me my sister.

✄

"WHAT'S YOUR NAME?" the driver asked as he stroked the side of my face with the rough pad of his index finger.

"Caroline," I lied, squinting through the darkness, hoping for a reaction. He blinked. His black eyes gleamed as he unbuttoned my top, sliding it off my shoulders and into a satiny puddle on the floor. He stretched his arms toward me, ushering me into the sleeper cab.

The smell hit me first. A combination of body odor and stale fast food permeated the tiny space. He sat on a well-worn mattress, pushing me to the floor between his legs. He turned his ball cap around so the bill faced the back of his head and drug a finger over my lips.

"Why don't you give me a taste of what I paid for, Caroline?"

Maybe it was my imagination, but I thought he stretched my sister's name out, raking it between his crooked teeth as if remembering her. My heart thudded in my chest as I unbuckled his belt and unfastened the fly of his jeans.

"Hang on a second, darlin'." A shot of adrenaline pumped through me as he reached into a darkened corner, his hand disappearing in the shadows for a moment, reappearing with a small, black bag. He slid it close to where he sat. "Wanna make this a little more fun?"

I tilted back onto my heels, eyes glued to the toiletry bag at his side. I'd heard horror stories, girls being hurt, even killed, by rough sex gone awry. That was the benefit of having Reed and Eli on our side. There was no question what they were doing with the girls they handled was wrong, but they did look out for us. Helped keep us safe from the wackos. Eli had pulled Caroline and I out of cabs more than once when he sniffed out a weapon or got a tip from one of the other pimps about a certain john. And until a few days ago, he'd kept us safe. But tonight I was on my own, with only the memory of my sister and a drive for the truth to keep me out of trouble.

I held my breath as the driver rummaged inside the bag, finally coming out with a palm full of small white pills. He held one up. Ecstasy. Caroline had tried to get me to take it before. *"C'mon, Carly. It'll loosen you up,"* she'd said. *"Helps you forget all the bad and focus on the good."* I'd refused then, and I'd refuse now.

"I don't do drugs," I said.

"Just say no, huh?" He threw his head back and laughed. A deep throaty laugh that rumbled into my bones, vibrating through me like the engine of the semi-truck. "That's too bad." He buried his fist in my hair. Leaned in close. "The last Caroline I had enjoyed my little mood enhancers."

He jerked my head back and pain screamed along my scalp. My mouth opened on instinct. His fingers filled the space, pushing pills to the back of my throat. I gagged, but he closed my mouth, clamped a paw over my lips and held my head to keep me from spitting the pills on the ground. I squirmed for a moment, but as the pills dissolved, so did my urge to fight back.

"Why don't you tell me why you're really here, darlin'." All play had evaporated from his voice. Before I could answer, he lunged, pinning me against the floor of the sleeper compartment. I screamed, but his hand still pressed against my lips, muffling the sound. I pushed at him. My hands balled into fists against his chest.

"Shh..." he hissed as he pulled away. "You're on the clock,

remember? And I'm a paying customer. Besides, what would sweet Caroline say if she found out you chickened out?"

"Where is she?" I fought against the grip he kept on my hair. My heart surged, adrenaline pumping.

"Why don't we take care of business first," he said, pushing his pants down with his free hand. He jerked me from the floor and turned me around, bending me over the console. I didn't fight. If I let him finish, we'd be done. I'd refuse to leave if he didn't tell me what happened to Caroline. Suddenly my plan seemed riddled with holes.

His breath was hot against the back of my neck as he struggled with my skirt, rolling it up to my waist before jerking on my underwear. He cursed as they ripped, ending in a lacy wad at my feet. My pulse pounded a staccato rhythm in my ears.

"Think of someone you like." Caroline's words haunted me. *"Close your eyes and imagine being with someone else. Who would it be, Carly?"* I never told my sister there wasn't anyone, not for the first eight months or so, not until I met Asher.

From the night he pulled me off the floor of the Truck-n-Go bar, his was the face I pictured to dull the pain, to make the inexplicable horror fade into a sufferable ache. But for reasons I couldn't understand, I didn't want to picture him now.

I squeezed my eyes shut against the violation. But the driver's hands were hot and rough against my skin. His breath stale in its rhythmic rise and fall as he thrust into me. I needed escape and his face came unbidden. Bright blue eyes staring at me, framed by thick brown lashes. "Asher," I whispered, the sound of his name on my tongue ushered away reality in exchange for a trickle of warmth through my veins. Or maybe it was the pills. I couldn't focus.

By the time my last conversation with Asher crept into my memory, taunting me, the worst was almost over. I made some obligatory sounds of pleasure, which the trucker seemed to enjoy, growling low in his chest with one final thrust.

He flopped back against the mattress, his chest heaving. I turned to face him, adjusting my skirt to a more respectable length and scooping my discarded blouse off the floor of the cab. I felt him watching as I shoved my arms in the sleeves.

"You look like her." His words stopped me cold. "Coloring's different. You're dark where she's light, but I see the resemblance."

He was still breathing hard as our eyes met. The corner of his mouth turned up into a smirk.

"That's why you're here, ain't it? You looking for some kinda proof?"

"I saw you talking to Reed. Watched you load her back into your rig. I want to know what you did with her. Where is she now?"

His eyes flicked to the toiletry bag still open by his side. He picked something thin from the bag and dangled it in the air between us. I blinked twice, trying to process what I was seeing. Caroline's necklace. I snatched for it, but he pulled it away, shoving it back in the bag and zipping the closure. "Me and Caroline had a good time. So good, in fact, I thought I'd keep a little souvenir. But as for where she is now ... that, I'm afraid I can't say. We took a little ride, sure. But after she left this cab, I got no clue what happened to her. You should check with your boys. Maybe they know somethin'. But seems to me you might be fucking the wrong man."

I stared at him while he adjusted his ball cap. Panic fueled frustration forced air in and out of my lungs in rapid succession. "Did you hurt her?"

He poked a couple more fingers into the toiletry bag and came back with two more pills. He pulled me closer. "I can show you what we did if you really want to know."

He pushed the pills into my mouth and waited for me to swallow. I blinked at the grungy man in front of me. Pictured Caroline trapped with him, taken somewhere, and ... what? Dumped?

He guided me low and I slid toward him, running my hand from his knee to his crotch. I rubbed—pushing his jeans toward his ankles with my free hand and waited until his eyes closed. His head tipped back. His breath hitched. Anticipation.

"Come on, darlin'," he breathed. I hiked up my skirt and leaned over him, straddling his midsection and nibbled the lobe of his ear as I spread one hand out to the side of the mattress, feeling for the toiletry bag with Caroline's necklace inside.

I whispered a moan into his ear as my hand wrapped around the smooth pleather.

"That's it," he responded before I jerked away, snatching the bag off the mattress.

I hopped through the opening to the front seat and tucked the bag into the crook of my arm.

"Whore," he spat as his eyes flew open. I struggled only a second or two with the door as he yelled threats and curses from the sleeper. I heard the familiar rustle of denim as he fought his way back into jeans now wound tight around his ankles, holding him captive just long enough to breed rage.

TWENTY-THREE

ASHER

For the second time that weekend, Asher woke to incessant thumping on his front door. This time, though, he groaned and rolled over, flinging the pillow on top of his head to drown out the noise.

Sleep was just beginning to reach its fingers for him when he heard the voice. Young, pleading. "Mr. Thompson, please. I know it's late, but I need to talk to Carly."

Asher lifted the pillow. Carly was supposed to be with Phoebe. That's what the note read when he got back from Jo's. *Christ, how stupid had he been?* He slung back the covers and slid into a pair of jeans, pulling a t-shirt over his head as he padded, barefoot, down the stairs.

Phoebe was still pounding—with more force than he'd given her petite frame credit for—when he got to the door. Asher hesitated, combed a hand through his hair and checked the appropriateness of his jeans. He pulled himself up tall, eliciting the best Mr. Thompson persona he was capable of—he checked his watch—three o'clock in the morning.

A look of shock streaked across her pale face when Asher swung open the door, leaving her fist poised mid-thrust.

"What are you doing here, Phoebe? Where's Carly?" Asher's voice was rougher than he expected. Phoebe's eyes reacted, pupils dilating even under the bright glare of the porch light. He cleared the sleep from his throat and tried again, softer this time. "You're going to wake up the whole neighborhood. What happened?"

It sounded like something his grandfather might've said. He cringed against the thought but glanced at the surrounding houses just the same. A light in the foyer window in the house next door sent a spike of irritation through his chest. He pulled Phoebe inside and closed the door.

If there was one thing he didn't like about small town living, it was the fact that everyone felt the need to know everyone else's business. And that particular neighbor seemed to have nothing better to do than dig up dirt on every other poor soul in the cul-de-sac and spout her gossip to anyone who would listen. The last thing he needed was her watching as he drug an underage student into his home at three o'clock in the morning.

"What is it?" Asher asked again, closing the door against prying eyes.

"I've been trying to call Carly all night. She won't answer and now her phone goes straight to voicemail."

"She left me a note, said she was staying the night with you." Asher did his best to loosen the ribbon of panic that threaded through his chest and into his gut. "Are you telling me you haven't seen her all night?"

Phoebe shook her head slowly from side to side. "I wanted to apologize, tell her it wasn't my fault. My dad found her drawings, took them straight to that detective."

"Moreno?" Asher asked, he pinched his eyes, rubbing to clear the fuzz of sleep.

Phoebe nodded, her eyes glistening with a sheen of barely contained tears. "I swear, Mr. T, I didn't know anything about it until it was all over." A new wave of moisture leaked from Phoebe's big blue eyes, cutting rivers down already splotchy cheeks. "Please, I need to talk to her. She needs to know it wasn't my fault."

Asher ran a hand down his face, frustration biting on already frayed nerves. His eyes met Phoebe's. If he hadn't been late getting back from Jo's he could have stopped Carly from going out. But instead, he'd slunk upstairs without so much as a call to her cell, further proof he wasn't father material.

"I hid her pictures," Phoebe managed between hiccupped sobs. "But I heard Dad on the phone. They're going to come for her, Mr. Thompson. They'll arrest her. You have to do something." Panic overwhelmed Phoebe's voice, pitching it up an octave as she sunk onto the nearby step. She'd lost the battle with emotion.

Asher squatted on her level. "Calm down, Phoebe. It's okay. Moreno was already here. He's giving us some time to sort this out."

"She—" another hiccup, "—already knows? What did she say? Is she mad at me?" Phoebe was shrieking now. "She thinks I sold her out, doesn't she?" Phoebe started rocking on the step, swinging her head from side to side like a deranged druggie. "I didn't tell them anything else, I swear. Oh, my God. She'll never talk to me again, will she?"

The questions came rapid fire. One barely had time to land before the next came barreling toward him. Each one a distraction from the most pressing issue at hand. "She'll forgive you," Asher soothed. "But we have to find her first."

Phoebe nodded. Her eyes latched onto Asher's. "She's really not here?"

Asher shook his head in silent confirmation. Part of him wanted to run up the steps and push open the guest room door, make sure it was empty. But that would be a waste of time. "Do you have any idea where she might go?"

"No." Another clot of tears accosted the teenager in front of him, redirecting her to the less important but just as dramatic, "She hates me."

"I'm sure that's not true, Phoebe. You're her best friend. She needs you right now." Asher was impressed by his ability to access nuggets of advice that sounded like they'd come from Jo. The teenage drama he was accustomed to didn't reach this magnitude within the confines of the classroom.

At school, he was a pro at diffusing situations, using humor to talk kids down from what was, more often than not, some trivial matter that served only to interrupt class time. But this was different. Carly–the girl who should have been asleep in his guest bedroom, for which he was solely responsible–was missing. And he sure as hell wasn't going to tell Phoebe that she was right–she ranked right up there with him on Carly's current list of people who'd let her down. Reality began to sink in.

"Wait a minute. Other than the drawings, what else did she tell you?"

"What?" Phoebe swiped at her nose with the end of her coat sleeve.

"You said, 'I didn't tell them anything else.' What else is there to tell?"

Phoebe's eyes grew unnaturally wide. Guilt.

Asher leaned in, fighting the heat of anger that bubbled through his core. "This isn't the time for games, Phoebe. Tell me. What else do you know?"

TWENTY-FOUR

CARLY

I sprinted from the cab of the semi toward the tree line. I didn't bother to slam the door behind me. It would take him a good thirty seconds to fasten his pants. Caroline's too big stilettos slipped from my feet as I ran across the pocked pavement and I left them where they lay. I wouldn't need them again–ever.

Shouts cut through the night air, piercing the low hum of idling diesel engines. Gruff accusations launched at me like arrows toward a target. One voice became two, three, maybe four. "Thief. Bitch. Whore." I'd heard them all before.

I kept running, snatching my backpack as I ducked through the chain link fence. My lungs burned and the growl of engines dimmed to nothing more than a buzz in the distance.

I imagined a mob of angry, overweight, or under-muscled truckers giving up their search for a girl who'd snatched a handful of pills and a dime bag of heroin from her john in the midst of a trick. I certainly wasn't the first. I wouldn't be the last.

I squatted along the path that ran the perimeter of the truck stop's parking lot and deeper into the forested state park. Packed with chattering stroller pushing moms and families of bikers during the day, it was deserted and silent this time of night. An owl hooted from a nearby tree, questioning, *Whoo? Whoo?*

I unzipped the man's black toiletry case. Using a stick, I pushed through the contents—needles, small white bags of powder, a scorched spoon, the white pills he'd shoved down my throat. I stopped when I saw it. The opal and diamond pendant winked up at me from the bottom of the grimy bag. The chain was broken, but there was no doubt in my mind. It was the same pendant my sister had worn every day since our mother's death. *Until her own*, the words filtered into my mind uninvited. I gritted my teeth. She wasn't dead. She couldn't be. She couldn't leave me here alone.

I reached in and pulled the opal from its hiding place, pinching the stone between my fingers. My chest ached, the pain of a heart breaking. The memory of my sister's body tumbling from the faded burgundy cab where I'd just spent the last half-hour reared in my mind. I could still feel the heat of his hands on me, his coaxing as I tugged his jeans to his ankles. The pressure of the sleeper cab carpet under my knees. *Had he killed her? Dumped her somewhere like Asher's Emily?*

My skin prickled with a chill that morphed into a wave of heat. My heart pounded. Panic. The surge of adrenaline quieted enough for my body to rebel against what I'd just done. My stomach churned as a wave of sickness rose in the back of my throat. I dropped the bag and lurched forward, expelling what was left of the Hot Pocket I'd microwaved just before leaving Asher's house into the weeds. *What had I done?*

"She went this way!" The voice rocketed into me from behind. The rustle of foliage echoed as footsteps closed in. I sucked in a breath, releasing it through tight lips as I fought a second wave of nausea. I punched my fists against my eye sockets, clearing a sudden surge of uncontrollable tears from my sight.

My legs trembled under my weight as I shoved the evidence into my backpack and slung it onto my shoulder. I had two choices. Forward, along the well-worn path, or down to the ravine below. I hesitated, pulse pounding and mind spinning. *What would Caroline do?* I couldn't stop the question from imprinting itself on my brain. I'd asked the same too many times before. Habit. But had those choices ever worked out for the best?

I ran forward a few steps, my bare feet slapping against the paved path. I didn't hear him. Only felt his hands gripping my bicep. I twisted free, hearing the rip of my blouse, feeling the icy bite of cold March air on exposed flesh. A second later he came at me from behind, shoving me forward so hard that I lost my balance, tumbling down the slight incline. Before I could rise, he was on top of me. His knee pressed into the center of my back.

"Got her." Hot breath sank onto the nape of my neck. He tangled a fist in my hair, pushing my head against the blacktop with enough force to make me wonder how much pressure it took to crush a human skull. "I think you got something don't rightly belong to you, sister."

He worked my backpack over my shoulder and slung it to the side before twisting my arms behind my back. Pinning them there with his other knee, he left me defenseless as two other men joined him, both panting loudly.

"Please, don't ..." I stopped myself. I didn't know whose voice that was. It couldn't have been mine. I didn't beg. Even the first time, when Caroline left me alone in the bedroom with Reed, I'd never begged. I refused to start now.

"What was that?" The hot breath came closer.

"Nothing," I said, my cheek pressed against the ground. I could hear the men rummaging through my bag before it hit the ground with a near-empty *thump*.

"We're good. I got it." A voice I recognized, the man from the burgundy truck, spoke.

In one swift movement, I was jerked from the damp coolness of the nighttime earth, back onto my feet. The second man shoved me forward, toward dark eyes and a hairy face, careful to keep hold of my hands as he did.

"I think you owe my friend here an apology."

"Go to hell," I managed through tight teeth. If they were going to hurt me, they'd have done it already.

The three men laughed. All of them. Their teeth shone like beacons in the shadows. Caroline's attacker took a step forward, stared at me.

"You want to know what happened to your sister? Ask the boys you work for." He leaned in. His breath hot against my ear. "But unless you got an Ouija board, you ain't never gonna talk to your sister again."

"She's all yours, Mac. I'm going back to the truck." Snakemaster103 backed away, tossing the words at the stranger holding my arms, rendering me defenseless.

My captor spun me toward a tree, scuffing my cheek against the bark before pinning me there. He pushed himself against me, already hard, and leaned in. He was still breathing hard and his breath stank of stale cigarettes and coffee, mixed with a hint of whisky. The combination hit my stomach, churning with the memory of what I'd done to get this far— what this man had planned for me. I lurched forward, losing what little there was left of my dinner all over his caiman cowboy boots.

The sting of his hand across my face came before I heard his curse, and I dropped to my knees, ignoring the searing pain in my shoulders as I fell. My arms twisted upward, still clutched in whisky breath's grip.

He shoved me to the ground and kicked once, landing a thrust worthy of a field kicker in my ribs. I groaned and pulled into a fetal position until the initial pain subsided. He continued a string of curses as he retreated back up the path, toward the lot, leaving me in silence.

Raindrops began to fall from the night sky. I heard the patter of them on the branches of the trees before I felt the cool pricks against my skin. The woods had gone quiet. For the first time since Caroline fell, limp and lifeless out of the burgundy International, I cried for her.

I crawled toward my discarded bookbag and slid it closer. My ribs stung in protest as I searched for the opal, although I already knew it was gone. I sniffed, the taste blood clogging the back of my throat. I coughed and pain radiated through my core, my ribs stabbing back in protest.

I swallowed against the ache, pulling my cell from the front pocket of the bag. A wave of relief that they'd left it muddied by reality. *Who was I supposed to call?* Phoebe? She'd sold me out, turned in the one piece of evidence I'd trusted her to keep. Who knows what else she divulged to Moreno. There were other drawings. Ones worse than the one Asher described. Ones that wouldn't just impact me.

I sat up and scrolled the near empty contact list of the burner phone. Asher? He wouldn't even look at me after what I'd done that morning. My fit had been effective. He'd barely made eye contact before leaving the house. No doubt he was cuddled up with Miss Harrison somewhere. I was the last thing on his mind.

My brain swirled. I couldn't remember Asher's number anyway. Everyone in my contact list was either dead to the world, dead to me, or wished I was dead. What difference did it make what happened to me now? Asher's story about the girl he called Emily seeped in as rain pelted from above. I imagined her laying out here, crying, desperate.

Voices echoed from the lot and jerked me out of the fantasy. The glow from the Truck-n-Go seemed to pulse, getting somehow closer. Whatever I decided, I couldn't stay here. I studied the rugged terrain that sloped toward the bottom of the gorge. A shelf of rock ran along the ravine about fifteen feet below the path I was on. I slid from the path, pushing myself in a seated position, down the embankment. Roots and rocks tore at my skirt and blouse. My legs grew slick with rain and mud. I gripped the trunk of a tree growing precariously out of the side of the cliff, my fingers clawing as I dangled my feet toward the safety of the ledge below.

Soft sprinkles turned into hard raindrops and multiplied against my skin. I stretched my arms, muscles burning, shortening the expanse of air between my feet and the ground below. My legs scratched against the rock wall, searching for a foothold. One foot scraped the edge of stone–slicing into my skin with knifelike precision. I sucked in a breath, blowing it out with the pain. I glanced down, the floor of the gorge spinning, a line of blood trailing from the freshly opened gash on my heel. I closed my eyes, mustering the courage to release my grip, and dropped to the shelf of rock below with a wet *thwap*.

I lay there a minute, waiting for the canopy of the woods to stop spinning, but it never did. Logic kicked in. If I could get to the bottom of the gorge, the main road was just a few hundred yards away. I could get myself home. Someone would pick me up. It wouldn't be the first time I'd had to find my way home alone.

I looked down at myself. Scratches mapped the skin on my legs. Blood gushed from the slit on my heel. The truckers had taken my sneakers from my backpack. My blouse was in shreds and my skirt was ripped, not to mention about six inches shorter than it needed to be. The people who'd pick *this* up were not the people I needed right now. I sucked in a lungful of cool night air, and turned to my side, stuffing down another wave of nausea.

I shuffled from the ledge and scooted down the incline, trying my best to ignore the throbbing in my heel and the Tilt-a-Whirl spin of the space around me. My phone weighed heavy in my hand. How I managed to hang onto it while I scaled the face of the gorge was a memory already lost. The rush of water below and the pitter-patter of droplets through trees echoed in my ears–louder with each breath.

I opened my fingers, staring at the phone in my hand. A swath of blood discolored the screen. I checked my hand to find another deep scratch at the base of my thumb. My fingers trembled against the smooth plastic case.

Dampness crept from the ground and into my bones as I sat on the bank of the creek. My mind lurched, my vision spinning out of focus. Memories–old and new–clouded together. Fuzziness dulled the edges of judgement as I tapped the phone's call button, stared at the keypad. Numbers blurred. I smeared blood from the screen with my thumb. Heard a shuffle to my right.

The shadow of a man pushed through the undergrowth toward me. Or maybe it was my imagination.

His form blurred at the edges and I leaned back, my head firm against a pillow of earth.

"You know you're not supposed to be out here alone, Carly." My name on his lips shot a spike of fear into me, and I blinked against the swirl of black, the heat of him as he leaned over me, took the phone from my hand. He said something else, but I couldn't hear, his words a jumble as forgotten memories played in my skull.

TWENTY-FIVE

ASHER

Asher wasn't quite so nice the second time he asked. "Damn it, Phoebe. If you know something that can help her–I don't care if she swore you to secrecy–you need to tell me."

"I can't, Mr. Thompson. Please. I just need to talk to her."

"You know I'm trying to do everything I can to help Carly, right?"

Asher waited until Phoebe nodded.

"Carly said she was going to your place tonight. Obviously, she never made it. Right now, that scares the shit out of me. So, if you know something ..."

Phoebe swallowed. Her blue eyes wide, probing. "I know why Caroline is missing. I know why Carly won't tell the cops."

Asher pulled back. He'd expected something about Carly's dad, not her sister. "Does Carly know where Caroline is? Is that where she went tonight?"

Phoebe shook her head. "She doesn't know where she is. But I think she intends to find out." Phoebe studied the floor beneath her feet. "I tried to convince her to tell the police about what Caroline was into. But she refused. She's worried if she tells, they'll hurt Caroline."

"Who? Who'll hurt her?"

Guilt radiated from Phoebe and slid along Asher's skin, pricking at him while he fought the pool of anger simmering in his gut.

"Aaron's son. His name's Eli. I met him a few times at Carly's, along with another older guy. Your age, maybe ... Reed, I think."

The name shot through Asher like hot lava. Coincidence. Nothing more. He stood, forced the panic from his brain, but his insides churned. Heat building.

"This Reed guy ... you know his last name?"

Phoebe shook her head. "Caroline and Eli had a thing going, at least, I thought they did." Phoebe shrugged, looking up at Asher through long eyelashes. Fear. "But Reed gave me the creeps. I only met him once, but the whole time I was at Carly's I could feel him watching me. Sizing me up."

I'll bet he was, Asher thought. Part of him wanted to run upstairs, fling Carly's door open and rifle through every scrap of paper, every memento he could find. Privacy be damned. The image of Emily climbing out of his father's cab slithered through his memory like a snake after prey. *This can't be happening. Not again.* Asher closed his eyes a moment, forced a deep breath. Fought to hear Dr. Morrison's advice over the pummeling images from a freshly sprung vault.

"And Caroline was involved with these guys? Worked for them? Carly told you that?" Asher mined for information he wasn't sure Phoebe possessed.

"For them, with them, whatever. I think it started out innocent enough. Looking back on it now, maybe it was the only way Caroline could get out of that house. Escape her reality, you know?" Phoebe wiped at a rogue tear. "But it all got screwed up somehow."

"Drugs?" Asher guessed.

Phoebe nodded, sniffing back a glob of snot. "Carly tried to hide it from me, but I knew."

"Carly was using?" Asher guessed. He detected the note of fear in his own voice. He wasn't sure if he wanted the truth. Emily's investigation came rushing back. The drugs in her system the night she died. His own father's admission to doping her up. He clenched his jaw, bracing for Phoebe's answer.

"No, not Carly. But Caroline was hooked. Heroin, I think. X, too. Carly never said for sure, but I could see it in some of her drawings. Caroline went from this golden beacon to a sunken gray ghost."

Asher sunk onto the step next to Phoebe. "How long have you known all of this?"

"I don't. It's just one puzzle piece after another. Gather enough of them and eventually they become a picture, you know?" Phoebe hesitated until the silence between them grew uncomfortable. "She told me about Caroline last night when she asked me to hold onto those drawings." Phoebe dropped her head into her hands. "I've known for a long time something in that house wasn't right. The way Aaron looked at her, like she was some kind of product to be sold. But when I went back through those drawings last night ... Mr. T, why didn't I do something? How could I be so blind?"

Full body sobs wracked Phoebe's frame. Asher wrapped his arm around her shoulder and pulled her closer. She wrapped her arms around him, clutching at the cotton of his t-shirt.

Asher let Phoebe be the first to pull away. She cleared her throat and shook her head, apologizing. "I need to show you this." She pulled her cell phone from the pocket of her jeans.

A few swipes later, Asher was staring down at a miniature

version of his worst nightmare. The very thing he hoped to save
Carly from had crept in and stolen what little she had left.
Asher's lungs were frozen in his chest. His heart hammered,
just as it had when he'd seen the photo of Emily's lifeless body.
Anger–he recognized it now–clouded his vision.

"Does Moreno have this?"

"No, this was from another time. I took a picture because I
thought it was amazing. I never dreamed it was real. I don't
know where the original is."

Asher fought the rage that roiled inside. He wanted to yell
at Phoebe, ask her why she hadn't told anyone about that drawing. How long had she had it? How long had Carly been
subject to what went on in darkened truck lots? There was no
question now. The Reed Carly and Caroline knew had to be
Reed Sutherland, the only man other than Asher's father that
deserved to die a slow and painful death.

"Are there more like this?" Asher asked.

Phoebe only nodded.

"Send them to me. All of them. Try Carly again on her cell,
I'll be back down in a minute."

Asher took the stairs two at a time, going to his own room to
snatch his phone off the nightstand before pushing open
Carly's door. The bed was made. Nothing left out on the
dresser. No scraps of paper to help him figure out where she
might be. He heard a series of beeps from the desk next to the
bed. He slid open the drawer, exposing Carly's ringing phone.
Texts and missed calls from Phoebe cluttered the screen.
"Phoebe?" Asher hollered toward the landing. "Does Carly
have two phones?"

His own phone buzzed in his other hand. Texts from
Phoebe. He was back to the top step when a number he didn't
recognize flashed across the screen.

"Hello?" Asher answered. The frightened voice on the other end of the line stopped him cold.

"I'm so sorry. I didn't know who ... please ..." Her voice was slurred, loose and unfocused. The words vibrated through him, gripping his heart in an inescapable vise. The image of her cowering somewhere cold and alone crept into his brain. Small. Hurt. Scared. A squeezing stab of panic sliced through his chest.

Asher didn't give her the chance to say more. His heart thundered against his sternum as he galloped down the stairs, pulled Phoebe up by her jacket and directed her outside to her car. He gave her a nod that said, *I'll get this figured out, give me some time.* Somehow Phoebe understood, climbing into her Audi and firing the engine.

Asher turned back to the phone at his ear, shrugging into his own jacket. "Tell me where you are, Carly. I'm on my way."

But the voice that answered no longer belonged to the girl who sat in his sixth period class.

TWENTY-SIX

CARLY

"Carly, look at me." Asher's voice.

I'd lost time. Wracked my brain for a memory that would stick. But each one was hard, hate-filled. Hurt. I squeezed my eyes closed. Felt his arms around me, lifting, warming my skin.

"You shouldn't have come." The words drifted together, light and airy. I opened my eyes, struggled to focus on what was happening around me. His eyes on mine, ushering me from the cold earth up the incline. He helped me into the warmth of his running Jeep.

"Just stay with me."

People always said that, but where else would I go? He slammed the door, leaving me alone in the dark for a moment before the driver's door opened. The interior light bit at my eyes, blinding me. The pain in my heel offered focus. I slid my gaze down my legs and onto my foot, blood leaked in a steady stream, pooling on the plastic floor liner beneath my feet.

Lights from infrequent oncoming traffic played against the gray interior of the car, bouncing from the upholstery onto

Asher's lightly tanned skin. The space spun. I closed my eyes again, ushering in a momentary reprieve from the weird strobe effect.

He reached behind him as he drove, pulled a towel from the top of the gym bag tucked behind the driver's seat. The action sparked a memory. He passed it to me.

"It's clean," he said, sliding a palm down his face, scratching at day-old stubble. I stared at the towel in my hands, my mind slowly working through what he wanted me to do with it.

"For your foot," he prompted, nodding toward the passenger floor. He hadn't looked at me since he picked me up. At least, I didn't remember it if he had. His eyes focused straight ahead, just like the beams of his Jeep's headlamps as we wound through back roads toward Brookside.

Blood leached into the white terry cloth as I held it to my foot. It would never come out. Even with bleach, he'd be left with a permanent reminder of me–a curious yellow stain in memory of this night. A surge of guilt lit inside my chest. How many lives would I have to ruin before I stopped? Everyone I touched ended up burned. Hot spikes of tears threatened the backs of my eyes. I swallowed them. Offered the only thing I had to give, "I'm sorry."

I felt him look at me. Heard him sigh. I knew what he was thinking. *How do I get myself into this shit? What the hell am I supposed to do with her now?* He was ready to get rid of me. Turn me over to the state. Why did he even come?

"You need stitches." I expected a lecture. Instead, I got this. "I'm taking you to the hosp–"

He didn't even finish before I yelled, "No!" The word echoed through the space between us, even the hum of tires on wet pavement proved no match for desperate teenage angst.

The interior swirled around me. My gut churned, threatening another eruption. I needed to get a grip.

Mr. Thompson glanced again at my foot. The towel was now almost completely crimson. He was right. I did need stitches. I closed my eyes. The car launched into a road worthy version of my own personal Tilt-a-Whirl. Hell, for all I knew, I might need a pint of blood.

I remained silent as the car rolled to a halt. We were nowhere near town. Of course, he was kicking me out. He had every right.

"Okay, Carly. Here's the deal. Give me one good reason why you were out here in the middle of the woods dressed like a prostitute and high as a kite or I will drive up to the nearest emergency department and dump you out on your ass."

I'd never heard him talk this way before. I swallowed the knot of fear that hung fresh and heavy in my throat. What choice did I have? I gripped the door handle, ready to pull.

He reached across me, pulling my hand away from the door.

"Look," his voice was softer this time–clouded with the hint of an emotion I couldn't quite place. Remorse? Guilt? "Phoebe came by tonight. She told me about Caroline. About Eli ... and Reed." He glanced in his rear-view mirror, lights from the truck stop would be pinpoints through the trees. "This is your chance to start over, Carly. Change the hand you've been dealt. Not for Caroline. Not for your mom or your dad. But for you."

He released my hand. Looked through the windshield. His jaw clenched and released. I noticed then how rumpled he was. His hair mussed, wearing jeans and a ratty Ohio State sweatshirt under his jacket. A white t-shirt peeked from the bottom of one side. If I hadn't been so doped up, it might have occurred to me that the man sitting in the driver's seat was the real Asher

Thompson, the one he hid under a costume of neatly pressed button downs and khakis.

"You've got too much potential, Carly. I don't want you to become one of them."

Any normal person would have asked, "One of who?" But I knew exactly who he was talking about, and by the dark expression and far-away look in his eyes, he did, too.

I don't remember answering him, but the car lurched forward, pulling away from the side of the road. My eyelids were heavy, but my body buzzed. Mile markers slid by the window, testing an already foggy brain. Memories of the night danced in my mind, flicking in and out of focus like the old television set Dad used to keep in our garage. One image fuzzed into another, none completely coherent. I squirmed against the friction of the cloth seat–my skin too sensitive–each position more unnerving than the last.

"Carly, we're here." Mr. Thompson's voice started soft and grew louder, permeating my consciousness until the words spiked through me like a jolt of electricity. *Where were we? Where had he taken me?* Panic surged in my chest as I opened my eyes.

He was already reaching in the passenger door. His hands on my arms, hot and smooth...gentle. A moan rumbled from my throat, the vibration pushing through clouds of fog. My eyes were open, but unfocused. The darkness beyond the car rolled, whirlpools flecked with standing lights. *A parking lot?*

"What happened?" Another voice now. A stranger. *Parking lots, strange men.* My brain grasped at the only frame of reference I knew. I pulled against the hands as they tugged me from the bucket seat. My heart pounded, thumping a rhythm that urged, *"Go. Get out. Run. Now."* But my legs were frozen, immobile. Every muscle burned when I tried to break free.

Cold air nipped at bare skin along my arms and legs, wrapping a cool cloth of consciousness around me. I shivered, nearly knocking the jacket that the stranger was draping around my shoulders out of his grip. He caught it just before it fell, blanketing my shoulders in blessed heat.

Arms came next. Two. One on each side of my waist, lifting, pushing, pulling me toward...*where?* Another surge of panic ignited my lungs—a hot volcano of fear. My own voice echoed, slurred and unintelligible. A grunt that could have been a, "No." A word too often outside of my vocabulary. One I should have uttered an hour, two hours ago ... *How long had it been?*

The fog dissipated for a moment as they steadied me on my feet. I jerked free, attempting to run, my bare feet slapping against rocky pavement.

"Jesus," I heard from behind—my body staggering forward. "Why didn't you tell me she was as high as a kite?"

A pain—no, worse than that—a knife twisted into the heel of my right foot, stabbing through my skin and into the muscle, radiating up my calf and into my thigh. I made it only a couple more wobbly steps before I fell. Hot tears stung my cheeks. My shoulders rocked with sobs beyond my control. I lay twisted in a knot on the ground. The cool of the pavement the only thing rooting me to reality.

Mr. Thompson's hands were on me again. Familiar. One on each shoulder.

"Carly, listen to me. You need help." He was looking at me now, into my eyes, forcing me to focus on him. As if he cared. "This is my brother, Ethan. He's a paramedic. Now, you can either come inside with us and let him help you, or I can drop you off at the ER. It's your choice. But you've got to stop fighting us, okay?"

"Something's wrong with me." I managed through the thickness in my throat. I gripped the lapels of Mr. Thompson's jacket, staring into his face, those blue eyes that bore into my soul. Our faces were so close. A vibration quivered in the pit of my stomach. The sudden desire to pull him close, cover his lips with mine, buzzed through me. The air hung in my chest as I leaned forward, just one more inch. He pulled back. Looked away. I remembered. That's right. Miss Harrison. He'd gone to her.

I closed my eyes. The pain in my foot pulsed. Damp coldness seeped into the flesh on my exposed legs. The second man kneeled. I squinted him into focus as the lights on the poles in the parking lot continued to dance, throb, around me.

"Sick," I whispered. Managing one word before the nausea won. I lurched forward. One of them held my hair. The other smoothed circles over my back and the borrowed jacket.

Getting from the ground in the parking lot and into Ethan's apartment was a blur. My limbs felt heavy and light at the same time. Every touch sent an electrical pulse straight to my brain that launched a panicked shudder in the pit of my stomach. I clenched my jaw, forcing myself to brace against it. Repeating, *Everything's okay. They just want to help,* on a loop through my mind. If this was what drugs made a person feel like, I couldn't see the appeal.

"Do you know what you took?" Ethan's voice was calm, caramel smoothing over the top of vanilla ice cream. I squinted against the pinpoint of light he shone in each eye, blinking as he moved on to the stethoscope wrapped around his neck.

"What?" I asked. The fingers of his question probed through the haze. Comprehension just beyond my reach.

"What drug?" he asked again. There was a softness, an understanding in his voice that I liked. He wasn't there to hurt me. I glanced at Mr. Thompson who stood a few feet away with his back pressed against a wall of kitchen cabinets.

"Get her some water," Ethan said. Jutting his chin toward the sink.

"Round." I remembered the feel of the pills on my tongue. I fought against the memory, taking the glass from Mr. Thompson with shaking hands. "Four of them. White."

I kept my gaze on the glass in front of me. The water rippled as my hands vibrated. I imagined Mr. Thompson turning away in disappointment. "I don't do drugs," I whispered, as if that mattered at this point. "He forced me."

I felt the tear slide down my cheek as I stared into the glass of trembling tap water.

"That part is pretty obvious." Ethan's voice was warm. "Ash, there are some sweats in the dresser in my room. Go get her some warm clothes."

The *click, whir* of the refrigerator was the only sound after Asher left the kitchen. I focused, without success, on making the water in the glass still as Ethan inspected the gash on my heel. I gave up, taking a gulp instead, closing my eyes as the cool ribbon of liquid sank through my chest.

"Carly," his voice melted into me. "Stay with me, okay?" Warmth from his hands seeped into my flesh. The glass I held slipped from my grasp, landing with a thud on the tile beneath my chair. My ears registered the roll of glass across the kitchen floor. My name came again. This time more urgent. I opened my eyes, a desperate attempt to regain focus. Ethan hovered over me, slipping his arms behind my back as the world around me faded.

TWENTY-SEVEN

ASHER

Asher sat in a tiny interrogation room at the Brookside Police Station with his head bowed. He scratched the back of his neck. The last time he'd been the target of an investigation was after Emily's body was discovered, complete with his phone number scrawled in Sharpie on her wrist. Asher straightened in the uncomfortable chair, working to free himself of the memory.

Ethan had called the squad as soon as Carly started seizing, before Asher even got back with the sweats. His only source of relief right now was knowing Ethan was taking care of her. His brother would make sure she got what she needed medically, but more important, she'd see at least a somewhat familiar face when she woke up. That is, if she had any memory of the last several hours, which was up debatable.

"Mr. Thompson." Moreno opened the door and stepped inside, holding the door with the flat of his palm while the second detective entered. "This is Detective Hastings. She's with our Special Crimes unit. I thought it might be best if she sat in with us this morning, considering the nature of what transpired last night."

Morning. Jesus, was it really still morning? Asher glanced at his watch.

"Somewhere you need to be?" Hastings glared at Asher.

"Sorry, no. It's been a long night. Just feels later." He'd have to watch himself more carefully. Everything he did from here on out would be scrutinized—the good minimized and the bad magnified. He didn't need to add any fuel to what was fast becoming a blazing fire.

"Why don't you walk us through what happened." Moreno situated himself at the table, opening a leather portfolio to reveal a yellow legal pad. He uncapped a pen and poised it over the naked paper. "When did you realize Carly was missing?"

Asher clasped his hands in his lap and relayed what he could. The phone call. A hike down into the woods to find Carly, curled up like an animal on the bank of the creek. The only thing he neglected to tell was the visit from Phoebe. He refused to throw another student under the bus before he knew the full extent of her involvement.

Hastings watched Asher with narrowed eyes, her arms crossed across her chest.

"You are Miss Dalton's teacher, correct?" Asher barely tipped his chin into the nod before Hastings followed it up. "Why didn't you take her immediately to the hospital when you realized she was hurt?" It was hard to miss the accusation dripping from the detective's voice.

Asher already regretted that decision. Watching Carly writhe on the floor of Ethan's apartment had been enough to lodge a permanent knot of guilt in his gut. He sighed through the tightening in his throat.

"Carly threatened to get out of the car when I mentioned

taking her to the ER. My brother is a paramedic for Brookside EMS, so I thought I was doing the next best thing. At first, I just thought she needed a few stitches, needed to sleep it off. I didn't realize ..." Asher let the words hang. He should have known better. Ignored her threat to run. Who was the adult here?

"What didn't you realize?" Hastings probed.

"I knew she was high, but I didn't know how much or what she'd taken."

"All the more reason to take her to the nearest hospital, is it not?"

Asher crumpled under the weight of Hastings's words. "In hindsight, yes."

"What *did* you know, Mr. Thompson?"

"I thought she'd been with someone. Someone who hurt her." Moreno's pen scratched across the paper, filling the room with its only sound.

"What made you think that, Mr. Thompson?"

"The way she was dressed. Carly usually dresses in jeans and sweatshirts. Tonight she wore a short skirt and a button down blouse. Her shirt was ripped. It was obvious she'd been ..." He wasn't sure how to finish that sentence.

"Having sex?" Hastings interjected.

Asher met the detective's gaze, returning her stare with hate of his own. "She had scratches on her face and along her arms and legs. I don't know about you, Detective, but that's never happened to me in the midst of *having sex*." Venom dripped from his voice.

"So you thought she'd been raped."

Asher nodded.

"Did you ask her what happened?"

"No. My first concern was getting her somewhere safe."

"How admirable." He didn't need to look to know Hastings was out for blood, scouring him for signs of untruth. There was a moment of reprieve as she leaned down, pulling a file from her bag. She flopped it onto the table between them and pulled a photograph from inside, sliding it across the table toward Asher.

"Recognize this girl?"

Asher held Hastings's stare. He knew what he'd find when he looked down at that photo, and it was the last thing he needed right now. The detective raised a neatly groomed eyebrow, lips pursed. Waiting. Judging.

Asher drug his eyes over the eight by ten. Emily. Her legs tangled. Blood-stained arms curled toward her torso. Unseeing eyes open on the stars above. Something inside him snapped, releasing a wave of heat through his core. A knot surged to his throat as he pushed the glossy back to Detective Hastings.

"I'll take that as a yes." She tucked the photo back into the folder. "The similarities between the two victims are astonishing."

"Do you have a question, Detective?" Heat pumped through Asher's veins. Anger built with each beat of his heart. He'd made mistakes. He couldn't deny that. He hadn't been there for Emily when she needed someone, and he sure as hell wasn't going to make the same mistake with Carly. Even if it meant reliving a past he'd rather forget.

"You were, what, eighteen when Emily Franklin was found dead?"

"Seventeen, but I'm sure your handy-dandy file tells you that."

"Your father was charged as a result of her case, is that right?" She flipped the file open and slid a pair of reading glasses onto the tip of her nose. "Aggravated rape, unlawful sexual conduct with a minor, sexual battery, among some other drug related misdemeanors."

Asher looked away from the detective, conceding defeat.

"Where was your brother during this time?" She patted the folder in front of her.

"Ethan stayed with Mom during the summers." Asher tried to mask the squint of regret that passed over his face. How many times had he wished he'd stayed home? "He took college classes the last couple summers of high school. Dad coerced Mom into letting him take me out on the road with him. I was able to make money at some of the loading docks. It was easier to go than to watch them fight."

"Did your mother know what happened when you were out on the road with your father?"

"She might have suspected. But she didn't know. Not until after Emily."

"What was it like–traveling with your father? You must have been exposed to his activities."

"It was hell. Is that what you want me to say?" Asher jutted his chin in the direction of the open file. "It's all right there in black and white. You want me to confirm what that file already tells you–that he bought girls, forced me to watch as he fucked them in front of me. But that's not it, is it? You want me to say I enjoyed it. That somehow I got off on his abuse. That maybe I had something to do with how Carly Dalton ended up in that hospital room. Well, I hate to disappoint you, Detective, but my father's influence died with him."

Hastings leaned back in her chair, palms toward Asher, feigning innocence.

"I just want to know what happened, Mr. Thompson." Her voice was calm and unaffected. "The research is clear on the tendencies of men exposed to sexual violence at a young age." A slow smile spread across the female detective's face. "I'm just curious why it took you so long to pick up where your father left off."

Logic dissolved into a red haze of fury. Asher lunged.

Before his hands could find their target, he was slammed from behind, landing face first on the table. The click of handcuffs echoed in his ears, followed by voices. *Assault.* He closed his eyes as Miranda rights were read. There was no sense in resisting the two uniformed officers who pulled him from the table. They led him from the interrogation room to the intake desk, helped him empty his pockets and shoved him into a holding cell.

He deserved this. The legacy of his father raining down on him. Payback for not standing up for the string of girls his father violated in the sleeper cab of his semi-truck. Revenge for refusing to help the one girl who'd cried out for him in desperation. Punishment for standing by while Carly became another statistic. He'd pledged his life to doing better, overturning the legacy of his father, but here he was cycling back, dangerously close to repeating a past he'd sell his soul to forget.

TWENTY-EIGHT

CARLY

The lights were too bright. A searing pain lit in my skull every time I tried to pry my eyes open. My mouth was dry, cotton-like. I cleared my throat and felt a hand on my arm. I squinted, bore the pain of the lights, and blinked through the fuzziness. The hand on my forearm was smooth, not the rough, calloused skin I'd grown used to. But the man attached to it was a stranger–almost. I shrugged away from him until a permeating pain in every muscle stopped my retreat.

"I know you don't remember me." He smiled. Brushed a hair away from my face. "My name's Ethan Thompson. Asher's brother. Do you remember what happened last night?"

I closed my eyes again, letting his voice flow over me. Warm. Safe. A tickle of a memory flittered at the edges of my consciousness, not yet close enough to grasp. "I don't remember," I spoke, but only managed a whisper.

"Probably for the best." He patted my arm, his fingers soft against my skin. I heard the door click, but I didn't open my eyes to see who had entered. Instead, I just listened, protecting my eyes from the pain.

"She asleep?" Miss Harrison's voice.

"In and out," Ethan answered. "Any word from Asher, yet?"

"Not since they invited him down to the station." I detected the frustration in Miss Harrison's voice. Heard the *fwump* of her body as she sunk into a chair. "My boss called, though. Had to do a lot of talking to keep him from removing me from the case. They're revoking Asher's guardianship."

I forced my eyes open, bracing against the slice of pain. "Why?" My voice was thick and rough. It sounded exactly the way I felt. "He didn't do anything."

"Oh, Carly." Miss Harrison leaned forward, her hand skimming along my leg. "It's policy. Our job is to make sure you're in the safest place possible. When something like this happens ..."

"But he didn't do this. I did." Desperation was creeping into my lungs, pitching my voice up an octave. A sudden lurch of memories pummeled me. A burgundy truck. An ill-advised trick. Mom's opal. I sat up, ignoring the burning pain of every core muscle.

Ethan stepped forward. His eyes flicked to a nearby monitor. "Take it easy, Carly. We'll get this sorted out."

"But ... where am I supposed to go?" The tears came without warning, and there was nothing I could do to hold them back. Whole body fatigue settled over me, rendering me incapable of the façade I normally kept on stand-by.

"We'll figure it out later. Everything will be okay. I promise." I checked Miss Harrison's eyes. She was trying for truth, but I read something darker. Guilt, maybe.

"He's in trouble, isn't he? Because of me?" I wracked my brain, trying to remember every element of the decisions I'd made, how any one of them could have been construed as his fault. I came up empty.

"The police just wanted to ask him some questions. They want to find out what happened so they can make sure it doesn't happen again."

"Then I'm the one they need to talk to," I said. Indignation built from within. "I'm the one who went to the truck stop. I'm the one who ..." *Who, what? Sold myself for a hundred-dollar bill?* I searched their faces. That's what it would look like to the people in this room.

"It's not your fault," Miss Harrison said as I settled back against the pillow. Standard line for the victimized. But I wasn't the victim here. That much I knew.

Ethan's phone trilled from his jacket pocket. He excused himself to take the call, leaving me alone with Miss Harrison. "You know that's not true," I said. "I did this. And I did it for the right reasons. Don't pin this on Asher."

"Prostituting yourself will not help us find your sister, Carly. You could have been killed last night. You know that, right?" She sounded like a mother scolding an insolent child. The image of her in the photograph on Asher's living room mantle flicked into my mind like a movie still. She'd make a good mom someday. Of that, I was sure.

"You're right," I admitted. "It doesn't matter anyway. She's already dead."

Miss Harrison's jaw hung open. Before she could pull herself together enough to form a response, Ethan stepped back inside.

"Jo, we've got a situation." Miss Harrison put a hand up in Ethan's direction, signaling him to wait.

"Give us a minute, Ethan." Her eyes stayed focused on mine, silently asking the question she couldn't voice.

"She OD'd with one of the johns last week. I saw him dump her from his cab, but then..." The pounding behind my eyes intensified. I sucked in a deep breath. *Just get it over with.*

"Then, what, Carly?"

"Reed tried to revive her. Gave her Narcan or something. But Eli took me home. I couldn't see." The words were coming fast now and I only hoped Miss Harrison wouldn't stop me to ask more questions. "I watched while Reed talked with the trucker, loaded Caroline back in. We pulled out before they were done talking. That's why I went back. I needed to know where he took her. I needed to know if my sister made it out of that lot alive."

Miss Harrison blinked twice, mute.

Ethan stood still in the doorway. "I'll be back in a few." His voice was soft, and I knew he'd heard. A slither of shame in my chest was squashed by the realization that it didn't matter anymore.

"And did she?" Miss Harrison asked. "Make it out alive?"

The trucker's words echoed in my skull, *"You'll need an Ouija board to talk to her now."* My sister was dead. The promise I'd made to my mother, broken. Everything I'd worked to keep safe, ripped away. I had no secrets left worth keeping.

"I don't think so." The words caught in my throat, constricted by desperate emotion.

Miss Harrison responded, pulling me into a hug, whispering hot sorrow-filled words against the side of my head. "No matter what happens, Carly. You'll never be alone. I promise you that."

TWENTY-NINE

ASHER

Asher sat in the silence of the cement block cell as the pool of anger he harbored for his father festered. His father spent summers grooming him. He'd had enough hours of therapy to understand that, now. If it hadn't been for Emily's death, his father's abuse would have continued. For how long? Asher scratched a palm over his scalp. His dad was dead, but there were other men to take his place. Men like Reed Sutherland.

"Still trying to change the past, Ash. How noble." The night rushed back at him, Phoebe standing in his foyer. Carly's voice, dissolving into incoherent mumbles on the other end of the line. And Reed Sutherland's threatening baritone taking over, launching Asher into action. *"Think you can make it to this one in time?"*

Asher punched the cot next to him, growling through the fury. How long had Reed Sutherland had his claws in Carly? How could he not have seen the signs? For the last seven years Asher had worked to forget the parts of his childhood that remained scars to this day. Pretending people like Reed Sutherland didn't exist–like a bogeyman from days gone by–was a coping strategy that had served him well ... until now.

Reed was still out there, turning lost girls like Carly and Caroline into victims, promising them a life they'd never live to see, just as he'd once promised Emily. And if history was any indication, he was damn good at his job. As long as there were lonely men out there with a taste for young flesh, guys like Reed would continue to exist.

Jesus, these girls were just teenagers. He sucked in a breath as the memory of Carly's breath so close to his ignited a wave of sickness in his core, replaced by a black wave of grief. He sunk onto the floor and buried his head in his hands. Hastings was right. He was no better than his father. No better than the men who preyed on the easiest targets, turning desperate girls into scarred prey.

The click of the lock engaged, triggering a memory. Asher jerked to attention.

"Hastings will have more questions for you later," Moreno said, nodding to the guard who closed the door behind him.

"But you have questions for me now," Asher guessed.

Moreno shrugged. "I want you to know I had no choice but to bring Hastings in. Once Carly was admitted to the hospital it was out of my hands."

"How is she? Carly?" Asher clasped his hands together, rubbing his left thumb over his right until it hurt, anything to keep the hot threat of emotion from erupting.

"She's a tough kid." Moreno lowered himself onto the cot next to Asher and the metal springs groaned. "How are you?"

"Why do you care?" Asher's voice sounded rougher than he intended, a knot of anger, guilt, and frustration caught at the base of his throat.

"I planned to tell you this the other morning at your house, but it didn't come up." Moreno sighed. "I cut my teeth as a rookie detective in a precinct just south of Columbus. Emily Franklin's case was the first one I caught. I'd been a beat cop for seven years before that. Seen a number of suicides. But I'll never forget that scene."

Asher squinted at Moreno. "Why don't I remember you?"

"You wouldn't. You were a minor. I was there when they brought you in, but my superior took your statement. Special crimes conducted your interview."

Asher nodded. A highlight thread of memories trickled back.

"Hastings might have pulled Emily's file, but I dug a little deeper." Moreno studied his hands. "Twelve domestic violence calls to the house you grew up in. Three child endangerment calls. Nothing was done about any of it." Moreno's coal black stare lifted to meet Asher's. "You started traveling with your dad when you were twelve-years-old. Why? And don't give me the bullshit about making money on the docks."

A constricted half-chuckle erupted from Asher's lungs. He wasn't ready to relive his past. Not here. Not now.

Moreno pushed a snapshot across the mattress toward Asher. "You were at the neighbor's when this happened."

Asher hazarded a glance at the picture. Ethan's swollen face stared back at him, dark purple bruises splotched his brother's normally fair complexion from hairline to collarbone.

"I thought that was sealed," Asher said, trying hard to pry his gaze from his brother's face.

"I called in a few favors," Moreno said, tucking the photograph into a jacket pocket. "Your turn."

"I promised Ethan I'd never let Dad hurt him again." The words drifted in the air, hung between the two men like a ghost.

"You were just a kid. The system failed you. And I think I understand what you're trying to do here–for Carly. But you've got to be careful. Hastings has it out for you."

"And you don't?" Asher tried to keep the sarcasm from his voice.

Moreno hesitated. "No. I don't."

It had been a long time since Asher had placed trust in the system that for years had seemed hell-bent on destroying him and his family. But there was something about Moreno. A darkness simmering beneath the surface that Asher recognized ... trusted.

The two men sat in silence for several moments, the drone of the police station blocked out by the metal door of the holding cell. Moreno shifted first, pushing himself up off of the cot.

"Carly wasn't alone."

The words stopped Moreno's retreat.

"In the woods, when she called, there was another voice. One I recognized."

"Who?"

Asher blew a thin stream of air through his lips. Speaking the name made it real. "Reed Sutherland. If you have my old files you'll find him mentioned."

Moreno's brows knitted together over his expression. "The Sutherlands were your next-door neighbors. Your dad drove with his."

Asher nodded, knotting his hands in front of him as his father's words clawed from the inside. *You're nothing but a snitch. Let me show you what happens to snitches.*

"What did Reed say? One the phone?" Moreno asked.

Asher cocked his head to the side, repeating the words in a whisper. "He asked if I was still trying to change the past. Then he shared Carly's location. Said, 'Let's see if you can make it in time for this one.'"

Moreno hitched one shoulder, exhaled a long uncomfortable sigh. "How would he know where to find her?"

"I don't know," Asher admitted. "The john, maybe?" He'd tried hard not to think about what Carly had done before he found her on the creek bed, but he wasn't naive. If Carly had gone looking for information from Caroline's last john, she'd have to offer something in return. He forced the imagery away.

Moreno nodded. "What about before last night? Have you had any contact with Reed Sutherland?"

"I haven't seen him since the night Emily died."

"I'll see what I can find out." Moreno rubbed his forehead as he turned for the door.

"Detective?" Asher waited for him to turn around. "What about Caroline?"

"I called in a few favors. Waiting for word. Right now I've got nothing. No leads. Nobody's talking. Carly said she was enrolled in classes at Ohio State, but they've got no record of her." He shrugged. "She's an adult. Took off on her own, maybe. We can't rule that out."

"Carly ran because of Caroline. Do you really think she'd take off and leave Carly in that house?" Asher challenged, standing as a ribbon of suspicion threaded up his spine.

"I don't know."

Asher appreciated the honesty and met it with a dose of his own. "Phoebe Anderson came to my house in the middle of the night. That's how I knew Carly was missing. She showed me more drawings, pictures she took of Carly's work. Ones that weren't turned over by Phoebe's father. Some of them are of Caroline. She was in deep, Detective. Drugs, prostitution, trafficking. Carly went to the only place she thought she could find answers."

"Truck-n-Go." Moreno stated the obvious, interrupted by three pounding knocks from the exterior of the door. "They're waiting for me," he said, thumbing toward the door. "Look, we've got officers searching for the driver she was with tonight.

Hoping he can shed some light on what happened. I'm working every angle of this. But in the meantime, keep yourself in check, Thompson. You can't help anyone locked up in here."

Asher glanced at the metal door, the top of someone's head was visible through the square window. Judging by height, it was Hastings.

"I've got some savings," Asher said, stopping Moreno before he could get to the door. "It's not much, but it's something. Could you tell Jo? Ask her to use it to get Carly set up someplace nice."

"If the judge sets bail, you might need that yourself," Moreno countered. His heavy brows came together above the bridge of his nose. If Asher didn't know better, he'd categorize the expression as worry.

"Please, just tell Jo. I never took her name off the account. Besides, the money was my dad's. It's about time some good came from something he touched."

Moreno stood in shocked silence for a beat before dipping his chin in a nod. "I can't promise anything," he said. "But I'll tell her."

The windfall had been a gift from the Gods of inheritance when his father died, a life insurance policy his mother had taken out on him when they were newly married, somehow left unseized. If anyone deserved to be the beneficiary, it was Carly, and girls like her.

Moreno disappeared into the hall, closing the holding cell with a solid *clank*, leaving Asher alone with the unwelcome trickle of childhood memories.

THIRTY

CARLY

"Carly, tell us about your relationship with your teacher, Mr. Thompson."

The woman detective–Hastings, I think–sat on the other side of the bedside table in my hospital room. I preferred Moreno to her. She gave off some holier than thou vibe that wasn't sitting well with me at the moment.

The doctors had signed off on my release that afternoon, but Moreno and his sidekick had arrived just after, holding me hostage in this sterile room of white. Neither one of the detectives had told me why their questions were so important that I couldn't go home to fresh clothes and a shower first. Why I couldn't answer them from Mr. T's living room couch was beyond me.

"Mr. Thompson is the best teacher I've ever had. He cares, you know?" I was sure they didn't. "I never would have the opportunity to go to Millbrook in the first place if he hadn't gotten me the scholarship. It's a good school. I'm grateful." The words sounded forced, unlike me.

"How grateful?" The unspoken implication caught me off guard.

"What?"

"Did he ever ask you to do him favors? Repay him in some way?" Blame sharpened the edges of Hastings's voice.

"No." The impact of the accusation slammed into me, knocking me off balance and twisting my stomach into knots.

"That's why I'm still here isn't it? You think he hurt me." I lowered my gaze and picked at the bed sheets. Jo had been right. They would never let me go back to Mr. Thompson's. He'd already been tried and convicted in their eyes. Nothing I said tonight was going to change their minds.

"It's my understanding you spent quite a lot of time with Mr. Thompson outside of school hours. Particularly in detention. Is that true?"

My heart pounded in my chest, thumping a staccato rhythm that navigated its way from my chest to my head. I glanced at Detective Moreno, the mountain of a man stood immoveable between my bed and the door. He refused to make eye contact.

"When can I go home? Where is Mr. Thompson?" I knew what happened from here–emergency placement. I'd only experienced it once. My dad had gone on a bender a few weeks after Mom's death, leaving Caroline and me alone at the house for more than seventy-two hours. Neighbors had called children's services.

Hastings scooted her chair back and stood. She smoothed her jacket and glanced at Moreno, who gave her a short nod. Familiar prickles started at the base of my neck. Hastings guided the wheeled table out of her way and leaned over me, pushing imagined strands of hair from my forehead. "It's over, Carly. You don't have to be afraid anymore. We're here to protect you. No more hiding from the truth. Mr. Thompson can't hurt you anymore."

My body buzzed with a mix of anger and frustration. "You've got it all wrong." My voice wavered, echoed in my ears. The prickles had reached my scalp, digging fingers of panic into my head like knives. "Asher never hurt me."

The detectives exchanged a renewed round of glances at my use of Mr. Thompson's first name.

"You don't know how many times we've heard that same thing from other victims of abuse," Detective Hastings said. "Fear is like a prison. It traps you. And I know this is scary. I know how alone you must feel. But there are people out there who want to help. You don't have to face this alone. But you do have to tell us what he did."

"He never touched me." I spewed the words, loud and panicked. "Miss Harrison?" I shouted toward the closed door. She knew Asher. She would make them stop. Force them to believe.

"She'll be along soon. Just a few more questions," Moreno's voice was full of calm understanding, the opposite of Hastings's piercing accusation.

But the pinpricks of panic intensified, burning at the base of my neck. "Who told you he hurt me?"

Moreno pulled something from a file under his portfolio. Encased in a plastic bag, I recognized the rough, unfinished edges of the high-end drawing paper Mr. Thompson had given me on my seventeenth birthday.

"Where'd you get that?" The memory of the bundle sitting on the corner of his desk as I entered detention that afternoon was fresh. Tied with a lavender ribbon, I could still feel the satiny softness between my fingers as I tugged the bow free. See the smile turn the corners of Mr. Thompson's lips as he lit a single candle on top of the chocolate cupcake he'd brought for the occasion.

The scent of hot wax had filled my nostrils as I made a wish, blowing out the flame in one puff. It was the first birthday gift I'd received in four years. And the first wish that had ever come true—at least, it had for a little while.

Moreno didn't answer, just held the bag out toward me. I knew which sketch it was before the whole paper was visible.

"We have all of your artwork, Carly. They're dated. Signed. You were smart to split them up. Some at home, some with Miss Anderson, a few with you. Frankly, you're talented. Altogether they're better than a diary."

I dared a look at the illustration—an imagined moment frozen in time. The lines of gray blended, meshing together, just like the image of Asher and me standing together, his hands on either side of my face, our eyes closed, lips locked in a kiss. I'd even named the sketch. Scribbled above my signature in the bottom right hand corner, *Bliss*.

"It's only a drawing." I defended, turning away from the incriminating evidence. "Art. Fiction. You can't believe everything you see."

He ignored me, nodding to the female detective.

"Is this 'only a drawing,' too?" She made air quotes around my meager defense and held another plastic-encased sheet toward me.

This time the air rushed from my lungs. I fought to replace it as my eyes combed over the image of Caroline's crumpled form. All legs and arms, tangled at the base of an old International.

"This is why you went to the lot." Moreno let the fact marinate in the air.

"I already told Miss Harrison. Mr. Thompson didn't have anything to do with me going to the Truck-n-Go."

Hastings lifted her eyebrows, one higher than the other, making her slim face appear gaunt. I recognized the look. Skepticism.

"But he picked you up. In the middle of the night. In an abandoned park. You expect us to believe he miraculously knew where to find you?" Her voice pitched higher.

"Take it easy, Amelia." Moreno's baritone cut in. His voice soft, but firm. My gaze ricocheted between them and the pain in my skull surged, like a knife between my eyes. I rubbed at the gouging discomfort.

"I called him." I didn't try to mask the unspoken, *I think*, in the statement.

"The call from your burner lasted less than ten seconds, Carly. We're waiting for records from the phone company, but there's no way you could explain your disappearance and tell him where to find you in that span of time."

A wave of panic seized my lungs, replaced by the growing heat of frustration. I fought through the fog of that night. I didn't remember dialing. I didn't remember hearing his voice. Had no memory of what I'd said to him, or what he'd said to me. After my slide down to the creek bottom, my brain locked in a drug-induced amusement park ride, my memory was spotty at best. None of the information I needed to exonerate the one person who cared was accessible.

A knock on my hospital room door cut through the tension in the room. Everyone turned, except Hastings. The heat of her stare bored into the side of my head even as I watched the door with hopeful expectation. A tired looking man in uniform poked his head in. "Miss Harrison is here for the transfer."

Moreno checked his watch and thanked the officer. He gathered his things.

"We'll continue this conversation later," Detective Moreno

said. "There's time. Miss Harrison will see you to your new placement."

"I don't need a new placement. I want to go home." The word felt foreign on my tongue, but the tears that sprung to the backs of my eyes were very much real. I rolled the word over again in my mouth. "Home." The sound of it warmed me from the inside.

"Asher Thompson's house was never your home, Carly. No matter what he might have made you think. He's a predator."

"Amelia," Moreno shot a warning to his partner.

Hastings ignored him. Narrowed her eyes on me as she pushed her business card into the palm of my hand. Her cool fingers sent a ribbon of anger down my spine, launching another round of tingles at the base of my skull.

"When you're ready to talk, give me a call. Otherwise, I'll see you tomorrow."

Moreno held the door as Hastings disappeared. I crumpled the card in my fist. Pointy edges carved into the flesh of my fingers.

"If Asher is innocent of the charges against him, we'll find out soon enough," Moreno said, lingering in the doorway. "Trust the process, Carly. It's in place for a reason. But right now, all any of us want is to make sure you're safe." Moreno nodded at me, holding my gaze for a beat before disappearing down the hall.

I wasn't sure why he was being so nice to me, buffering Hastings and her inborn bitchiness. But his words did little to soothe the panic that coursed through my veins. Mr. Thompson was in trouble. Worse than that, he'd been accused of crimes that would impact every part of his life. Professionally, he'd be done. Personally, I had no idea how Miss Harrison might react. And it was all my fault.

I ignored Miss Harrison as she lowered into the chair across from mine. I kept my eyes glued to my lap until I heard the squeak in her voice as she tried to speak. I recognized that squeak. She cleared her throat. Her eyes were rimmed in red. Her porcelain complexion splotched with the tell-tale signs of tears.

"They arrested him because of me, didn't they?"

"Not because of you, Carly. None of this is your fault."

"Bullshit." I huffed the word under my breath.

Miss Harrison pretended not to hear, shuffling a stack of papers in her hands. She slid a trifold pamphlet toward me. I read the title, *New Dawn Renewal & Rehabilitation: A safe haven for healing. A fresh start for a new life.* The cover sported two girls, one my age, one a bit younger, with their arms around each other, smiling at the camera. I pushed it back toward Jo.

"You'll like it, Carly. It's a nice place. You'll share a house with a few other girls. Have your own room. They offer therapy sessions, in-house tutoring."

"No more Millbrook?" Of course not. Word would be out. Mr. Thompson would be canned and I'd be the cause. I'd never be welcomed back.

"This is better for you right now. You'll be with people who can help. Girls who have been through the same things as you. It's what's best—"

"How do you know what I've been through?" The anger rose so fast I had no control over the fire that burned in my words. "You're as bad as the detectives, jumping to conclusions."

Miss Harrison breathed my name, reached her hand to cover mine. But I jerked away.

"Never in all your visits did you ask what Caroline and I had been through. It was easier to just turn away, wasn't it?"

Jo leveled a stare on me. "I'm asking now."

A stab of guilt worked its way into my chest as I headed for the door. I turned it into defiance. "You still have no idea, Jo." I paused, fingertips poised on the door handle. "Our well-being was your *job*, and you never bothered to ask."

"I'm sorry," Jo whispered, words clouded by the sniff that accompanied them. "You're right. It was my job to protect you and I turned a blind eye because I was too afraid to see what was right in front of me. But this isn't all my fault." Jo rose from the chair, closing the distance between us. "Would you have told me what was happening if I'd asked?"

I swallowed the lump in my throat. We both knew the answer.

"Please, Carly, I can't help you if you don't let me in."

THIRTY-ONE

ASHER

It was dark as Asher rode silently in the passenger seat of Ethan's Honda. He'd already delivered the obligatory thank-yous and I'm sorries required of someone whose kid brother just bailed him out of jail.

"How's Carly?" It was really the only thing that he could think of to say as they pulled into Asher's driveway.

"She'll be okay. Had a rough morning. Doctor said it's good we brought her in when we did, but she seemed to bounce back okay. Jo took you up on the offer. Got Carly settled into a facility this afternoon. It's called New Dawn, about an hour from here."

Ethan pulled to stop behind Asher's Jeep and killed the engine.

"Look, I know what you're trying to do here, Ash. I'm not blind. But you can't let the tragedies in this girl's life unravel yours. Nothing can change what happened to Emily. Sometimes you just have to cut your losses and move on. Girls like Emily ..." Ethan hesitated. "... Carly ... sometimes they don't want to be saved."

"Carly's different."

Ethan sighed, palmed the steering wheel in front of him. "I know you see Emily when you look at her, Ash. I know you just want to do what's right. Make up for whatever it is you think you didn't do back then. But this obsession you have to help her, it's not healthy."

"I'm just her teacher." Asher forced his way into Ethan's speech. "Anyone in my position would do the same."

"Maybe." Ethan paused, watching his brother. "You've overcome so much, Asher. Don't let this one girl tear your life apart."

"Are you done now?" Asher bit back the irritation creeping into his voice.

"For now."

"I know who did this, Ethan. It's Reed. He's behind all of it–Carly, her sister ... what happened last night ... everything."

Ethan sunk back at the mention of the name. "Reed Sutherland." He whispered it as if voicing it aloud would open some portal to hell. "So it's true then?"

"What do you mean?"

Ethan shrugged. "That's the second time I heard that name tonight. Carly told Jo what happened to Caroline. I overheard her mention someone named Reed." Ethan tapped a thumb against the steering wheel. "I thought we left the Sutherlands back in Columbus."

Asher's heart hiccupped. "Jo knows?"

Ethan nodded. "Some of it anyway. Did you tell the cops about Reed?"

"I told Moreno. Hastings has already made up her mind about me. They've dug into the old files from Emily's investigation. My interviews. Old domestic violence calls to the house. She's convinced I followed in Dad's footsteps. That I put Carly up to this."

"Guess she doesn't realize Reed was the son Dad always wanted but never had."

The glow of headlights from a car in the cul-de-sac illuminated Ethan's face. Asher read the hatred in his little brother's eyes. The years of neglect. The two of them had had to pull together growing up, look out for one another. Just like Caroline and Carly had to do. It was the reason Asher climbed into his father's cab every summer–refused to let his dad scar his little brother the way he'd scarred him.

"Are they looking for him?" Ethan asked.

Asher nodded. "Moreno is. He's also trying to figure out what really happened to Caroline."

Silence spread in the space between them, broken by the trill of Ethan's ringtone. He pulled it out of his pocket and answered, offering it to Asher.

"It's your boss."

Asher glanced at the screen, sucking in a breath as he drew the cell to his ear.

Principal Baum's voice on the other end was louder than necessary, booming through the smartphone speaker and forcing Asher's head to the side. "Sorry to call this way Thompson. Detective Moreno said I could reach you at this number. Just calling to let you know we won't need you in the classroom tomorrow."

Asher let the words sink in, grate through his chest and into his gut.

"You've been placed on administrative leave effective immediately. The board will review the circumstances surrounding your arrest, including allegations of improper conduct with students. The board meets Saturday. I've got to say, Thompson. You've disappointed me."

A surge of heat shot through Asher's core, replacing the bone deep defeat. If Angus Baum was looking for an apology he wouldn't get one from Asher. "Understood," he managed. "Appreciate the heads-up, Angus."

Asher pulled the phone away from his ear and pressed the end call button with the pad of his thumb before Baum could say anything else.

"I'm sorry," Ethan said, his voice full of quiet resolution. "Promise me you won't let this derail you. Just sit back for a bit, let the cops do their job, Ash."

Asher aimed the remnants of anger at Ethan, but softened. His kid brother, just shy of sixteen when he'd pulled into the driveway after driver's ed one night to watch cops cuff his big brother and haul him off to jail. There'd been fear in Ethan's eyes that night, just as there was fear in them today. But today's fear was masked by something else–sorrow.

"He'll talk to me," Asher said.

"Who? Sutherland?" Ethan shifted in his seat, facing Asher the best he could in the confines of his Accord. "I mean it, Ash, stay out of it. You can't go after Reed on your own."

Asher surveyed the darkened house in front of them. A house that once held promise, now just a shell. "He knows Carly called me from the woods. I'm already involved. You know as well as I do he'll come after her again." Asher allowed the silence of the car to close in for a beat before continuing. "I can't lose anyone else, Ethan. Not to him."

THIRTY-TWO

CARLY

Almost a week at New Dawn, and I could already name the best part–the playground. I'd sit and swing for hours, watching the activity between houses in the small circular community. I used to have a swing set kind of like this one when Mom was alive. Stained wood, with swings on one side and a fort and climbing wall on the other. The highlight was a big yellow slide that resembled a curly fry on the opposite side of the fort. It brought back good memories, which was probably why they let me spend so much time out here.

The worst part of New Dawn was knowing why my nine-year-old roommate, Taylor, was there. I couldn't imagine having sex with a stranger at her age. I'd been fifteen, just a few months shy of my sixteenth birthday, when Caroline first asked me to join her at the party that changed my life. My sister's words echoed in my memory as I swung. *"It'll just be Eli and a few of his friends."* Her voice clung like ivy in my mind, full of the hopeful expectation of young love mixed with desperation. Oblivious to every counter-argument I ever thought to make. *"Come on, Carly. It'll get you out of the house for a while."* She should have led with that incentive. Getting out of Aaron's house, even for a little while, was always priority number one. Until ... it wasn't.

Looking back, I should have been able to read the reckless glint in her eyes, unpack the fact that her interest in me was more than sisterly concern. Should have known when we got to Reed's place, when he locked the door behind us, that there was no going back. But when you're watching your sister morph into a woman you no longer recognize, you'll do just about anything to get her out. Even if that includes offering yourself up as sacrifice. Little did I know it rarely works that way.

That first night—that party Caroline dragged me to, the time I spent alone with Reed, locked in his bedroom—will forever be burned into my memory. I didn't want to imagine a nine-year-old girl going through what I'd gone through. Pain. Humiliation. Fear. Every time I saw Taylor, my heart squeezed, and I counted my blessings.

"Hey, Carly. Mind if I join you?" Taylor's voice cut into my thoughts.

"Course not." I nodded toward the empty swing next to mine. Late afternoon sun streamed down through the budding leaves of the giant maple tree that shaded the area from the mid-day warmth. Not that there was much this time of year. The spring sun mottled the deep caramel of Taylor's arms as she pulled the swing back.

"You should be wearing a coat," I said. The mother hen in me pecked her way out.

Taylor just shrugged. "I'm not cold." She pushed up off her tip-toes, launching the swing into its pendulum motion. "You coming to group tonight?" Taylor asked, pumping her legs back and forth, working for momentum. She glanced over her shoulder at the ever-present guards not far from the edge of the playground. Curls blew in thin ropes across her face.

I shrugged. I hadn't gone yet. Why start now?

"You should. There was a girl in the office today while I was working. She was asking for you. Pretty. Blonde. You know you can't have visitors until you join the group."

"Thanks, Tay. I'll think about it."

"Who was she?"

I hesitated, not sure how much of my life I wanted to share with these people. Taylor looked up at me with deep, chocolate eyes. "It sounds like Phoebe. My *ex*-best friend." I stressed the *ex*. Detective Hastings had been quick to tell me that my best friend had stepped up, done the heavy lifting for me and turned in my teacher.

Little did Hastings know that Phoebe was playing her just as she'd played me. Phoebe was the one to turn over my drawings. I could have forgiven her for that. But accusing Asher just to make herself look like an angel in her father's eyes was beyond betrayal. And Hastings had soaked it all up like a fresh paper towel.

The corner of Taylor's mouth tipped up and she focused once again on swinging. "You're lucky. None of my friends ever come to see me."

My heart seized, ached for the little girl next to me that had never been able to be just that ... a little girl. It was in moments like this when hatred crept in. "That's okay, Tay. My sister never comes to see me, either. Maybe it's better that way."

The two of us sat in silence, both lost in our own thoughts. Me, of a sister I was afraid I'd never again see and a teacher I owed. I sucked in a breath of the warming spring air. It wasn't a bad idea, going to tonight's group session. I'd been putting it off since I'd been here. But if I went, I'd miss the opportunity to scope the place out at night–research. Find out where there were cameras and where there weren't. I needed to learn when the day shift guards switched with the night shift.

A couple birds called from the trees planted at specified intervals around the green space. Taylor's swing squeaked, her weight pushing and pulling against the chain as she gained lift. She leaped when it reached its summit. The seat flopped back and forth, falling jerkily back into place beside mine. The jingle of the chain silenced the birds' song.

Taylor tossed a quick, "I hope you'll come," over her shoulder and trotted away, dark hair shining in the sun.

I studied my feet and spun in a circle, twisting the chain above my head into a tight braid. When I was satisfied, I closed my eyes, extended my legs, and leaned back. The momentum of the braid turned me faster and faster until I finally slowed, jerking to a halt. When I opened my eyes, Detective Moreno stood in front of me, hands in his pockets...waiting.

"Afternoon, Carly."

I returned the greeting.

"Looks like you're settling in well. I was hoping we could talk, clear up some loose ends. Think you could find the time?"

I didn't know if he was being sarcastic or was trying to make a joke. Since coming to New Dawn, the only thing I had was time.

"Where's Hastings?" I asked, cocking an eyebrow. Moreno had to know there was no love lost between me and the female detective. I hated her. And we'd spent more than enough time together over the past week for him to see it.

He glanced off to the side. "I'm off duty, Carly. She doesn't know I'm here."

I studied the dirt under my tennis shoes, squeezed my hands around the chain, focused on the metal digging into my palms. The reality of blessed pain.

"Shouldn't you be talking to my lawyer?" I tilted my head so I could watch Moreno out the corner of my eye.

"I should be." He licked his lips, looked away, nervous. "I thought you deserved to know what was going on without the interference of counsel. And I thought you might be able to help me wrap my head around it myself."

I hopped off the swing and stepped toward the detective. His frame dwarfed mine, but instead of making me feel small and vulnerable, it had the opposite effect. We'd gotten off to a rocky start, the two of us, but it was clear now that we both wanted the same thing...truth. I just wasn't sure how much of that I could give.

"Let's take a walk," Moreno said, eyeing the empty courtyard. His gaze lingered on the guards stationed along the perimeter.

"You feel safe here?" he asked. A slither of nervousness snaked its way into my lungs.

"Most of the time. Why? Who are you looking for?"

Moreno shrugged off the question. "They tell me you've been avoiding group sessions."

"I don't need to hear everyone's sob story, Detective. They certainly don't need to hear mine."

Moreno didn't respond. Shoved his hands deep into his pants pockets.

"We all have scars, Carly. Sometimes it helps to know we're not alone."

I squashed the urge to ask what scars he had. And he must have felt the tension, because he changed the subject. "There's been a development. A witness came forward."

I stopped walking and gripped the detective's jacket at the elbow, turning him to face me. "A witness to what?"

The boa around my lungs loosened. The thought of someone besides me reporting Reed and Eli was magnetic. A thread of some strange emotion–relief, maybe–trickled through me before reality yanked it away.

Moreno slid his cell out of his jacket pocket and swiped a few times, turning it to face me. "Do you recognize this man?"

Hateful eyes, greasy hair, stained t-shirt. The memory slammed into me. I tried to speak, to refuse, but nothing came. Moreno shoved the phone back into his pocket.

"State Highway Patrol picked him up just shy of the state line. We're holding him on drug possession. He identified you. Claims you spent some time in his cab that night." Moreno's eyes were laser focused on mine.

I clenched my jaw and stepped away, turning to watch the breeze play with the now abandoned swings. Moreno followed.

"You're not in trouble, Carly."

"Prostitution's illegal, right? Wouldn't it be easier to arrest me, get me out of the way?" I spat back, daring to confront him. "Whoever's footing the bill for this place could get their money back."

Moreno's body deflated. His shoulders sagged and the lines on his forehead scrunched and deepened. "That's not why I'm here."

"I'm listening." My eyes burned at him.

He reached for his back pocket and just when I was about to take off at a sprint, the threat of handcuffs looming, his hand returned, palming a worn leather billfold. He flipped it open and pulled a photograph from behind his ID.

"You see this girl?" Moreno waited for me to acknowledge the young dark eyes staring back at me.

I nodded.

"My daughter, Lidia," Moreno said, eyes still fixed on the aged photo between us. "She went missing from a friend's party when she was fifteen. Missing persons put in about six months worth of work before the case went cold. She was trafficked.

Found her photographs on the dark web. But her handlers were always one step ahead. Her body was found in a field sixteen months later."

Moreno's words stopped up my throat like a drain. I'd watched girls come and go. Had wondered where they went. But no one ever asked, just went on about our business as if nothing had changed. The same thing happened once Caroline was gone. Emotion tugged at the corner of my lip, threatening. "Why are you telling me this?"

Moreno sighed and pocketed his billfold. "Because I want you to understand that I'm on your side. I have a stack of pictures just like this–young girls, like my daughter, like you. The men who do this know what they're doing, know how to mess with your mind. I know what's going on here, Carly. But I need your help to stop it."

"Look, I'm sorry about your daughter. I really am. But I don't know what you're talking about." The programmed response came without effort.

Moreno cleared his throat. "Our trucker friend says you stole drugs from him. So he followed you into the woods, took what was his, and left you there."

He wanted confirmation. But I refused. Moreno exhaled and pressed on. "Says he passed someone as he was coming out of the park. Someone he thinks you might have known."

Hope evaporated from my body and I froze. "Who?" I barely recognized the squeak of the question as my own.

"Reed Sutherland."

The name singed my skin, burned against me like a branding iron. It took a moment for me to force air back into my lungs.

"The driver says he's seen you with Sutherland's boys at the Truck-n-Go before. He identified you. Said you called yourself Caroline."

I swallowed the knot in my throat, tried to keep up with the puzzle pieces Moreno placed.

"What happened after you left the lot, Carly? Was Reed Sutherland there? Did you see him talk to Mr. Thompson?"

Images flashed in my memory. Nausea and fuzziness, fear and pain. I remembered the constriction of fear as he approached, sliding down to my camp at the base of the rock wall. I felt his hand over my mouth as he pulled my cell phone out of my hand, glancing at the screen with one side of his lip curled into a snarl.

His voice echoed in my mind as he spoke into the handset. *"Asher Thompson, still trying to change the past?"* I must have blacked out after that, because it was the last memory of the night I had until Asher turned up on the bank, pulling me off the ground and into his arms so he could wade back across the creek to his Jeep. By then, I barely remembered Reed had been there at all, chalked it up to a drug induced hallucination. I rubbed my forehead, the first pricks of a potential headache from hell spiking into my skull.

"I don't remember what happened," I said, wisps of fear creeping into my voice. "But I know he was gone by the time Mr. Thompson came."

Moreno stopped walking and took my hands. "What *do* you remember, Carly? I know Asher didn't hurt you. And I'd like to believe you didn't have anything to do with your father's death. But I can't help either one of you if I don't know the truth."

I stared at Moreno. His round face, dark chocolate eyes, the lines that tugged around his eyes and forehead. Some might call them laugh lines, but I knew better now. They cut through his skin at downward angles, the hallmarks of grief.

I spoke softly, afraid of giving voice to the truth. "I went alone. I just wanted to find my sister. That's all."

Moreno nodded. "And Reed just left you there?" His eyes narrowed, an attempt to understand.

I nodded. The knot in my throat too big for words to squeeze through.

"Carly?" Moreno's voice, soft encouragement. "Is Reed Sutherland your handler?"

I swallowed.

Moreno unfolded a piece of copy paper from the back of his notepad. He pushed it in my direction, but I didn't need to look. The breeze lapped at the edges of my drawing, threatening to pull it from his fingers. "Is this what he did to you?"

The knot of emotion in my throat dissolved with the heat of anger as my eyes combed over my interpretation of that first night–my *initiation*. Reed's body on mine. My pain. His laughter. My tears. His pleasure. My fear.

"He told me he'd kill her if I ever told anyone. Caroline needed me. I know it was wrong, but I couldn't abandon her. She was already into drugs and I had to make sure she was okay. It's my fault she's gone."

"No, Carly, listen to me. This is not your fault." Moreno shoved the paper in his jacket pocket. Freeing his hands to hold my shoulders.

The tears fell without warning. "No one cares what happens to people like us, Detective. Caroline and I are expendable. And Reed Sutherland knew it. He turned my sister into someone I barely knew.

Tears blurred the kindness in Moreno's face. I squeezed my eyes to clear my vision but each time I did only one face broke through. The cold earth against my cheek as he held me down.

"He's the only one who knows where Caroline is. If he finds out I told you ..." I couldn't finish the sentence. He'd what? Kill her? She was already dead, the driver assured me of that. The driver. Thoughts jumbled in my brain. "Did you ask the driver about my sister?"

Moreno's body sagged. "He claims he slept with a girl matching your sister's description a couple weeks ago. Said she OD'd in his cab. His story matches the one you told Miss Harrison, except, he claims he left Caroline with Sutherland."

"Reed has her?" The words spiked from some desperate part of me I'd hidden away for too long. "No," I whispered. "He'll know I talked."

The muscles in my body turned to liquid. But strong arms enveloped me, catching me as my knees buckled. Detective Moreno sank to the ground with me, holding me while tears seeped from my eyes onto his shoulders.

His voice on a loop, repeated, "It's okay, Carly," followed by the one phrase I'd waited years to hear. "You're safe now."

THIRTY-THREE
ASHER

Asher stood at the edge of his deck looking out into the woods. He'd spent the last several days keeping to himself and trying to piece together why Reed Sutherland would be using girls from Brookside to fund his business ventures. Even now, the only reason he could come up with involved a long-held vendetta between former friends. He sucked in a breath of the unseasonably warm afternoon air, grateful that spring had finally broken through the long, gray Ohio winter.

He heard Jo's voice before her first footstep on the wooden decking.

"I tried to call. I hope it's okay that I'm here." Jo shrugged a shoulder. Her cream-colored sweater lifted against her neck, a stark contrast to the warm bronze of her skin. A trickle of warmth unleashed in Asher's core, lifting the hairs on his arms.

"The cops still have my phone. I haven't bothered to get another one yet."

Asher had only talked to Jo through his attorney, helping arrange funding for Carly's stay at New Dawn. He wasn't sure she wanted to speak to him considering Hastings's allegations, let alone be in the same room with him. The fact that she was standing three feet from him right now seemed more dream than reality.

"I owe you an apology." Her voice slid over him like caramel.

"You don't owe me anything, Jo." He swallowed the hot threat of emotion that started a slow creep toward his throat.

"I know you couldn't hurt Carly, or Phoebe. You wouldn't."

There was a "but" coming. Asher could feel it.

"But what Hastings said scared me. She was so sure. She's been rambling on about your dad's crimes—about what happened the night Emily Franklin died ..." Jo's gaze sank to the boards beneath her feet. "How genes play a role in violent crimes."

Asher turned away from Jo, unleashing an irritated chuckle into the night. "She must be writing a thesis. Tell her to let me know if she has any other questions about what it's like to be born a rapist."

"Ash, that's not—"

"It's fine, Jo. I know who I am, where I came from."

"You're the good to your father's evil. You paid for New Dawn. Moreno's looking into Sutherland. Carly finally talked, Ash."

His body tensed as Jo stepped closer. Her fingers skimmed down his bicep and along his forearm, coming to rest on his hand. He watched as her fingers laced through his.

"Carly is getting the help she needs now because of you." Jo stepped into his space, pulled his fingers to her lips.

Asher tugged his hand from Jo, turning away. "I'm still my father's son, Jo. That's never going to change. You'll always have that little voice—wondering, doubting—whenever something goes wrong." He kicked the toe of his tennis shoe lightly against one of the wooden spindles, gripped the railing along the edge of the deck, prepping for a confirmation that never came.

"I know *you*, Ash. I know you have secrets. I know you'll tell me what they are when you're ready. I know what happened to Emily Franklin scarred you. But I've read the file—cover to cover, actually." Jo huffed a nervous laugh into the evening air. "Her death was not your fault. Just like the way your father lived his life was never your responsibility."

Asher felt the heat of her against his back. "Why are you here, Jo?" The words came out with more accusation than he intended. But they had their intended effect. She stepped away.

Her voice was quiet, a balloon of emotion, when she spoke again. "The other night ..." she started. Stopped and regrouped. "Do you ever wonder what would have happened, with us, if things had turned out differently?"

Every day. The words echoed in his skull, but he didn't answer.

Jo took up position at the rail, looking out at the view they'd once shared over morning coffee. She broke the silence. "When I was a little girl, about eight, I guess, I had a classmate who moved around a lot. I think she was only at my school for about a year. But I still remember her. Her hair was usually matted and tangled. She'd come to school at least three times a week with some new bruise or injury. That year, I invited her to my birthday party."

"Did she come?"

Jo nodded. "A man brought her. Stayed in his car outside our house the whole time. Watching all us girls play. Looking back, I know it was strange. But back then, I didn't think anything of it. That day, at my party, was the first time I think I ever saw that little girl smile. I mean really smile. Two days later, she was gone. I never saw her again."

Asher shifted to look at Jo, from where he stood he could smell a hint of her sweet honey and jasmine shampoo. "I'm sorry." It seemed like the right thing to say.

"My point is, Ash, she's why I do what I do. Just like Emily is what drives you to protect Carly. I get it. That girl's shadow lurks in every case I take, Carly's included. We all have moments that shape us—people who change us. And as long as we use those experiences for good, then we've already won."

"Carly hasn't won."

"But she's safe now. She's getting help. You've done everything you can."

"Why are you saying all this?"

Jo turned to meet his gaze. "Because I want you to know that I believe in you." She reached for him, skimmed her fingers down the side of his face.

Her touch sent a spiral of warmth though Asher's core that he didn't deserve. Guilt bubbled to the surface, but he chased it away, leaned into her touch.

"Nothing's been right since ..." She stopped short of bringing up their baby. "I'm not the person I want to be when I'm not with you."

"Jo," he started to object, but her finger against his lips shushed him.

"Don't overthink this, Asher." She gripped his hand in hers and started for the house, pausing at the sliding glass door. "For once, just do what feels right."

His heart thrummed against his sternum. Every voice in his mind screamed at him to stop as her lips met his. But he couldn't. He'd never been able to say no to Jo. She pulled him farther into the house, toward the bedroom they'd once shared.

He pushed at unwelcome memories. Dark images of Carly's abuse morphed into vignettes of memory—Emily and other girls, strangers, he'd been powerless to save. He focused on Jo's hands, pushing his t-shirt up his torso and over his head. The hunger of her kiss melted into him, chasing away the ghosts of failure.

Her sweater and his shirt puddled on the bedroom floor, their bodies pressed against each other. He did as she asked, gave in to what felt right. And nothing in that moment felt as right as her hands hot against his skin, her softness firm under his own fingertips. But one question refused to relinquish its grip.

"Why are you doing this?" he whispered. She pulled away, confusion coloring her features. "Why now?" he clarified, fear that his words had the power to destroy crept in.

In that moment, their heat shifted, cooled in the silence. Jo lowered onto the edge of the bed in front of Asher. She stared at the floor, her brightly painted toenails neon against the light gray rug.

"Moreno talked to Carly yesterday afternoon."

Asher worked to make that piece of information fit their current situation. "I'm gonna need more than that."

Jo grabbed her sweater from the floor and shrugged into it, crossing her arms over her chest. "You were right. The whole time. I thought Carly was okay in that house. I thought Caroline was looking out for her, keeping her safe, fed, cared for. But neither one of them were okay, Ash. I was so wrong."

"You didn't know. Caroline was an adult. Carly told you everything was fine. You had no reason not to believe her."

"I had you."

Asher joined Jo on the edge of the mattress.

"Moreno used the term, 'forced prostitution.'" She spat the words like they made her sick.

"You followed protocol, Jo. You did what you could."

When she looked up at him her eyes were moist, tears threatening to spill free. "Moreno thinks Reed still has Caroline. He wanted to set up a protective detail for me. Said if Reed finds out I'm still working Carly's case, then he might come after me."

Some shadowy part of Asher, the bit of him that snapped and gave way to darkness when push came to shove, ignited inside of him. He recognized the distinctive clench in his chest. The heat roiling just under his skin, itching to claw its way out.

"He wouldn't do that," he managed. The grit of his teeth sent a spike of ache through his jaw. He forced out a balancing breath. "But that still doesn't answer my question."

Jo sat in silence for a moment, finally uncurling her arms and sliding one slender hand down Asher's thigh. "This past year has been the worst of my life. And these last weeks, seeing you, talking with you. Those moments have made me realize that I never should have left. We could have–should have–worked through all that loss together. I shut you out, but I never stopped loving you, Asher."

Asher's insides churned with a mixture of unresolved grief, hate, and love. Grief over the loss they shared and never had a chance to mourn as one. Hate at Reed Sutherland for his role in Carly's abuse. And love for the woman next to him, who'd chosen to put herself out there, raw to the possibility of rejection.

"You're quiet." Asher could hear the waver of nerves in her voice. "What are you thinking?"

As Asher exhaled, an unexpected peacefulness fell over him. The turmoil of emotions replaced by one singular strand of complete contentment. He smiled at Jo. "I'm just wondering why you didn't say all that in the first place."

THIRTY-FOUR

ASHER

Asher's lawyer, Jeff Bohrman, turned up on his doorstep later that evening with good news, adding fuel to the afterglow Asher was already experiencing after Jo's afternoon visit. Asher had been out on bond, but this was the news he'd been hoping to hear. Thanks to Carly's chat with Moreno, all criminal charges would be dismissed.

The possibility of a civil suit brought by Phoebe Anderson and her father still remained, but Bohrman seemed certain that the dismissal of the criminal charges would persuade the Andersons to rethink their options.

"None of this could have happened if you hadn't come forward with that name." Bohrman shrugged, lowering onto the living room couch. "It helped that Moreno was receptive. All we needed was enough evidence to draw some doubt. We had the phone records from that night and Sutherland's history, but Moreno did the hard work, convinced the girl to talk."

"How is she—Carly?" Asher asked, imagining what it must have took for her to name Sutherland, place blame at the risk of her sister. "Have they found her sister?"

Bohrman lifted a shoulder and let it drop, an obvious but silent, *"What does it matter now?"*

"What about Sutherland?" Asher carved the words into the silence, his eyes laser focused on the neatly pressed frat boy in front of him. "Where is he?"

He and Jeff Bohrman never would have been friends in school. The more time Asher spent with him, the more obvious it was that they ran in completely different circles. Bohrman would've been part of the popular crowd—the kids who got invited to post-game parties and dated cheerleaders. Asher never quite made it that far up the social ladder.

"Moreno didn't have to look far. According to probation records, he's back in his old neighborhood in Columbus. Hard to tell how accurate that is, though. Guy's got a rap sheet a mile long. Always manages to snake his way out of doing any hard time." Bohrman drew a stack of paper out of his briefcase and passed Asher the hefty packet of stapled pages.

"Always has." The words slipped out as Asher flipped through the brief history, his eyes holding on the last known address–617 Presley Avenue, Columbus, Ohio–an address Asher knew too well. He turned a few more pages, glanced at more recent dates–a DUI on I-70, some minor drug possessions charges, both in Ohio–Sutherland knew better than to do the dirty work himself. There was nothing more sinister, nothing on paper indicated he could have been responsible for Caroline Dalton's disappearance, or Carly's abuse.

"You said Carly named him–told Moreno that Sutherland was responsible?"

"That's right."

"What is he doing about it?" Asher itched to call Moreno himself, find out exactly what was being done to get Sutherland off the street.

Bohrman leaned forward in his chair, his suit jacket crumpling in rolls at the shoulder. "Look, I've read the reports from the Emily Franklin case. I know there's history. If there's something you know ..." He sucked in a breath, let the words drift. "Moreno is in our corner on this one." The lawyer rolled his eyes to the side, one brow jutting up. "I'm not exactly sure why or how, but he is."

"I haven't seen Sutherland for over six years," Asher admitted. "Maybe he's clean."

Bohrman was quiet for a moment. Asher felt him studying him, the heat of his gaze sizing him up. "Do you really think that?"

"No." Asher pushed the papers back at the lawyer. "But I've got no proof. And I'm going to walk into an executive school board meeting tomorrow morning expecting the people who hired me to overlook *my* history, to give me the benefit of the doubt. According to karma, I should do the same for anyone else, right?"

"Guess so," Bohrman responded. Confusion weighted his words.

Asher sighed and leaned back against the sofa. "Have you ever felt completely out of control of your life, Jeff?"

Asher waited for a response but didn't get one.

"Like the world is spinning around you. The people you care about are coming and going, revolving in and out of your life on their own trajectory, and you are powerless to stop any of it? You can yell for them to stop ... To stop running, stop hurting themselves, stop putting themselves in harm's way. But they don't hear you. No matter how loud you yell, you're just..." Asher searched for the right words. "Invisible."

"Asher..." Bohrman's mouth hung open, gaping twice like a fish out of water. "I see you. The court sees you. You're a free man now. No case hanging over your head. A chance to get your job back. I thought that's what you wanted."

"Jesus Christ, Bohrman. I do want those things–a stable job, a life with Jo, Carly safe, her sister found." The heat in Asher's chest reached a boiling point. "But more than anything right now, I want Reed Sutherland to pay for what he's done. I don't fucking care what happens to me."

THIRTY-FIVE

ASHER

Asher walked up the steps to the entrance of Millbrook Academy Saturday afternoon for his dismissal hearing, in the same suit he'd worn for his interview. The fabric wasn't as fine as Jeff Bohrman's, didn't pucker in all the right places when he sat, but it was all he had, and until today, he'd been proud of it.

Asher wasn't sure what to expect. Small town news moved fast, especially when that news involved a teacher accused of assault and inappropriate conduct with students. He wasn't sure if the fact that the charges against him had been dropped would matter. There was no evidence that he'd done anything to directly endanger Carly's life. Phoebe had withdrawn her statement. The pendulum could swing either way. But he wasn't oblivious. He would still be considered a liability in the eyes of the school board. And no matter what the courts said, public opinion remained.

Ethan slipped into the conference room just as Baum readied to address Asher. Asher had asked both his brother and Jo not to come. But now that Ethan was here, Asher's thoughts focused on Jo. The weight of her absence sunk through his chest like lead. They hadn't talked since she'd left his house yesterday afternoon, and let's face it, they both knew how what happened here this afternoon might impact her own career just as much as his. And seated now, in front of six angry-looking school board members, Asher wished she'd ignored his request. He could use all the support he could get.

Baum cleared his throat. "Let's get to the business at hand," he began. "A legal matter's been brought to our attention involving one of our Millbrook teachers, Mr. Asher Thompson." Baum nodded at Asher, and six pairs of accusatory eyes locked on his. "Some of the accusations against Mr. Thompson involve improper relations with minor students, in particular, Phoebe Anderson and a scholarship recipient named Carly Dalton."

"Those charges were dropped," Asher forced the words through the clench in his throat.

Baum paused, eying the papers in front of him. "Yes. I see that." He passed the documents down the line to the other board members. Asher watched their faces. The downward tip of their lips. The furrow of their brows. All of it proof of the only acceptable ruling a school board could make under the circumstances.

Baum narrowed his gaze on Asher. "And where is Miss Dalton now, Mr. Thompson?"

"I can answer that," Moreno cut in from the back of the room before Asher could respond. "My name is Detective Vic Moreno, with the Brookside PD. I've been the lead detective in charge of this case. Miss Dalton has been placed in a residential facility thanks to the generosity of Mr. Thompson."

Baum leaned back, crossing his arms. The chair creaked under his weight. "Was she, or was she not, staying in Mr. Thompson's home prior to the incident in question?"

"She was."

"And you felt she was safe there, Detective–a seventeen-year-old girl with a twenty-four-year-old man?"

"Both her case worker and I felt it was the right decision for Carly at the time."

"Carly was my student," Asher cut in. "She'd just lost her father and her sister is missing. I thought I could help."

"Help?" Baum echoed.

"To provide some stability, nothing more." Asher fought the bead of irritation at Baum's implication. He pulled himself up straight in the uncomfortable metal chair. "As the record indicates, both the Brookside Police, and the courts, found in my favor."

"But there is something else, Mr. Thompson. This isn't the first time you've been investigated for a sexually motivated crime, is that right?"

"If you're referring to the incident regarding Emily Franklin, those charges were also dropped." Asher deflated. Could hear the murmur of the small crowd behind him. Baum was doing this for show now.

"In spite of the rulings of the court, this school board's number one priority is the protection of our most valuable assets, our students. As such, we are unanimous in our decision to terminate your contract with Millbrook Academy, effective immediately. Mr. Albertson will walk you down to your classroom where you may take the next fifteen minutes to gather any personal effects you may have left. Thank you."

There was a rumble from the onlookers as the elderly custodian, Mr. Albertson approached Asher with outstretched hand. His eyes were kind as Asher stood.

"This meeting is adjourned." Baum's voice echoed as Ronnie Albertson pushed open the conference room door. The gavel rapped against the wooden table, sending an involuntary shudder through Asher as the custodian led him into the empty hall.

"I put a couple boxes on your desk, Mr. T.," Ronnie said as they approached Asher's classroom. "I'm sorry about this. Truly." Ronnie scrubbed a worn hand over his curly gray hair. "I'll give you a few minutes."

"Thanks, Ronnie." Asher slipped inside the semi-darkness of his empty classroom, still processing what this would mean for his future, when Ethan showed up.

"You could fight this, you know." His little brother's voice jerked Asher out of the Tilt-a-Whirl his mind had created–spinning from one possibility to another.

Asher nodded, picked up a book from the clutter on his desk. "What's the point?" He loosened his tie, slid some books into the empty box on his desk. "Maybe this is for the best. Maybe I was never cut out to be a teacher."

"You care more about those kids than any teacher I've ever met. Christ, Ash. I wouldn't be here if I didn't believe that. Forget Baum and the board members. Because of you, Carly's safe. She'll get the counseling she needs. She'll have a chance at a future. That's all because of you, brother."

Asher was quiet. Listening as his kid brother ripped a falsely motivational poster from the cinderblock wall.

"The board wasn't wrong about everything, you know."

Ethan turned. Eyes boring into the side of his brother's head.

Asher shrugged. "When Carly was staying at my place, she came onto me–twice. I must have done something to cause that, right? I deserve this, Ethan. The school district is doing the right thing." Asher sunk into the chair at the front of the room.

His mind spun through possibilities. Memories of Emily flickered with the voice of the past he'd heard on the other end of the line when Carly called from the woods. Carly's crumpled body lying motionless on the bank of the creek. The drug induced convulsions that forced the call to 9-1-1. Betrayal. Guilt. Jo's forgiveness. The perfection of the afternoon they'd spent together.

"What if all I've done is cause more pain, Ethan?"

"Ash, you haven't. You gave Carly a chance. You protected her. Fought for her."

"But I didn't fight hard enough did I? Not for Jo, not for Carly, and definitely not for Emily. Reed's still out there, Ethan. If Reed is responsible for this, I failed them all. I should have turned him in when I had the chance."

"Maybe. But what's done is done." Ethan stood with his hands on the desk, leaning into Asher's space. "If you need someone to blame, blame Dad. Dad failed Emily. For God's sake, Ash, Dad failed *us*. It's not your fault you got caught in the blood spatter."

THIRTY-SIX

ASHER

Asher left the boxes of his former life in his Jeep and took the stairs to Jo's apartment two at a time. He'd called twice on the way over, her phone going to voicemail both times. But he needed to see her, needed her to tell him that everything was going to be okay. But when he rounded the corner of the second floor his feet slowed, his brain working to process what he saw.

A sliver of light fell in a thin line onto the gray indoor/outdoor carpet of the shared hallway in front of him. He followed the glow to Jo's front door, cracked just enough for the rays of soft white interior light to escape in a fight against daylight. Asher glanced across the hall. The apartment on the other side was silent, a spring wreath encircling the peephole. He sucked in a ragged breath, a vise clamping around his lungs. Worry pricked the hairs along the nape of his neck—a chill he couldn't shake.

"Jo?" He called her name and pushed the door inward, the chill creeping from his neck and traveling down his arms and spine.

Asher called her name once more before the disorder of the room sucked the air from his lungs. The chairs near the breakfast bar were tipped over, laying at odd angles on the laminate floor. The cushions of the couch where he'd sat with Jo the last time he was here were slashed, their cotton batting strewn across the floor like small drifts of snow.

His eyes darted around the room, kitchen cabinets opened and violated, their contents now splayed across the countertops in helpless heaps. Shock wore off just enough for his eyes to focus on the hall. Asher stumbled past the kitchen toward the back of the apartment, kicking his way around a displaced ottoman and overturned end table. The lamp it once held safely, now smashed into shimmering pieces on the ground.

He surged toward Jo's bedroom, his lungs burning against what-ifs and how-tos. Her door was locked. The tongue of the latch stuck out from the side of the mechanism like a thirsty dog. The door hung open, splinters of wood near the handle and along the frame told him the story. She'd locked herself in here. He fingered the scorched wood along the edge of the frame. Whoever was here had shot their way in.

This room was as trashed as the rest of the house. Her intimate space invaded, jewelry armoire tipped, its contents strewn like glittering Mardi Gras beads. But that wasn't what caught his attention. A small pool of deep mahogany spread in a nearly perfect circle on the side of the bedspread. He sunk to his knees. His chest tight. Lungs on fire.

"Jo," he whispered, fingers trailing the edges of the cooled pattern of blood. The spatter of dark against the light gray softness of Jo's comforter burned into his memory. A surge of adrenaline shot through him, masking panic and heating his core as his fight or flight response kicked in. He jerked his cell phone from his pocket and punched three numbers he swore he'd never use again. 9-1-1.

ASHER SAT on the curb outside of Jo's apartment. Magenta and electric blue lights swirled from the squad cars, contaminating the quiet of the apartment complex and reflecting against white siding as the sun slipped behind the western clouds. Neighbors were now gathered outside of their homes, lining the sidewalk across from Jo's building.

Asher kept his head down, ignoring the buzz of voices from across the stretch of asphalt. The cop squatting next to him was committed to asking the same stupid questions the first officer on the scene had posed. "When did you arrive? How long were you in the apartment? Did you see anyone exit the apartment? How do you know Jo Harrison? Was she expecting you?"

Asher answered each query with staccato beats until he couldn't take it anymore. "What the hell does that matter?"

"We're just trying to get a full understanding of what happened here tonight." The officer seemed unfazed by Asher's outburst.

"There's a pool of blood inside her bedroom, the door of which was blown halfway off its hinges, and you're worried about whether or not I was an invited guest?" Asher's voice rose above the din of onlookers, prompting a hush from the crowd. "Jesus Christ," he breathed, returning to his bowed position on the pavement, hands clasped hard over the back of his head.

"I'll take it from here." The voice was familiar. The shadow cast by Moreno's approaching figure gave Asher a momentary reprieve from the strobe of lights. Asher felt it in his chest first, the unclenching of the knot of frustration that coiled around his heart and lungs. For the first time since the authorities arrived, he rose from the curb. Thankful for a familiar face.

Moreno palmed Asher's shoulder, escorting him away from

the throng of police and rubberneckers toward a quiet gazebo about thirty yards from Jo's apartment building.

"You should have called me first. This is a circus."

Asher didn't respond. Waited for Moreno to ask all the same mundane questions the other officers had. Except, he never did.

"Preliminary look at the scene suggests robbery. I think you and I both know that's not what happened here tonight."

"Where's Sutherland?" Asher asked, hatred boiling through his core.

"You know I can't tell you that."

Asher clenched his fists, soothing the urge to hit something.

"I didn't get a chance to say it earlier, but I'm sorry about the board meeting." Moreno groaned lightly as he sat, motioning to the bench seat next to him.

Asher nodded and sat. Cool evening air skittered across exposed skin, lifting the hairs along the back of his neck. "I can't do this," Asher's voice floated on the breeze, a desperate whisper. "I can't lose her."

Moreno clapped a palm over Asher's shoulder. "We'll do everything in our power to find her. You have my word. But right now, it's important to stay open, level-headed."

"You mean don't jump to conclusions," Asher sat straight, shrugging out of contact.

"It's important to go about this the right way." Moreno answered, lifting from the seat next to Asher.

"I'm sure Hastings would love to pin this on me. I was in the apartment. I think I touched ..." Asher looked at the tip of his index finger, just a tinge of red remained.

"You let me worry about Hastings." Asher detected the note of regret in Moreno's voice. "This is a question I have to ask. Is there any connection between Jo and Reed Sutherland that you can think of?"

Asher blinked through the realization. "Just me," he admitted, knotting his hands between his knees.

Moreno nodded.

Asher watched the detective silently survey the scene across the lawn. Cops in and out. The crime scene unit van had arrived and was entering the building with satchels of equipment.

"What happens next?" Asher asked.

Moreno exhaled loudly. "We find Jo. Keep an eye on Carly." The detective paused. "Stop Sutherland from doing something he can't undo."

Asher didn't respond right away. The weight of Moreno's words sank into his gut, twisting.

"Where is he?" he asked again. He already knew Reed was behind everything, from Carly's abuse to Jo's disappearance. But he didn't know why.

"Columbus," Moreno stated simply. "I'm waiting on a warrant."

"How long will that take?"

"It's not as cut and dry and you might think. All I've got is a cold case suicide with no solid evidence and a statement from a girl who's been known to be less than truthful with police."

"And a missing case worker."

"With no connection to the suspect," Moreno added, pointedly. "But I'm on it, Thompson."

Asher sucked in a long breath. His lungs ached.

"I went back through Emily's case file. You gave us his name the night we brought you in. And if he was here tonight, we'll find out." Moreno set his eyes on Asher. "We failed Emily. But we won't fail Jo."

Asher swallowed the knot in his throat. "This was him, Moreno."

The detective nodded, returning his gaze to the activity at Jo's apartment. "We'll find her, Asher. You have my word."

THIRTY-SEVEN

CARLY

O nly one girl in my house at New Dawn had phone privileges. But she was easily bought for the pack of cigarettes I'd found hidden in my mattress the day I arrived. She brought the handset to me after group on Saturday night.

"Phoebe?" I cupped my hand over the mouthpiece. "I needed to hear your voice."

The line was silent, but only for a moment. I heard the click of a door in the background. "They told me you couldn't have visitors. That you didn't have phone privileges, yet."

"I don't. I'm ... borrowing," I admitted.

"I need to see you, Car. There's something I need to tell you—something you need to know."

"Can you come get me?" No way was I mincing words. Who knew how long before they checked the cameras and realized I was on an unapproved phone call.

"When?"

"Tonight, eleven-o'clock."

Silence stretched on the other end. "My dad, he's ... he's not happy with me right now."

I rolled my eyes. I didn't fucking care whether or not daddy's little angel had tarnished her halo over the past couple weeks. I needed a ride, and if I couldn't get one from her, I'd beg, borrow, or steal enough money to get a cab.

"Please," I breathed into the phone. I really need to see you, Phoebe." I listened. Heard her breath hitch.

"Okay. I'll be there. Eleven."

"Pick me up at the corner of Bethel and Glenview. There's a COTA stop there. I'll be in the bus shelter, it'll hide us from the cameras." I ended the call just as the night nurse tapped on the door.

"Lights out," she said in her sing-song voice. No one should be that happy here, not even a nurse. I glanced over at Taylor's already sleeping form, and my heart softened, blooming in my chest like a flower. Tonight wasn't just about me or Caroline. It was for all the other Taylors out there.

I shoved the handset of the phone under my mattress and sunk under the covers. I didn't bother undressing. What was the point? I glanced at the clock on my nightstand as the nurse's voice echoed down the hall, humming a tune I didn't recognize. I closed my eyes, content in the understanding that she was just as mad as the rest of us.

⨵

I CLIMBED in Phoebe's car just as the clock on her dashboard turned from 11:07 to 11:08.

"Sorry I'm late," she blubbered. "Dad was still up and I had to sneak out my bedroom window to get out of the house. Almost broke my ankle jumping from the porch roof. You're lucky I made it at all."

She reached for my hand as I pulled the door closed. I gritted my teeth, forced myself not to pull away.

"Where are we going?" She smiled at me, that bright beaming smile she'd flashed the first day we met. That smile that put me at ease, didn't ask too much or expect too little. From day one, she'd been my friend. I felt the pull of regret in my face. Even as she laced her fingers through mine now, I knew it could never be that way again.

I sucked in a breath and rattled off the address as she pulled away from the curb. I expected push back—at least a few questions—but there was no sound. Just the bob of her throat as she swallowed, her skin illuminated by the dashboard lights.

I drew her hand to my lips, watching for her reaction as my breath skimmed along her fingertips. She closed her eyes, relishing the moment. I pressed my lips together to keep the smile at bay and sat back in the warm bucket seat. Reaching into her cup holder I snatched her cell and broke contact to type the address into the map app.

Phoebe glanced at the phone when the computerized voice announced, "Forty-nine minutes to your destination."

Her eyes caught mine in the semi-darkness. A question she was too afraid to voice tamped down by desire. If there was one thing I'd learned in my time on this earth, it was that sex could get you just about anything. Men had been using it to their fullest advantage for the past century, why not me?

A bubble of guilt threatened as I watched Phoebe, her blue eyes wide as we drove in silence, the computerized voice directing her to the edge of Brookside and onto the interstate. I wondered when she'd ask me why we were going so far. But silence stretched.

I slid my hands over the smooth leather of the seat. Like most kids at Millbrook Academy, the brand new Audi had turned up in Phoebe's driveway on her sixteenth birthday, complete with a big, pink bow. The whole idea of receiving a car as a birthday present was ludicrous to me. Even if Mom had still been alive and Dad had been able to keep his job with the bank, I felt certain a car would never have been within the realm of possibility on my sweet sixteen.

I listened to the quiet hum of tires against pavement. The high-dollar car blocked out nearly all the road noise, so unlike the van Eli drove to the lot three times a week. The dash lights reflected against Phoebe's porcelain skin, and I remembered my last ride in Eli's van—alone and scared. Our worlds seemed a million miles apart. How had we ever become friends? What would she think when she pulled up to the duplex Reed called home? I shook the thought away. It didn't matter what she thought.

The hum of the car lulled me. A memory of Caroline clear as day. She'd baked me a cake on my sixteenth birthday. Well, she'd tried anyway. It was complete with blue and purple flowers, my name scrawled across the top in wavy, unsure letters. I squinted against the memory, remembering where I was. The heat of tears threatened the backs of my eyes and I sucked in a silent breath, holding it in my lungs until they burned. I could see Caroline looking at me, her blue eyes demanding an answer, *"Why are you doing this?"*

"For truth," I exhaled, the choke of a sob catching on the final syllable.

"What was that?" Phoebe glanced at me, removing her right hand from the wheel long enough to cover my own. Her touch was warm, gentle. "We could turn around, go back home. I don't know where you're going or what you're planning to do, but I know you, Carly. You're not okay."

"Just drive, Phoebe." I pulled my hand from her cocoon of warmth and directed my attention out the window.

She didn't say another word. Left me to battle demons in a fitful sleep. I woke when Phoebe's GPS pinged, signaling the turn onto Presley Avenue. Only then did I begin to question my decision.

"That's it. Up ahead on the left." I pointed toward a run-down old row house. Swaths of graffiti swirled illegible designs under the partially boarded front window. The houses around Reed's were dark, appearing empty, but only a few of them actually were. Condemned, maybe. But that didn't stop the squatters. I focused on Reed Sutherland's place. Lights glowed from inside number 617.

Phoebe pulled into an empty spot along the curb across from the house and killed the engine. I followed her gaze toward the door, the reflection of the lone streetlight flickered on her face and neck. Her eyes widened as the door to the house swung outward. A man staggered out, laughing. He gripped the handrail, rocking back and forth, navigating the steps toward the sidewalk. Once there, he threw a wave toward the house. I squinted to see who it was, but I didn't recognize his face.

Phoebe turned to face me. "What is this place?"

"It's where I think Reed took my sister."

"You've been here before?" Phoebe asked. Her voice wary.

"Just once," I admitted. *Initiation.* The word screamed in my skull.

"Please, Carly. Let's go back home. We can tell the cops about this place. Let them handle it."

"Like you let them handle Mr. Thompson?" My words bit at the air. Left Phoebe speechless. "They have Caroline. I can't wait for Moreno to get his shit together. As soon as Reed knows I talked, he'll kill her. I can't let that happen."

Phoebe's lips parted, her eyebrows scrunched. "She might already be dead." Phoebe acted as though the words were painful to say.

"I have to know. Besides, it's okay. I know these people. It's really not as bad as it looks."

The lie pounded against my eardrums. But I sounded more convincing than the knot in my chest gave me credit for.

Phoebe only nodded. A tear trickled from the corner of her eye as she stared at me. "I'm sorry, Carly. I'm sorry my dad got a hold of those pictures. I'm sorry for leading them believe that about Mr. Thompson. It wasn't fair. I never meant to hurt you."

I took a chunk of my bottom lip between my teeth, coercing the return of anger. I reached to brush the tear from her cheek. When was the last time someone had cried over me? The knot in my chest tightened as I popped the passenger door. The cool night air seeped in through the crack, sending a shiver down my spine.

"Call me when you find Caroline. I'll come get the two of you."

I nodded, unable to speak through the threat of possibility.

"Or I could wait for you, right out here."

I glanced up and down the nearly deserted street, considering her offer. A squat brick building sat off to the right. Maybe an old school. It was too run down now to tell. But I could see the shadows of lurking figures, pinpoints of light as they drew in a hit of whatever they were smoking. They'd already noticed the car. The last thing I needed on my resume of responsibility was a car-jacked best friend.

"Go home, Phoebe. I'll find a ride."

"Wait," Phoebe dug around in her purse, coming out with several crinkled bills. "Here, just take this. Get a cab or something, okay?"

I grabbed the cash and swung open the door. The group of shadowy figures had already started a slow saunter toward the electric blue Audi shining under the one operable streetlight.

I leaned my head inside. "You need to go, okay?" I flicked

my head to the side, an indication for Phoebe to check out the group approaching from the lawn behind me.

She nodded as I slammed the door. The engine roared to life as I took off across the pavement. Fueled by the squeal of her tires at the end of the street, I took the stairs two at a time, hesitating at the front door. Phoebe's car disappeared around the corner and I raised my fist to knock on the door of number 617 Presley Avenue just like I'd done once before.

THIRTY-EIGHT

CARLY

I checked over my shoulder for the thugs, but Presley Avenue was clear. They'd dispersed, slinking back to the shadows. The cold night breeze washed over my skin, brushing my hair away from my face and neck. I raised my fist, ignoring the phantom pressure of Caroline's hand against my spine, her whispered words, *"You can do this Carly ... for us,"* and knocked. Three quick thumps, loud enough to chase away the ghost of the first night I'd come here.

A man I didn't recognize answered the door with a head to toe scan. I must have passed his litmus test because he swung the door wide, nodding me inside.

"Got a visitor," he hollered toward the back of the house. He ushered me into the house with his palm splayed against the small of my back. I swallowed against the involuntary clench in my chest, the first hint of the rising thread of panic.

I blew out a ragged breath, thankful for the Xanax the doctor at New Dawn insisted on prescribing. I'd gotten pretty good at hiding them in my cheek when the nurses came with our meds. I wasn't the only one who spit their pharmaceuticals in the toilet or, like Taylor had shown me, stockpiled them for later use. Tonight was bound to be a good night for anti-anxiety medication, and I'd already popped two of them while waiting for Phoebe to pick me up.

"Is Reed here?" I asked, bolting my feet to the floor. The room reeked of marijuana and cigarette smoke, and I was barely in the door before some unknown waif with hooded eyes offered me a hit. She trailed a finger through my hair. "Pretty," she slurred, making it obvious she was rolling on more than just weed.

The doorman nodded and waved toward the back of the house, abandoning me to wrap a hand around the girl's waist and take her up on the offer. She moaned as he pinched the joint between his fingers and buried his head in her neck. I stepped around them both, glancing back once when she giggled, his hands grabbing her ass as he ground against her. That was an image I wouldn't get out of my head for a while.

The door to the kitchen swung both ways like an old saloon door. I'd been knocked with it when Caroline brought me here that first night. I hung back with my hand extended, ready to catch the slab of wood if it swung toward me. I pressed with my fingers and it gave easily, so I shoved inward.

Reed was seated at the kitchen table with Aaron's son, Eli. Eli minced white tablets into a fine powder with a razor blade, while Reed packaged Eli's dust into tiny little packages, wrapped in cigarette paper.

"Where's my sister?" My voice sounded hard, forced.

Eli stopped mid-cut, surprise flickering over his features, while Reed finished his wrap without looking at me. His lips curled into a snake of a smile.

"Carly Dalton, I wondered when you'd find your way back home." Reed pushed his chair out, wood on wood grating against my eardrums. I forced myself not to back away as he came forward, battling the fear that locked my lungs in a painful clench. He grabbed my chin in his hand, turning my face from one side to another. "Looks like you're no worse for wear. How's the foot?"

"Fine," I managed.

Buried memories of his appearance at the truck stop trickled into my brain. Moments I'd hoped had been figments of a drug-induced overactive imagination now solidified into reality. "You were there. In the woods."

"You should know better than to interfere with business, Carly." His eyes darkened. His lips curled. "Somebody had to make sure you didn't do something stupid now that Caroline's not around."

Faint memories seeped in—hands on my skin, heated breath against my ear, weight on top of me. I fought to assign Reed's face to the memory, but it wouldn't come. I stepped backward.

"Where is she?" I glanced at Eli, who kept his head down, let Reed take the lead, just as he had the night Caroline disappeared.

"Carly, we've been over this." Reed closed what little space there was between us, positioning himself between me and the closest escape route. He pushed my hair back from the sides of my face, cupping my cheeks in a hard squeeze. "And frankly, I'm getting tired of the drama."

Reed hadn't changed since the last time I'd seen him. Shaggy light brown hair hung in half-curls over his forehead and around his ears. The beginnings of fine lines hinted at the corners of his eyes as he squinted, cocking his head to the side. He was probably Asher's age, but he looked much older.

He slid one hand from my cheek to my waist and pulled me against him. My chest tightened, a cocktail of hate and fear heating my veins. The rhythmic *click-click* of Eli's razor blade hiccupped and slowed.

"The police know what happened at the truck stop. I told them everything. They're looking for you, Reed." At this point I wasn't sure what Moreno believed and didn't believe. But I needed leverage. "You can't hide forever."

Reed gripped the collar of my shirt and pulled me in. His breath seethed in my face. "Don't fuck with me, Carly. I will destroy you the same way I destroyed your sister."

His face flushed red and nostrils flared. The gun he kept tucked in the back of his pants wagged near my midsection. I winced against the jab of the barrel into my ribs, once, twice, stabbing harder each time. My eyes watered. My hands instinctively wrapped around his wrists.

"Do it," I dared. "I've got nothing to lose."

Wood scraping wood ended the standoff. "Let her go, Reed. She's not worth it." Eli stepped between us, his hand on Reed's chest, pushing him away. "You've already got Caroline's death on your hands do you really need to dip your hands in more Dalton blood?"

It was the word "death" that got my attention—confirmation of what I already knew was true. I stared at Eli. The man who had played up this business to Caroline. Who had pretended to love her. Had sworn to protect her.

"Your hands are just as dirty, Eli." I didn't mean to speak, but the words came like the wave of a tsunami. "Where were *you*? Caroline trusted you, and you left her to die."

Eli's green eyes darkened, his voice soft. "He was a regular, Carly. I thought she'd be safe."

"Safe?" The knife's edge of a scream bit against my throat. "You think I don't remember the first time she went with him? He drugged her up so high she didn't know her own name. This time he used her up and tossed her out. And you left without her."

"That's not how it happened."

"Your *regular* even took her necklace, or were you too busy screwing around with the new girls to notice?"

Reed's fingers dug into my shoulders as I raged. I pulled against his grip, stepping closer and closer to Eli. All this time I'd blamed Reed. But it was never his fault Caroline was dead. That was on Eli. Eli sucked her into the game. Eli was there that night. Eli turned her over to Reed. If any one of those decisions had been different, my sister wouldn't be dead.

"Caroline loved you, Eli." The tears choked me, climbing up the back of my throat and solidifying into a hardened knot. "Was it really only about the money for you? Please tell me there was more."

His eyes softened in the silence. Pain. Regret.

Reed pushed Caroline to turn more tricks, but Eli was the one who brought her drugs, promising relief from the pain of abuse until the Caroline I knew disappeared, became one of the girls hunched in a corner at the end of a long night, leaving me to battle the memories alone.

Reed spun me around, a deep phlegmy chuckle erupted from some dark nook of his soul. A shiver slithered down my spine in response. He waved toward Eli. "You want to blame him for what happened to Caroline. But seems to me you need to take a look in the mirror. Caroline only stayed because of you."

"Shut up," I warned. I couldn't listen to this.

Reed stepped forward as I fought his grip. "But to get you out for good she needed money—a way to put a roof over your head. You know as well as I do, she couldn't afford that. Not without me. What was she supposed to do?"

He wanted an answer, but I wouldn't give him one. I twisted my wrist against his fist until it hurt, tender skin screaming in protest.

"Reed, let her go, man." Eli's voice broke through the background noise. The hard ledge of the countertop dug against my spine.

But Reed continued. "All she wanted was a better life for her little sister."

Crooked teeth sneered at me from under dry lips. I struggled, his fingers digging into my flesh.

"Reed," Eli's arm snaked its way onto Reed's shoulder before the bigger man shrugged it off.

"The work took its toll, Carly." He traced a finger down my jawline. "Caroline wasn't hard like you. She couldn't do it without some prefab courage."

Reed picked up a little wrapped ball from the countertop and held it out toward me. "A little of this, and she never thought twice. She'd go all night." He glanced at Eli. "We all benefitted. Even if Eli's slow to admit it."

The heat of tears threatened the backs of my eyes. I blinked them away. "What did you do with her?" It was weak—a whisper wrapped in sorrow.

"No one cares what happens to a used up hooker, Carly. Let it go."

He stepped into me, jerking my hands up and pinning them against the upper cabinetry. The weight of him held me tight, just as it had that night in the woods. I closed my eyes and steadied my breath. It had always been about control for him.

Reed leaned forward. Inhaled against my ear. Spikes of fear clawed at my skin as he released his breath, lips skimming the hollow at the base of my neck. I yearned for the bite of cold steel against my skin. Anything was better than this.

Reed's jaw tightened as he leaned over me. The heat of his body firm against mine as he maneuvered me toward the nearest solid wall, the basement door from what I could tell. The peak of his hairline, the darkness of his eyes ushered in another unwelcome memory.

My first night at Reed's. My hand in Caroline's as she led me up to Reed's room. *"Initiation,"* she'd called it. *"Don't worry, Car. He won't hurt you if you don't fight."* She'd squeezed my hand. *"Just do whatever he asks. Don't ask questions."*

Pinpricks of anxiety began a slow march across my scalp as he leaned closer, grinding against my pelvis. His breath fell hot and wet against my cheek as he whispered, "Your sister owed me, Carly, and I plan to collect."

"Jesus," Eli cursed, grabbing once more at Reed's shoulder, his grip just enough to throw Reed off balance.

"Go to hell." I kicked as Eli pulled, my knee connecting with Reed's groin with satisfying accuracy. Reed dropped to his knees, hands hovering protectively over his crotch. He rolled to the floor, gasping for breath between promises to kill me. I took off at a sprint for the back door, shoving chairs aside to get there.

Eli reached for me, his hand securing a grip on my elbow, wrenching me toward him. I jerked away once before the look in his eyes caught my attention. Worry. Regret. He shoved me toward the door, and I stumbled, my knees colliding with the dingy hand scraped pine plank of the floor. His hand wrapped around my waist, lifting me free.

"Run," he whispered.

The word echoed in my mind as I stumbled down the back steps and into the yard, dodging an obstacle course of lawn furniture and empty beer cans. I kicked one and it ricocheted off the privacy fence with an empty *clunk*. I grabbed for the latch, twisted the lever and pushed it open. The angry creak of hinges replaced Eli's voice as the gate swung open, emptying me into the darkened alley.

THIRTY-NINE

CARLY

"Run," Eli's voice repeated in my mind. But fear froze me in place against the neighbor's section of splintery fence. My heel throbbed, not yet healed from my tumble down the ravine. How I ever thought I'd manage a foot chase was beyond me.

"Carly?" Reed's voice called from the yard less than fifty feet away.

"I couldn't catch her." Eli worked the words in between faked heavy breaths.

"You let her get away." Blame dripped, permeating the quiet of the night. I held my breath, strained to hear Eli's response. But the moment was silent. Punctuated by the first sickening thud of hardened fist on flesh. Eli's guttural protests. One man beating his frustration out on another.

Sudden silence broken by the metallic jingle of a locked gate, forced me into a lopsided run, pain be damned. My tennis shoes pounded out a rhythmic chant against the gravelly pavement of the alley. My breath grew ragged, my feet slowed.

Tears choked my throat as grief clawed at me, the ebb and flow of waves against a rocky shore.

Caroline. My sister had been my protector. Imperfect, maybe, but it was through her I gained strength. Voices raged in my mind. My father yelling. My sister shouting in return. The slam of the door as she left. The same voices that haunted my dreams. Truth hit me like a wall, halting forward momentum. I was the reason she'd gone out that night. Caroline was dead because of me.

Tears clouded my vision, and I stumbled. On all fours, pebbles biting against the palms of my hands, the darkness of broken streetlights closed in. Droplets of rain pelted my skin, dotting my shirt with expanding circles of moisture. I pulled myself to my feet, staggering toward—what? There was nowhere to go. I looked back. I'd only made it a few more houses down by the time the skies opened. Cold slices of icy rain stung my face. My hair slapped in wet strands every time I forced myself into a hobbled run, checking over my shoulder for Reed.

I turned the corner into an adjoining alley, stopping some-where in the next block. I tucked myself in the shadow of a dilapidated garage, the overhang my only shelter against the storm. I bent over, sucking in uneven breaths. Blowing out puffs of wet air, I worked to calm my burning lungs and racing heart. The pounding of my heel and the taunting truth in my skull, though, were binds I couldn't shake.

Thunder rumbled overhead and lightning split the sky, illu-minating the alley for a second—empty. I stood, jeans sucking at my legs and my t-shirt plastered against the damp skin of my chest. As I rested against the garage door, a low rumble vibrated from the ground near my feet.

The bottom of the door was cracked, just enough for a pink and brown nose to poke through. I knelt to get a closer look just as the animal on the other side lunged, rattling the overhead door in its tracks. Teeth glistened with the next bolt of lightning. The dog strained against the door, clawing and snarling at the broken cement at my feet. Barking and growling overtook the soundtrack of pounding rain.

I backed away, crossing the pavement to the other side of the alley, limping from one garage to another, flattening against the cold block walls of the single car sheds that dotted the darkened pathway.

The glow of lights from the main street was just one more block away. I'd almost made it. I dashed once more, but this time, as I crossed, I heard laughter. I poked my head from under the overhang, straining to make sense of what I'd heard, as a final rumble of thunder crackled through the sky.

The human sounds came from the other end of the alley again, this time followed by a single word, "Please." A sob of panic.

Phoebe.

"Please don't." Her choked cry came again, striking me like a punch to the chest. I stepped from the shadows, the rain running in rivulets from my scalp to my chin, trickling onto the exposed flesh of my neck.

In the dark, I could make out two figures standing in the glow of a lone streetlamp where the alleys met. Tangled in some kind of dance, their bodies locked in a struggle one of them was sure to lose. I squinted through the too-black space. Breath seized in my lungs as they disappeared around the corner and into the shadows. Reed's maniacal laughter my only clue they were still there.

I glanced over my shoulder. Cars whooshed by on wet pavement. One good sprint would get me there. I could get help. Call the police. *You're a runaway from a home for kids with emotional disorders, Carly. Who would believe you?* The voice came unbidden.

A piercing cry. Pain. The slam of a body against fence boards. Familiar whimpers. I knew those cries too well, but Phoebe's face in that world didn't mesh. Getting help was no longer an option. By the time I made it back it would be too late.

"Stop," I yelled and started toward the sounds in a half-hobble. Pebbles crunched under the soles of my tennis shoes. Everything went silent for a moment. No laughter, no sobs. Only tiny shards of ice pelting my face, the ground, popping up before settling into their spot in the gravel.

My heart ratcheted up a gear, the silence deafening, and I ran, focused on the uneven slap of my shoes against crushed rock and ice. "Reed!" My voice echoed against the surrounding fencing, bouncing from one lot to another, the note of hidden panic more evident with each bounce.

"Looks like someone came to save you after all." Reed's voice penetrated the darkness. He dragged Phoebe from the shadows as I rounded the corner, back into the round circle of streetlamp light. His fist twisted a thick rope of Phoebe's long blonde hair as he jerked her to her feet. "Come on out, Carly," he hollered. "Let me introduce you to your replacement."

His eyes scanned past me. It hadn't occurred to me until then, but in the shroud of darkness I was invisible. My chest clenched and I stopped walking. I glanced at the nearby garages. I could use them as cover, sneak up behind him. Have the element of surprise. The idea choked me, tightening its fingers around my throat. A shiver quaked down my spine. From cold or fear, I wasn't sure. I'd done the unthinkable, confronted Reed and lived to tell about it. And now I was going back.

"Carly?" Phoebe's voice split me in half. I couldn't leave

her here. Not with him. I sucked in a breath. What was the worst that could happen? *He'll kill you.* Caroline's warning trickled in. What did it matter? Death wish or not, Reed would not victimize Phoebe's life as he had mine.

I tiptoed forward. Forcing calm when the snarling demon in garage number three started in again. The door was still nearly closed. I drew a breath through aching lungs and kept walking.

"Please don't hurt me." Phoebe's arms were pinned behind her back, and she hiccupped a tiny scream as Reed jerked her head back, running the barrel of his gun down her neck, pressing it hard against her chest.

"What'll we do if she doesn't come back for you?" Reed asked as I stood–waiting, watching–just outside the halo of light.

"Run, Phoebe," I felt the scream in my chest. "Please, just run."

But she didn't. She couldn't. And she knew it. She'd get two steps before Reed would splatter her brain all over the gravelly pavement. I'd seen it happen. She was nothing to him. At least I was an income source.

I took another step toward the glow of the streetlamp. "Let her go." I sounded more confident than I felt. My hands shook at my sides, and my teeth chattered unless I clamped my jaw shut tight.

Reed looked from Phoebe to me, holding her in front of him as he squinted through the darkness. A smile crept onto his lips, sending another whole body shiver down my spine. They stood directly under the lone streetlamp, but its illumination barely reached the patch of gravel on which I stood. One more step.

Phoebe's mascara-lined face tore at me. Her blue t-shirt was ripped at the collar, exposing one creamy shoulder. One cheek was scuffed and reddened. Neither of them was soaked through, not even Reed. Beyond them, past the gate to Reed's house, the distinctive blue headlights of Phoebe's Audi shone in the darkness. The driver's side door hung open. Anger simmered alongside guilt. *Damn it, Phoebe.* I'd told her to go home.

One more glance over my shoulder toward freedom—instinct more than desire. Eli's voice hung thick in my brain, remorse turning like a spit in my stomach. Caroline had sworn to me she'd never let them take me out without her. It was our rule. Never turn tricks alone. Even when she was too high to care, she knew what cab I was in. And once she'd cleaned herself up, she turned her tricks and pretended—for me. Always for me. I shook away the thoughts of my sister.

"It's okay, Phoebe," I soothed, taking another step toward the pair. Phoebe's knees buckled when she saw me, and Reed kept hold of her hair as she hit the ground, knees first.

"Aw, now. Ain't that sweet." Reed mocked, a cockeyed grin splitting his face into a visual representation of evil.

"She hasn't done anything to you. Let her go."

He aimed his grin at me now. Phoebe's eyes widened as I stopped a couple feet from Reed.

"Untie her."

"Maybe she could help you work off your family's debt."

"That's between you and me, Reed. Phoebe has nothing to do with it."

The two of us stood in silence, like gunslingers in the old west movies I used to watch with my dad, except in this film only one of us had a gun. I swallowed a knot of fear. If he wanted to kill me, he would have done it already. But Reed didn't want me dead. I knew that much. I was too valuable. I choked on the sob of realization lodged in my throat. Turning tricks was the only thing I'd ever been good at.

"Let her go, and I'll stay. I'll do whatever you need me to do."

Reed cocked an eyebrow. "Anything?"

I nodded in answer. Too afraid to speak. I'd never let him see me cry.

Reed paused, contemplating my verbal consent. And I held my breath until he kneeled, fiddling with the ties at Phoebe's wrists while she murmured something unintelligible through tears.

She jerked away from him as soon as she was free, crawling on hands and knees until she reached me. I slid my hand through her hair, pulling her into my side. She gripped my leg like a monkey, hands tight, clawing at the wet denim of my jeans.

I wound an arm under her shoulders and held her to me. If anything had ever represented a moment of separation between her life and mine, this was that moment. Her eyes shown full fear, while I knew mine wavered between the dull ache of acceptance and grief.

I grabbed her hand, pressing the money she'd given me earlier against her palm. It was soft and wet from the rain, but it would spend. I brushed a blonde curl away from her face. He breath still rose and fell in rapid huffs. I hugged her against me. Reed was watching.

"Go back to your car," I whispered. "Go home, Phoebe. You weren't here tonight. I'm not here. Do you understand?"

She shook her head, snot bubbled from her left nostril.

"Please," I added as Reed's shadow fell over both of us. "There's no more time."

Standing in a dark alley, preparing for the torture to come, I pulled my best friend back onto her own two feet and set her free.

FORTY

ASHER

It was a little past midnight when Moreno climbed the steps of Asher's back deck.

"Thought I'd find you out here." He tossed something oblong toward Asher. "Thought you might be able to use this."

Asher caught the phone, turning it over in his hand. "In other words, you need a way to keep tabs on me."

Moreno didn't answer, just lowered into the Adirondack chair next to Asher.

"Do you have news?" His heart raced. He'd tried to sleep, but scenarios involving Jo ran circles through his brain, one possibility more evil than the next. He exhaled slowly, smoothing his thumb over the dark screen of his iPhone.

"When's the last time you saw Phoebe Anderson?" The question pricked at him, raising wall of defense that ebbed and flowed in Moreno's presence.

"The night Carly went to the lot." Asher forced the words out slowly. "Why?"

Moreno sucked in a sigh. "Phoebe's father reported her

missing. Last time he saw her was this morning. She told him she was going out to study with some friends."

"What does that have to do with me?" Asher asked.

Moreno lowered his voice and looked out over the lot and into the black smudge of trees. "I placed a call to New Dawn at Mr. Anderson's request. Carly is unaccounted for as well. I thought–hoped–you might have heard from one of them."

Asher sunk back against the tall wooden chair. Breath stuck in his chest. First Jo, now Carly. His heart thrummed an irregular rhythm against his sternum.

"I haven't," was all he could manage.

Moreno nodded. "Mind if I ask you a question? Off the record?"

Asher rubbed his forehead, kneading the tension from his temple. "Sure." His voice was tight, unsure.

"Why'd you get involved?"

"With Carly?" Asher asked.

Moreno dipped his chin in a nod, the glow from the porch light magnifying his features. "You risked your job. Your relationship. There has to be more to it than the ghost of Emily Franklin."

Words tumbled, unspoken, on Asher's tongue until he finally set them free. "I could have stopped him."

"Sutherland?" Moreno clarified.

Asher nodded.

"And he would have killed you." Moreno's words pricked Asher like ice. "Look, I've been doing this long enough to know what retaliation from men like Sutherland looks like. You had a family to protect." He paused, a gust of cold air, heavy with the threat of rain billowed around the corner of the house, rustled the trees. "So why now? Did you know Reed Sutherland was responsible for trafficking Carly Dalton?"

"That doesn't sound like an off the record question," Asher

started. "But, no, I didn't. Not until the night she called me from the woods."

"But she reminded you of your past."

"Of course. Doesn't she remind you of yours?" Asher's words landed with more force than he intended. Moreno's face squinted in a grimace. Asher backpedaled from the weight of their conversation. "Where are you on the warrant?" he asked.

"It's not looking good."

Asher's skin creeped with the answer, fury roiling beneath the surface.

"The woman I love is missing," he said into the night. "The student I tried to help is now an apparent runaway. And her best friend is gone from under her father's fancy roof. Please tell me the legal system understands the seriousness of this trifecta."

"I do," Moreno managed, guilt seeping from the words.

"I know how this works, Moreno. I've watched Jo go through the same thing. Fighting her way through rolls of bureaucratic red tape that protect the guilty more than the innocent. If you can't do something, just say the word, and I will." Asher stood, looking down on Moreno's hulking frame. "At this point what do I have to lose?"

Moreno stood. He wrapped his jacket tighter around his midsection, before turning to face Asher. He stuck out a hand in silence. Asher took it, pumped once. The folded slip of paper tucked in Moreno's palm bit hard against his flesh.

Asher unfolded the slip of paper and read. *617 Presley Avenue, Columbus.* "What are you saying?"

Moreno sighed, his voice full of painful resignation. "I'm saying my hands are tied. Anderson is coming after you with the full support of the D.A.'s office. Thinks you're responsible for Phoebe's disappearance and Hastings is his number one on this. Look, Asher, I'm not going to pretend to know everything that happened to you as a kid. But I do know guilt when I see it. And I see it in you. You'll never be able to change what happened to Emily, just like I can't change what happened to my daughter, but we can change what happens to Carly. With or without permission."

"Your daughter?" Asher asked, working his way through Moreno's words.

"Found dead in 02. She'd been abducted. Trafficked."

"I'm sorry. I didn't know." Asher lowered back onto the chair, Reed's address gripped tightly in his fingers, allowing the silence of the night to move in.

"It was easy," Asher started, "to help Carly from here, as a teacher. There was enough space between that life and mine. But now, I don't know if I can go back there." It may have been the most honest statement Asher had ever spoken.

"She needs you, Thompson. You can put the demons to rest—hers and yours. This isn't the end."

"What about Jo? Is Anderson blocking that investigation, too?" Fury clipped Asher's words.

Moreno's phone hummed beneath his jacket. He checked the screen and declined the call. "I should go."

The muscles in Asher's core tightened. A clap of thunder ricocheted in the distance. "Jo?" What was meant as a hopeful question came out flat—a statement.

"You know I can't tell you that." Moreno turned and trotted down the stairs.

Asher stepped back into the shadow of his porch. His heart hammered in his chest. "Find Jo," he said, voice tight. "I'll take care of this."

Moreno stopped at the foot of the stairs. "I know you will." Dark eyes locked on Asher's—a silent exchange of secrets—before Moreno disappeared into the night.

FORTY-ONE

CARLY

I could still feel the finger bruises on my upper arm where Reed had grabbed me after Phoebe ran, forced me back into the house and onto my knees. I don't remember what happened after that. An ache in the side of my head pulsed, offering a clue. But there was still just a wedge of blank where a memory should be.

My eyes blinked open in time to the thump of a pulsing beat as it hiccupped from the front room of the house. I was propped against the kitchen cabinetry. That, or I landed this way. I squinted against the pain in my skull when the nearby space erupted into cheers. I tried to bring my hand to my head, but felt resistance instead. The cold bite of plastic into the flesh at my wrists and ankles holding me hostage.

The rhythm grew louder, the walls of the old house throbbing. I didn't even hear the screech of the door swinging open as Eli entered. I blinked as he came closer, kneeled in front of me. He checked once over his shoulder before grabbing a dishtowel from the sink and pressing wet strands of my hair between his cloth covered palms.

His blue eyes latched onto mine. I could almost see what my sister had first seen in him. A mop of shaggy blond hair hung over his eyes, just enough to give him that purposely disheveled look, and his eyes pierced with an internal kindness that, in spite of his role in all this, somehow made him the good half of Reed's evil.

The knot in my throat swelled as he looked me over, checking for obvious injuries. His eyes stung me with pain, pity, sadness. I squinted against the scrutiny, an unwelcome tear sliding from the corner of my eye and skimming down my cheek before Eli wiped it away.

Footsteps sounded from beyond Eli. "That girl knows where we live. She's bound to tell. Cops'll come looking."

Eli wasn't talking to me, but he continued drying strands of my hair, calming the march of prickles.

Reed's voice broke into my thoughts. "We've got time. Let me worry about the big picture from here on out."

Reed shoved Eli with his shoe, toppling him off balance.

"I make the decisions. Got it." It was a threat, not a question. And Eli nodded, turning away as Reed disappeared up the stairs toward the bedrooms on the second floor.

"It's gonna be okay," Eli whispered. The dishtowel hung limp in his hand, too wet to do any good against my still damp skin. I braced against the shiver that started in my shoulders and vibrated downward.

Eli stripped out of his hoodie and wrapped it around my shoulders, tying the arms together in a loose knot.

"Bring her over here." Reed's voice echoed as he reentered the room, breaking through the persistent thump of music. He passed Eli and me, opening a mahogany door at the base of the stairs. When Eli's eyes left mine, I followed his gaze. A rectangular black hole stood like a gaping mouth where the door had once been.

Reed jerked his chin toward the opening. "Come on, Eli. Get her settled and we can deal with the other issues."

Eli stood, his hand firm on my shoulder. His lips moved in a whisper that grew as the pounding of the music swelled. "She's just a kid, Reed. You don't need to do this."

"No? She's my property, Eli. Collateral. I own her." Reed snorted a laugh. "I think Caroline made you soft. Man up, Carver. We've got a business to run."

"Fine." Eli's voice carried over the music, heated by anger. "If you don't want to let Carly go, fine. But put her upstairs, not the basement. There's an empty room. She's wet and cold, Reed. She'll freeze down there."

The two men stared at each other while my heart throbbed giant pulses in my chest. The rhythm of music thumped, the cabinets at my back jumped and rocked with the beat.

"Bring her here, Eli. Now."

But Eli didn't move.

Reed pulled the gun from his waistband, and cocked the hammer, pointing it at my skull. "Bring her here, or you can clean up her pieces."

I could feel the anger rolling off Eli as he bent in front of me. He sliced the bindings at my ankles with his pocket knife. His hands slid under my legs and back, hoisting me from the floor. The hard length of his closed knife slid into one of my back jeans pockets.

"I'll be back," he said into my ear, his breath warming my chilled skin. "I'm so sorry, Carly."

Reed jerked me from Eli's arms at the top of the darkened stairs and shoved me forward. I reached a foot forward to feel for a step, but there was none, just air past the threshold where stairs should be. Reed gave me one last thrust, plummeting me into the abyss.

I cycled my legs, but instinct or centrifugal force kept them glued to the doorsill, my toes gripping the only solid object I could see. My body twisted in the air, but without arms to catch me, my cheek met the broken concrete of the cellar floor with a sickening crack. The moan I heard in the darkness was my own. Pain radiated from my cheekbone and into my temple as I jackknifed forward, coming to rest in a crumpled heap.

I sucked at the damp air, tears seeping from the corners of both eyes. I struggled against the pain, groaning like a caged animal. I pushed at the tape on my lips with my tongue, but it held tight against my skin with no release.

I rolled onto my back just in time to see the light from the doorway disappear. The slam, followed by the click of metal on metal—locks being strung in place—echoed in already tender ears. A thin seam of light remained, coating everything around me in inky blackness.

Panic sucked at my lungs. I closed my eyes against it and focused on my breathing. *One in ... one out ... two in ... two out* ... In time, and as the silence around me grew, the breaths came more easily. The percussive thump of pain in my skull dulled to a manageable ache as long as I made no sudden movements.

Having overcome the initial shock of the fall, my sense of smell exploded, retaliating against the musty, rancid odor of the place. Part death, part animal feces, all consumed by the watery stench of a crumbling foundation in the aftermath of an early spring storm. Dragging in a full breath became a new challenge, my lungs and throat fighting to keep out the contaminants.

I tucked my head down into the protection of Eli's sweatshirt sleeve, digging my chin into it, I forced it over my nose and mouth and rolled to my side. I pulled my knees to my chest, extending my fingers like probes toward my hip pocket. No knife. I tried the opposite pocket just to be sure, but it wasn't there.

I coughed through the swollen knot climbing into my

throat. Rolling back and forth against the ground, my hands and body tuned to every lump and bump along the crumbling surface, searching for the small folded chance at freedom.

FORTY-TWO

ASHER

A sher never thought he'd set foot in his old neighborhood again, let alone drive up to the house that was the setting for so many of his childhood nightmares. The storm had ceased, blanketing the Columbus skyline in the gray gloom of a mid-March morning.

Asher sat in his car for a moment, watching the duplex. It didn't look quite so menacing with the ghost of daytime hovering, but even so, no one belonged here. Asher popped open the door of his Jeep. Lingering dampness from the nighttime storm crawled in over his legs. He swung one leg out as his phone rang, breaking through the silence like a child's cry in church.

Asher cursed and silenced the phone—just Ethan—and drew one final drag on the cigarette he'd nursed since arriving—it would be the last one, he swore. He flicked the butt into the nearby gutter. The windows of the house he'd once called home were dark. The corner of a yellow condemned sticker on the front door flapped in the breeze.

The blinds in the front window were drawn, but he could hear the dull thump of music. A stray shadow zigzagged back and forth in front of the window at odd intervals, or maybe it was all his imagination, at this point it was hard to tell.

Asher couldn't imagine Reed still living there. Both his parents were long gone, Asher knew that much, but Reed, still living in that house with those memories–the shiver walked in cold fingers down his spine.

He should have told Moreno everything–about his childhood, his one time friendship with Reed. Should have waited out the warrant, Anderson's threats, let the PD find Jo, deal with Reed. But who was more likely to get Sutherland to talk–a hardened detective, or a childhood friend? And if Jo was here. Asher stopped the train of thought. She wasn't. She couldn't be. He sanctioned off a corner of his thoughts for Jo, this life and hers should never coexist, let alone intermingle.

He scanned the street for faces from his past, but it was too early in the day. The windows in the row houses gaped at him, as if asking why he'd come back. *You got out,* they said. *Once you get out you should never come back.*

Asher stood across from the houses, the sense of déjà vu washing over him as he closed the driver's side door. A stab of memory sliced through him. The two of them, Asher and Reed, lying belly down, peeking through floorboards, as Reed's dad plied girls with MDMA. Hiding in Reed's room, they'd watched the girls roll, smiles creeping onto perfect cupid's bow lips. Reed's father always started slow, massaged their bare feet, working his way up young skin until they were high enough not to fight his full-fledged assault.

Asher clenched his eyes closed. He'd been so young–seven, eight when his father first introduced him to the Sutherlands, forced him into their world. He didn't know better. His stomach churned, guilt threatening to empty the egg McMuffin he'd forced down on the way. He was grown up now. And he had a better name for it–rape.

Asher lost count of the number of nights he and Reed had fallen asleep to the sounds of sex drifting from downstairs. But those nights changed Asher. Opened his eyes. While Reed slept, Asher schemed. He'd stare at the ceiling, plotting scenarios in which he'd help the girls escape, never to return. Only when the noise quieted was he able to sleep.

Reed had only picked up where his father had left off. Living in this hell-hole it was bound to happen. Same thing would have happened to Asher if he'd stayed. But this time was different. He'd never let a Sutherland go free again.

His phone buzzed from his pocket for the second time and he pulled it free, ready to ignore another call from his little brother. But one glance at the screen stopped him cold— Moreno. Asher's heart pitched into overdrive.

"We found Jo."

Some guttural sound akin to relief punched through him. Asher's gaze went back to the decrepit duplex, still shrouded in the mystery of morning. Whatever went on in that house was no longer his concern. Moreno could take care of this. His place was with Jo.

"Turned up in a county emergency department about thirty miles west of the city," Moreno continued. "She's being treated for dehydration, some minor lacerations." Moreno's voice was detached, distant. "She's asking for you."

The bubble of anxiety that Asher had bottled up in his gut since finding the blood in Jo's apartment, popped free.

"What about Carly?"

"Still looking. You?"

"Nothing," Asher said. Moreno didn't need to know he never went in.

"We've got a team going over security footage from New Dawn as we speak. I've offered to take Jo home when she's released. I told her you'd meet us there."

Asher thanked Moreno and trotted back to the Jeep. He skimmed the house once more and twisted the key in the ignition, coaxing the engine to life. Another imagined shadow passed by the front window. A girl, about Carly's height. Asher shook his head and looked again–nothing. His mind was playing tricks on him.

Asher clenched his eyes closed and revved the engine. He pulled away from the curb, glancing just once in his sideview mirror at his childhood home. A blueish flash in the alley beyond caught his attention–the blue halo of daytime running lights on a high-dollar car. Out of place in this neighborhood.

He slowed. Looked again. But again, there was nothing, just his mind playing games after days of stress-induced sleeplessness. He sucked in a breath. Jo was waiting for him. *Sweet, Jo. Where have you been?*

FORTY-THREE

ASHER

The haze of spring sun reflected off Jo's apartment windows as he pulled into the lot of her complex. He breathed a sigh of relief. He'd passed Moreno on his way in. No cruisers in the parking lot, no suspicious sedans, meant a morning free of interrogation. He could use the break, especially after Moreno's revelation about Hastings and Anderson painting a target on his back. He took the stairs two at a time, shoving the memory of the last time he'd been here to the back of his mind. Jo was alive–well–and right now, that's all that mattered.

She answered the door slowly. Checking the peephole and asking who it was before cracking the solid entry door. A thread of worry climbed through him, twisting the relief in his gut into fear. He forced a smile as she opened the door.

"Detective Moreno said you were on your way," Jo said, stepping away from the doorway so Asher could enter. The smile on Asher's face dissolved when she turned to face him. A busted lip, black eye, and a neat row of stitches near her hairline. He reached for her chin, but she turned away.

"What happened, Jo?"

She shrugged, gesturing to her face. "Stupid really." A forced laugh. "I was gathering some stuff to take to my parents' and I tripped. Hit the side of the nightstand on my way down."

Asher studied Jo, gauged her reasoning for the obvious lie, then drug his eyes pointedly around the destruction surrounding them. That story only worked if she attacked the sofa, kitchen cabinets, and bedroom furniture with a machete on her way to the floor. "Is that the story you told the cops?"

She joined him in his scan of the room. "It didn't look like this when I left."

Another lie. "Jo." The tone of his voice said what he didn't know how to explain. Disbelief. Hurt. Understanding. A request for more information.

"Don't, Asher. Moreno already took the report. Let it go." She retreated to the kitchen, moving a few displaced items back to their proper position. "Can I get you something to drink?" She pulled a bottle of wine from the fridge. "This okay?"

He glanced at the clock on the wall, not yet nine A.M. "How about I make some coffee?"

"Of course, yeah. Right." She knocked the side of the wine bottle on the edge of the countertop on the way back to the refrigerator. It didn't break, but Asher could see frustration building. Her shoulders slumped and she propped herself against the edge of the counter for a beat before launching in again. "What about eggs? I think I have some bacon." She reached again for the stainless steel handle of the refrigerator door. She was babbling. Nervous.

"Sit, Jo." Asher slipped behind her in the kitchen. He skimmed his hands down her arms, and she flinched. His jaw tightened. He took the bottle from her hands. Spoke softly, "I'll take care of breakfast."

A half-hour later they were sitting next to one another in

the living room couch. She'd pushed her scrambled eggs around on her plate long enough to make them soggy and congealed. He'd eaten half of the toast he'd made, afraid to add more eggs to the churn in his gut. Neither of them had said a word since sitting on the slashed sofa.

"You can talk to me, you know?" The silence was caving in on him. Thoughts of what might have, could have, even did happen to her warred inside his brain. He picked at the remnant of napkin draped across his knee.

Jo propped her fork against the plate noiselessly. Took a too big sip from her second cup of coffee.

"When I got home from your place the other night, she was waiting for me."

"She?" Asher felt his brows scrunch. It wasn't what he expected.

"Phoebe Anderson. She said she had information that could help Carly. Wanted to show me. I told her I needed to meet her in the office." Jo's words, innocuous at their face value, injected a dose of anger directly into his core.

"And what did Phoebe say?"

"Said she knew who was after Carly. Said if I didn't come, they would hurt her, take her from New Dawn." Jo tucked her bottom lip under a top tooth, staving off tears, and picked at the cuticles of her left hand. "I should have listened to her. I should have gone."

"But you didn't?" He was trying to slide the puzzle pieces together, but the edges wouldn't fit.

Jo shook her head. The first tears spilling free.

"Come here," Asher slid his hand over hers, pulling her gently toward him. He was ready for her resistance, and was prepared to let go. But she slid closer. Her leg brushed his, just once, before she resituated, putting an inch of space between them.

"Maybe he wouldn't have come if I had just done what Phoebe asked."

The heat of anger radiated through Asher's core. "Tell me who it was, Jo. Please."

"Why, so you can beat the shit out of him, like you did Aaron Carver? Stan?"

Asher had no regrets about Carver, but he flinched at the reference to Jo's innocent colleague. How was he supposed to respond to that? "Okay. I deserved that. But this is different, Jo. Someone hurt you." Asher longed to touch her, to smooth his hand over the softness of her skin.

Her gaze lifted, and she looked at him. For the first time since she'd let him in, she really looked.

"I'm sorry, Ash. I didn't mean that. I'm just ..." Her eyes glistened and she blinked away the second wave of tears.

"Hurt. Frustrated. Worried. Scared." He listed the emotions already obvious in her expression.

"I don't know his name. I'd never seen him before Friday night."

"Where did he take you?"

"I don't know. A house. But I don't know where." The ache in Asher's chest grew, stabbing from the inside out. He skimmed his thumb lightly over her cheek, drying the trail of tears. This time, she didn't pull away. "I tried to call Moreno as soon as Phoebe left. But I never got through. I think I was still scrolling my phone for his number when ..."

Asher nodded, not sure he understood. "Someone else showed up at your door?" he guessed.

Jo nodded, swallowed. "He had a gun. Threatened me. I dropped my phone. Moreno said his team found it under the credenza." Her eyes drifted there, holding as if lost in a memory. Her voice softened. "I didn't check the peephole. Some part of me thought it might be you, you know?"

God, if only it had been him. He could have been here. Could have stopped the monster that had haunted him for the better part of the last decade. Better yet, why hadn't he convinced her to stay at his place that night.

"Everything happened so fast. I locked myself in the bedroom, but he busted his way in. We struggled. I did fall against the nightstand. That wasn't a lie." She said it as if the words were proof of her innocence–as if Asher blamed *her*. "But he hit me with the gun." She touched the gash near her hairline. "I blacked out after that. I woke up blindfolded. I never saw the house, but I remember him hauling me up a flight of stairs. There were voices." Jo's brows pinched. The next assault of emotion clear in her features.

The question Asher most wanted to ask weighed him down like an iron blanket. Possibilities sunk into his skin. Poking. Prodding. Jeering at him. "Did he ... tell you his name?" Giving voice to the question wasn't as easy as he thought it would be.

Jo shook her head.

He swallowed, restarted, the words tight. "Did he ... hurt you?"

Another tear skied down Jo's cheek before she lifted her gaze to meet his. "No. Not like you mean."

Asher blew out a relieved breath.

"But he hurt them," Jo whispered.

Asher closed the gap between them. His hands cradled her head, thumbs tracing arcs over the hollow in her cheeks. "Who did he hurt, Jo?"

"Women. Girls. Some of them sounded so young. One of them cried as he ..." She choked on a sob. "He made me listen," she whispered.

"Was it just one man?"

"Two at least. Three maybe. But only one forced them ..." Jo choked on the words and Asher held her close.

She sighed and started again. "Their voices blurred together the longer I was there. I tried to tell them apart. But it was cold, I got confused."

"Were you in a room?"

"No, a basement. I busted my lip when he threw me down the stairs."

A memory sparked in Asher's skull, but he forced it away. "Jesus, Jo. You have to tell Moreno. He could track these guys down, before they do it again."

"I told him. But it's too late." She was sure. Too sure. "They have what they want now. It's why they let me go."

Asher pulled her close, nestling her head against his chest. Tears pierced the cotton of his shirt. The heat of them singed his skin. "How do you know that?"

Another wave of sobs racked Jo's whole body. Asher pulled a quilt off the back of the couch and wrapped her in it, folding her cocooned body against his. He'd never let anyone hurt her, not like this, ever again. Her warmth seeped into him—comforted him—banished some of the panic.

"She's supposed to be safe, Ash, but it was her. I'd know her voice anywhere. I heard the men talking to her. She wanted to know what happened to Caroline."

"Carly," the name slipped through his lips like a whisper on the breeze. Dissipated terror seized back, full-force. "Carly was there?"

"Yes," Jo hiccupped, launching into an explanation that Asher didn't need to hear. He'd been there. He should have gone in.

"She knows them, Asher."

"How'd you get out?" His voice was hardly more than a whisper, all he could manage with the guilt billowing inside him.

"There was a fight. One man came back. He pulled me out

of the basement, put me in a car. Told the driver to take me to Memorial Hospital. We were in the middle of nowhere when he pulled over, took the ties off my wrists and ankles, my blindfold off. But he was armed. Told me to keep my eyes down. And I did. I kept my eyes closed the rest of the way. I was a coward, Ash. I didn't want to give him a reason to hurt me like they hurt those girls."

Jo paused. Her fingers clawed at his clothes, skin, forcing him to look at what she'd become. "I was supposed to protect her, Asher. And instead, I sacrificed her. I left her with monsters."

Asher held her while she cried. Guilty words bubbled inside, threatening to break free. *But I sacrificed you both.*

FORTY-FOUR

CARLY

The house breathed in the quiet. I listened to the benign creaks and moans as I lay in the fetal position. Hard-packed earth scratched at my cheek. The cement on which I'd landed only extended so far, giving way to a trough of rocky dirt. I'd lost track of time. And my clothes had dried in sections, molding to my body, the denim of my jeans now hard and unforgiving when I tried to extend my legs, giving me a new appreciation for the magic of fabric softener.

I'd stopped convulsing with cold, my body somehow adjusting to the frigid temps. That, or I was in a stage of hypothermia I didn't know existed. The tips of my fingers felt fat and immobile, circulation strangled by the ties on my wrist. Every few minutes I pulled against them, trying to break the bond. But my skin screamed as the plastic dug in, forcing tears down my cheeks.

My eyes had adjusted to the darkness, though. Small lumps of cloth scattered here and there, old blankets or towels maybe. A shoe in the far corner. Farther away, a slab of something–bare mattress? I huffed through the constriction in my lungs, the tape on my mouth halting an easy exhale. What happened upstairs was hell enough, the ghosts of what Reed did to his prisoners down here was purgatory.

A creak against an upstairs floorboard jerked me to attention. I wiggled, inchworm style, toward the door, moaning incomprehensibly through the gag at my lips. More creaks, heading away. *No, please come back.*

Silence.

Soft feet padded across the floor above my head. Light and fast. A woman. I released an exhale. The jostling slide of a key in a lock, the tinkle of metal against metal sent a new rush of gooseflesh along my arms and legs. *How? Who?* It didn't matter. Someone was coming for me.

"Carly? Are you down there?" Her voice. That precious, sing-song voice. *Phoebe.*

I groaned–screamed–against the tape, my mind forming the words. "Please help me." My lips unable to comply. I wiggled toward the slice of light that filtered from the newly cracked door.

Those big blue eyes widened. Horror. Pity. This time I didn't care. I pushed my forehead into the cement and knelt at the foot of the should-have-been stairs.

"Hang on, Car, I'll get you out." I watched as she searched the room for something, anything, that could lift me from the dungeon.

That's when I saw it, in the light from the kitchen. A wooden ladder propped against the cinderblock wall near the opening. I lunged for it, jostling it enough with my shoulder that it danced in the glow from upstairs.

I hit the ground with a thud, my head bouncing once against the cracked cement. When I opened my eyes, it was there. The knife Eli slipped in my pocket nestled against the foot of the ladder. I raised up, stars dancing, forcing me back against the cold of the earth. But the effort worked, Phoebe noticed the ladder and reached in, grabbing the top rung and pulling it toward the door.

I don't remember her coming down, but I felt her hands on me–hot against my face. My eyes flickered open onto her wide-eyed innocence. She ripped the tape from my lips. I winced against the sting, my tongue darting out to lick the stickiness that remained.

"What are you doing here?" My voice scratched my throat, raw to my own ears.

Her lips curled in an almost smile. "I could never leave you here alone."

She pulled me into her. I could hear her heart thrumming in her chest. Feel the warmth of her seeping into my skin. She grabbed the knife from the floor and flipped it open, slicing through the zip ties on my wrists.

Every part of me ached as I sat on that floor. I checked the flesh at my wrists. Other than a few angry stripes of dried blood, most of the skin was intact, unlike the picture I'd painted in my head of zombie flesh hanging from bone.

She shrugged out of her jacket and wrapped it around me.

"We can't stay down here." Planting my feet under me, I clawed at the ladder, forcing frozen muscles into action. "Is your car outside?"

When she didn't answer, a spike of hot panic raced through me, buzzing in my muscles and prickling along my scalp.

"Reed sent me back, Carly." Her voice was low, calm, dark. "To take care of you."

I swiveled my head to look at her. The barrel of Reed's gun pointed at my temple.

"You. Know. Reed." The words were a staccato whisper.

Phoebe smiled. "How do you think he finds girls like you?" She tipped her head.

Almost memories swirled in my brain, gray and fuzzy against the backdrop of reality. The day she'd asked me to sit with her. Invited me to her house. Promised to keep my secrets. Cover for me. Never asked questions. The pieces clicked into place.

"You used me."

"*I* used *you?*" Phoebe laughed, her lips twisting into a wicked smile. "Remember that first day you came to Millbrook? Why do you think I talked to you? Invited you to sit at my table?"

I shrugged. Glanced toward the ladder, not sure my muscles would hold if I made a dash for it. The pain in my jaw, once numbed by cold, ached.

"Because Reed asked me to. You were already involved, but Reed knew you were different. Always looking for a way out." Phoebe slid a hand down the side of my head, threading my hair through her fingers.

I jerked away, the sudden motion threatening a wave of nausea.

"Of course, the drugs did the job on Caroline. They always do. But not you. And Reed wanted *you.*"

"Why?"

Phoebe lifted a shoulder, light from the kitchen reflected off the barrel of the gun. "I don't ask questions, especially when his plan works in my favor. See, what Reed didn't know was that *I* wanted you, too." Phoebe lowered her voice, leaned in, "Carly, it could have been so much worse. You could have ended up like Caroline—used up and tossed aside. But I *protected* you."

Cold steel slid down the side of my face. Images from the night flashed in my memory—Phoebe's whimpers, Reed's hand tangled in her hair, his willingness to let her go. "I didn't need your protection, Phoebe." My voice was calm and even, a shock to my own ears.

"How can you say that?" She stepped closer, wrapped her free hand in my hair. The gun looked heavy, out of place in her small hands. "Your father *sold* you. And your sister let him."

"My sister tried to get me out, Phoebe. That's why they were arguing." I barely got the words out before Phoebe interrupted.

"Did she? She took you to Reed's. Forced you into initiation. She may have been your sister, Carly. But she was guilty—focused only on the money, the drugs. And you followed her blindly. Almost got yourself killed." Neither of them cared about *you*, Carly."

Her thumb skimmed the side of my face, brushing away a tear I didn't know I'd shed.

"Neither of them deserve your tears."

I swallowed against her touch. The barrel of her gun pierced the hollow below my collarbone.

"What do you want from me, Phoebe?"

Her blue eyes flicked up and to the side, as if she was conjuring up a reason for her behavior on the spot. "One word, Carly, appreciation."

I backed up, the rungs of the ladder colliding with my spine.

"You never appreciated me—all the things I did for you. All the times I saved you from the worst of the johns, put Caroline in your place."

My head spun, working to make sense of the words that streamed from Phoebe's cherubic lips. "You couldn't," I exhaled the words.

"Oh, and your drawings!" A maniacal chuckle erupted from her chest. "My God, Carly, those drawings were perfect. Laid everything out. When I saw them, I knew exactly what I had to do."

"I don't understand," I said. But I did. I choked back the clot of tears in my throat.

"I did exactly what you wanted, Car. You wanted someone to save you. I took over when Caroline failed. It was only a matter of time before her demons took her down. But your dad? Your dad was never going to let you go. So I got rid of him." Phoebe eyed me. "Come on, don't act surprised. A little of Reed's best heroine and he was already passed out on the couch. He hardly moved when I stuck the needle in his arm. Without the two of them, we could be together." The corner of her lips curled into a sneer, transforming into a dragon snarl. "But then Mr. T stepped in. Of course, taking care of him was easier than I thought. Small towns love good gossip."

She paused, tilted her head to study my reaction. "Just like that, you were free, Carly. No more paying off your father's debts. Free to be with the one person who truly loves you."

"Caroline is the one who loved me, Phoebe. And Reed's not going to just let me go. He wants what he's owed." I glanced at the ladder.

"Reed?" Phoebe laughed at his name as if he was the nerd in science class she flirted with to get homework. "Even now you don't get it, do you? I went out of my way to make sure Reed went slow with you. He never treated you like the other girls, Carly." She poked me in the chest, forcing me back a step. "But you were too selfish to notice. Too caught up in your little infatuation to see how much I'd done for you. It's a shame it took me so long to see it. But I watched you, Carly. I followed you, and I realized, it was too late. You'd fallen in love with *him*." Phoebe said the word as if it made her physically sick.

Part of me wanted to ask, "Who?" But the effort seemed pointless. I slid my foot backward toward the first rung of the ladder.

"He moved you into his fucking *house*, Carly. Do you know

how hard that was for me?" Her eyes darkened, a sneer pulling at the corner of her lip. "You'd been through so much, though, so I gave you one last chance. But I saw it in your eyes, Carly. I felt it when we kissed." Phoebe brought her free hand up to my mouth, skimming her thumb along my bottom lip. Her voice softened. "You used me."

My breath hung tight as she leaned in, brushing her lips against mine. I kissed her back, reaching for a grip on the ladder. My fingers grabbed at the rough edges, never landing with enough control.

Phoebe pulled away, her lips still moist from our kiss. "You still love him, don't you?"

I shook my head, fear climbing through me and clotting in my chest. "Asher belongs with Miss Harrison." The calm had left my voice and I sounded like a child, scared and out of control.

Phoebe's eyes darkened. "He does, doesn't he?" She checked her watch, slinging the gun haphazardly as she did. "I'm guessing right about now, the last thing on his mind is you."

I lunged for the gun, my hypothermic fingers twisting uselessly against the strength of her grip. She released an animal scream as she tore it away from me. Her body collapsed onto mine, her nails digging like claws into my shoulders.

The gun clattered to the cement and I reached to the side, fighting Phoebe's weight, fingering the cold cement for the mass of metal, but found nothing. She sat on top of me, her fingers digging into my shoulders, my neck, my hair.

"You did this, Carly," she seethed through clenched teeth, her hundred-and-ten-pound frame pinning me against the ground. My hands reached for flesh, grabbed, scratched. My legs kicked. I screamed through the raw remains of my throat, but she clung like a parasite, fighting back.

She lifted my head by the hair and slammed my skull back down against the earth, just shy of the cracked concrete. "You're so good at playing the victim." *Jerk. Slam. Pain.* "But it's time for you to take responsibility. *You* caused it all. Caroline. Your dad. Asher." She paused, her fist still tangled in my hair as she pressed my head against the cold dirt. "Even Miss Harrison."

A flow of adrenaline opened up inside of me, spilling into my core, replacing the tremble in my muscles with the fire of hate.

"They're using you," I growled the words, forcing them through the throb in my head.

She repeated the procedure. *Jerk. Slam. Crack.* Blinding pain ripped through my skull. Blackness threatened the edges of my vision. I felt the trickle of blood, saw it on her own hands as she readjusted her grip.

"What makes you think I'm not using *them?*" Phoebe leaned over me. Loosened one hand to reach for the abandoned gun. I lurched, clawing with hands that could no longer land a blow. My muscles flailed, drained of strength, as the room swirled. I clung to her, one index finger caught in the chain around her neck. In the semi-dark it glistened, taunting me. A fresh wave of hatred surged, but my limbs remained useless, my brain no longer capable of sending instruction.

The gun scraped noisily over cement. Her lips tipped into a smile. All in the haze of slow motion.

"They say it's bad luck to wear an opal if it's not your birth-stone." The words slid from Phoebe's lips as I fought to maintain consciousness.

"Where'd you get it?" It came out as a moan, slurred and unintelligible. Gritty fingers of darkness reached into my voice, my vision, threatening to take over.

"Caroline was born in July, right, Carly?" Phoebe

unhooked my finger, letting my arm fall to the ground before readjusting the familiar pendant.

I watched Phoebe with blind eyes. Sent every last ounce of strength to my fingers. They stretched, slowly, outward along the ground, searching for anything I could use to defend myself. Hate dammed the flood of tears burning the backs of my eyes.

"Guess that old wife's tale is true." Phoebe pulled the gun from the cement, eyed it, and clasped her hand around the barrel.

One more extension, as far as my hand would go. My fingertips brushed the weight of Eli's knife. I closed my fingers around the blade. It dug into my skin, blessed slices of pain. I worked my fingers down the handle until the chill of smooth antler hit my palm.

"Caroline's necklace was a gift." The words were only in my mind, a clause in the October birthstone superstition, but it didn't matter.

Phoebe raised the handgun high before hurling the grip in my direction. I closed my eyes. Slung the open pocket knife toward her midsection. I braced for the weight of impact. Heard Phoebe's surprised grunt when my blade penetrated the soft skin on her belly, ripping through like shears in fabric.

I opened my eyes. My vision swirled, flickered, as the gun dropped from my best friend's hand. Her body pitched forward. Her moans deepened, while I drifted. My limbs heavy. My eyes blinked, no longer able to focus. But I saw the shadow. Heard the voice–soft, familiar. I felt his hands–warm, kind–before the breath I held in my lungs loosened. Air seeped from my lips. No longer replaced as I lost myself in darkness.

FORTY-FIVE

ASHER

Jo's inner turmoil lost the battle with exhaustion by noon, and she slept, curled next to Asher. He stroked the side of her face with his index finger while childhood memories raged inside him. Sitting in his dad's truck with a blanket over his head, trying to mute the sounds coming from the sleeper cab. Encounters that started as innocent exchanges–money for sex–got rougher as Asher got older. The girls got younger as the wrinkles in his father's face deepened. And the demands of his father trickled over into the off season, the house next door fulfilling his father's need when his mother refused, or was too beat up to comply.

Asher had promised to stay with Jo as long as she needed him. Promised to protect her from the monsters that terrorized her dreams. She'd woken twice, both times it had taken him ten minutes to convince her she was at home, safe in his arms. But Carly. His own demons cackled and jeered even while he sat awake.

Phantom pain bloomed in his jaw with the memory of the night he'd refused to watch his father abuse yet one more girl.

He'd just turned fourteen, and that's what they were now–girls, not much older than himself. But his father didn't like the word no, and Asher found out just how much that night.

He'd never told Dr. Morrison about that fight with his father. And in spite of the beating, he'd won. His father no longer insisted he stay in the cab–no longer forced him to watch. All that mattered to Asher was that he'd been allowed to escape. And it made life on the road with his dad manageable–until Emily.

Asher planted a kiss on the side of Jo's face and slid from under her. His thumbs pounded out the text to the only person he knew that might understand.

ASHER: CAN YOU COME OVER TO JO'S, STAY WITH HER UNTIL I CAN GET BACK?

SHE'S SLEEPING.

Three gray dots pulsed in the corner of Asher's screen then disappeared, the display of the phone going dark. He was about to give up when the phone pinged, the screen surging back into color with a new notification.

ETHAN: GIVE ME THIRTY. EVERYTHING OKAY?

ASHER: I'LL EXPLAIN WHEN YOU GET HERE. THX

✍

"WHAT THE HELL IS GOING ON?" Ethan asked as Asher stepped into the hallway outside Jo's apartment.

"It's Carly." Asher pulled the door closed quietly behind him. "She's missing. And I think I know where she might be."

Ethan's smile dissolved. He stared at his brother until Asher couldn't help but look away. "This is a bad idea, Ash."

Asher nodded. "I know. But he took Jo to the house. And from what Jo said, Carly's already there."

"What house?"

Asher didn't answer.

Ethan stepped away and ran a hand through his close-cropped hair. "Jesus, Ash." He paced the hall. "The Sutherland house? You can't go back there. Is Carly working for him?"

Ethan didn't leave time for answers, but his last question was one that Asher didn't want to think about. He knew what happened in that house–had happened for decades. And he couldn't allow his mind to cast Carly in the role of victim anymore. An image of Emily's body, bruised and broken, filtered into his brain in Carly's place.

"Never mind," Ethan said. "Don't answer that. Of course, I'll stay. But I'm giving you two hours, Ash. If I don't hear from you by then, I'm calling Moreno."

"He already knows. Court is balking on the warrant."

"Why?"

"Because of me. Anderson wants an indictment."

"You? Even after what happened with Jo?"

Asher nodded.

Ethan lurched forward, gripping his brother to his chest. "You don't need to do this," he whispered.

"You know I do," Asher said.

Before Asher could step out of Ethan's embrace, the half-closed front door of Jo's apartment squeaked open. A disheveled Jo stepped out into the hall. "You're not going anywhere without me."

"No way, Jo." Asher shook his head hard, but his voice was soft. "I'm not taking you back there. Not now, not ever."

Jo's gaze drifted to Ethan, looking for support.

"Ash is right, Jo. You should stay here. He knows the house, he'll be in and out in no time." He glanced at Asher. "Right, Ash?"

"I promise," Asher said.

Silence stretched in the hall, but Jo's eyes asked the questions she never could. *"How did Asher know that house?" "Why was he so familiar with the hell hole where she'd been kept?"* Maybe most importantly, *"Had he ever been one of the monsters she'd left Carly to confront alone?"* Asher vowed he'd answer them all, just as soon as he knew Carly was okay.

Jo finally dipped her chin in a nod. "Two hours," she whispered, "or I'm coming after you myself."

Asher pulled Jo into a hug, pressing his lips against the warmth of her forehead.

"I'll be back," he said, turning for the stairs.

"Watch your back," Ethan called after him, the same words his little brother had uttered when Asher stepped up into the cab with their dad that final summer. Asher nodded, disappearing down the stairs and out into the night.

⚔

AN HOUR LATER, Asher was pulling onto Presley Avenue for the second time in less than twenty-four hours. He'd called Moreno, but the detective's cell went straight to voice mail. It only took one radio news briefing for Asher to understand why. Phoebe Anderson was missing. Her car had been found near a dam just outside of Brookside.

Asher switched off the radio. The report only stoked the fire of rage that was burning in his gut, the clear difference between the haves and the have nots when it came to law enforcement resources. No wonder Moreno had passed him the address. He was stuck in the middle of it all, forced to perpetuate the hypocrisy.

He ignored his previous survey of the neighborhood and climbed the porch stairs with purpose, skipping the third step, the one that used to squeak when they were kids. By the looks of things, it'd still squeak today.

He didn't bother knocking. Just gripped the handle of the door and turned. At this house he knew exactly what he'd find inside. Sex. Drugs. Prostitutes either sleeping or working on the high they'd need to make it through the night. He'd seen it too many times before.

The door creaked on its hinges as he pushed it open. A lamp in the corner of the room cast shadows. Three girls on the couch, two in an overstuffed armchair, two more huddled together on the floor, all either asleep or passed out. Asher stepped closer for a better look. He pulled a blanket from the face of a raven haired teen–girl, really–even younger than Carly. But none of them were her. He sucked in a deep breath. Letting his lungs expand with the tiny bit of hope he had left.

FORTY-SIX

ASHER

The house was dark except for the light of day filtering through dingy windows. Asher slipped from the living room of the rundown house, down the hall and into the kitchen. The familiar *thwap, thwap* of the door as it came to rest behind him sent him back in time to his own childhood, coming to this house to play with Reed. They used to barrel through that very door, laughing as Reed's mom scolded them for stealing snacks from the kitchen.

He ran a hand across the seventies era table, green laminate trimmed with a silver metallic edge. He expected what was left of last night's stash to be piled in the center, along with a hefty roll of bills. He could remember coming over and finding Reed's dad counting money at the same table. He'd toss Asher a couple bills and a, "Don't spend it all in one place." The memory sent a stab of guilt into Asher's gut. A reminder of all the things he should have done, but didn't.

"Jesus Christ, what the fuck are you doing here?" a man whispered from the landing that led upstairs and Asher jerked, too lost in his own daydream to hear footsteps on the risers.

"Who are you?" Asher asked without hesitation.

The stranger glanced back up the stairs before answering. "Carver. Eli Carver."

Asher wasn't surprised. Eli hadn't been in the picture when Asher left town, but if he had to guess, he'd say being the son of Aaron Carver had to be a bit like being the son of Jack Sutherland. Asher closed the distance between them, stared down the stranger on the stairs.

Eli descended the rest of the stairs, setting the stack of blankets he was carrying onto the edge of the table. He grabbed Asher by the arm and turned him around, glancing up the stairs behind him. "You can't be here. Do you know what Reed'll do if he finds you?" A hint of panic colored Eli's voice.

Asher jerked away. "I'm not opposed to finding out." He combed his eyes once more over the empty space, unchanged from when he'd last stepped foot inside almost a decade ago. "Where's Carly?"

Eli ran a hand through his shaggy mop of wet hair.

"I know she came here last night. Just show me where she is and I'm gone."

"Man, you know I can't do that." Eli's face scrunched and Asher recognized the expression, guilt.

"Did Carly work for you last night?"

Eli shook his head, and a bubble of hope expanded in Asher's chest. "We didn't make it out last night. Partied here instead." He motioned toward the living room. "When Carly showed up, Reed lost it."

"What did he do?" Panic sucked out promise.

"Let it go, man. This doesn't have anything to do with you anymore."

"Anymore?" Asher echoed. "How do you know who I am?"

Eli shrugged. "I was there."

Asher worked to place him. The puzzle piece finally

clicking into place as the night he lost Emily came back into full view. Eli had been there all right–with Reed and the others. He'd got a good right hook in if Asher's memory served. But he'd been a kid–fourteen, fifteen maybe.

Eli must have read the recognition on Asher's face because he stepped away, ruffled a hand over his shaggy head.

Asher stepped forward. "This place, this life, has had something to do with me since Reed and I were teenagers. Since the day I said, 'No,' to him and his father. Once this life puts its claws in you, it doesn't let go."

Eli backed away, his eyes darkening. Asher moved in, grabbing the collar of Eli's t-shirt. "Tell me where she is."

Eli remained silent, but his eyes flicked toward the door tucked under the stairs.

"Jesus," Asher breathed through the curse and released Eli, pushing him backward. A thread of horror piped through him, twisting into an evil knot. *The basement.*

Asher swung his head toward the slab of mahogany, out of place in the run-down, chipped Formica kitchen. History gripped him. Raw fingers of his past clawed their way into every orifice. Flashes of repressed memory. Asher had been locked in that basement himself a handful of times over the years. The booming voice of Reed's father, criticizing him for some manufactured crime, followed by the pounding slam of a lock ricocheted against his eardrums.

He glanced at Eli whose face morphed, from the smooth young man in front of him to craggy deep cracks and hard lines. *"Your dad says you don't wanna play with the big boys. Sounds like it's time you learned the rules,"* Jack Sutherland's voice echoed in Asher's skull. Hard hands on his shoulders. Pressure giving way to pain. Asher stumbled back against the countertop. Lungs fighting for breath, for something real.

"You okay, man?" Eli's voice, distant–eyes, concerned.

"Look, I had to wait for Reed to crash, but I came down here to check on Carly. Bring her some blankets. Food maybe."

Eli's voice. *Carly.* Reality. *Thank God.* The images dissolved into fog.

"I tried to stop him from throwing her down there, but you know how Reed gets."

Asher pulled himself together, brushed the trickle of sweat from his forehead. *Christ. What just happened?* He coughed through the constriction in his chest and fingered the locks–two new, one just as he remembered. He put his ear to the door, listening for some sound, any sound.

"Can you open this?"

Eli pulled a keyring out of his jeans pocket. "I got lucky. Reed's sleeping it off with a new girl. I slipped in and took them off his nightstand." Eli stopped midway through the string of locks. "That's weird."

"What?" Asher pushed forward.

"Only the top three are locked. Reed always locks all five." Eli slipped a key into the second lock and twisted.

Every moment the two men stood at the door brought Asher dangerously close to his past. The rebounding wave of blinding anger at Eli for allowing Jo to be stuffed in a trunk and brought here, washed away by the remorse of knowing exactly what Eli had been through. Back and forth, ebb and flow. The tide mixed with guilt. Painful realization that Reed's vendetta was the spark that ignited Carly's abuse, Jo's abduction. The truth deepened already ragged scar tissue.

Eli struggled with the third lock, releasing it with a final twist of the key. They both listened. Deafening silence rose with frigid air from the darkness below. Eli clicked on the flashlight he'd carried from upstairs, sucked in a breath and cursed.

Asher shoved forward, pushing Eli aside to peer into the hole. "Carly?" He didn't dare more than a loud whisper.

Eli glanced at the stairway, keeping watch and stepped away from the gaping hole, allowing a spear of light from the kitchen into the space below. Asher's heart lurched, pounding an erratic rhythm in his chest.

Exposed skin along Carly's shoulders and chest reflected the light, alabaster against the dark, packed earth of the ground underneath. Asher jumped into the hole, the toe of his shoe catching a smear of blood from the stagnant pool near her head. Her arms lay outstretched on either side of her body, one palm caked in bloody residue, the front of her shirt so saturated with blood that Asher knew she must be dead.

"We need an ambulance." Asher called to Eli, no longer caring if Reed could hear.

"Are you out of your mind?" Eli responded in whispers. "She was okay when I left." The words were broken. "I swear."

Asher kneeled at Carly's head. "Come on Carly, hang in there. I'm here. I'll get you out of here." He brushed blood-matted hair from her forehead and face, unprepared for the cool clamminess of her skin. He slid his arms under her shoulders and behind her knees, watching her face as he lifted her into him.

Her lips had taken on a bluish tint, and as Asher held her to his chest, her body was limp and still against his. A whimper of a breath escaped through dry lips giving Asher undeserved hope.

Dampness seeped from Carly's clothes into his own, the steam of anger he'd been fighting, set into a full-blown boil. *They left her here to die*, Asher thought. *All of them. Eli is just as responsible as Reed. He let it happen, just like you.*

The final words echoed in his skull. A grim reminder that guilt was shared–for Emily, Carly, Jo–all of them. Asher stared into the shadow of Eli's face. The ladder was propped against the opening, as if all Carly needed to do was wake up and walk out. Asher checked its stability, holding Carly close. *One–two–three steps.* He lifted Carly to Eli's waiting arms.

Old voices flirted with the edges of memory as Asher hoisted himself out of the dungeon. *Did Reed still call it that?* Mrs. Sutherland never let them down there. *"Just my canned goods,"* she'd say, scooting them off to play in the backyard. Asher only found out what really happened in the dungeon when he was thirteen, one week after Reed's mom left his dad for good. *Focus.*

Hate colored Asher's vision as Eli settled Carly on the rundown loveseat in what was once a breakfast nook. But Asher could see through the anger enough to know that the worry in Eli's eyes was genuine. Reed's lackey draped one of the blankets over her, tucking it gently in around her legs.

Asher knelt beside the couch, studied the repeated blows to the back and side of Carly's skull. "How'd she end up like this?"

"I don't know." Eli paused, eyebrows scrunching. "Reed sent me to get rid of Jo. By the time I took care of that he'd found Carly in the alley. She was half conscious in the kitchen when I found her. Reed made me dump her in the dungeon. But I gave her my sweatshirt, slid my knife into her pocket. Thought she might be able to cut herself free. I'm sorry." A half-sob cut through Eli's throat. "I didn't know what else to do."

Asher pulled Carly's hand from under the blanket and sandwiched it between his palms. Her fingernails were ripped. Jagged edges sliced against the skin of his palm. She'd fought, hard. But, who? He swallowed the knot of hate, rubbing his thumbs over the soft skin on the back of her hand.

"I'm calling 9-1-1." Asher said, sliding his phone from his pocket.

"Are you fucking kidding me?" Eli lunged, knocking the

phone from Asher's hand. They both watched as it skittered across the kitchen floor. "Look around, Asher. You ain't callin' no squad."

Asher worked to satiate the lava boiling inside. He held it in, clamped inside like a caged lion, and waited for the right time to explode. "She needs to go to the hospital." His voice was calmer than he expected.

"What the hell would we tell them?" Eli stage-whispered. His eyes flicked toward the stairs and back to Asher.

Asher swallowed. Eli was right, but not for the reasons he thought. Asher could care less about the prostitution and drug charges waiting for them on the other side of a 9-1-1 call. But waiting for a squad took time. The chances of waking up Reed multiplied. Asher couldn't take the chance of his one-time friend going off the rails and finishing Carly before he could even get her out of the house.

FORTY-SEVEN

ASHER

Carly whimpered on the sofa. A shiver rolled over her body, curling her muscles. A tinge of pink replaced the blue in the center of her lips.

Asher slid a palm over her forehead, her once warm skin cool to the touch. Her thunderstorm eyes were closed, thick lashes fringing the corners, one matted and glued into pointy spikes by half-dried blood, creating a subtle homage to *A Clockwork Orange.*

The rough fabric of the couch cushion pressed into her cheek, mottling her complexion as a trail of deep red dribbled down the back of her neck, pooling into the outdated orange and black tweed upholstery.

"I need to get this bleeding stopped before we move her. How long before Reed wakes up?"

Eli glanced at the ceiling, listened. "Hard to tell. Not long, I'd guess. He was rolling pretty good after ..." Eli motioned to Carly. "But the guy's like a bloodhound. He can sniff out trouble."

Eli turned to the kitchen, running the water a bit before

returning to Asher with a warm cloth. Asher thanked him, swiping the terry cloth over Carly's bruised cheek in gentle swaths, using his fingertips to test the ridge of bone.

"Is it broken?"

"I don't think so." Asher parted some of the hair at the rear of Carly's head. Her scalp mapped with lines of broken skin. "She needs stitches. Probably has a concussion." The words were soft. Meant more for himself than for Eli's benefit.

"That blood, on the basement floor, is it hers?" Eli asked.

Asher swiveled to face Eli. "How the hell would I know that?"

Eli glanced at Carly, winced. His face screwed into an uncomfortable frown. "There was no blood when I left her, I swear."

For reasons he couldn't explain, Asher believed him.

"You said she came looking for Caroline." Asher said. "Where is she?" He kept his gaze on Carly, ignoring Eli, who sat back on his heels and pushed up from the floor.

Eli coughed, a poor disguise for the twist of emotion in his voice. Asher was familiar with that trick.

"I tried to help Caroline get out. But Reed found out. I don't know how, but he knew. She got accepted to Ohio State's psychology program was supposed to start this summer. I helped her find a job near campus. But before she could even enroll Reed set her up. Told her he was taking Carly out to this one john. Caroline knew he was bad news. She'd had a run in with him before. She wouldn't let Carly go alone."

Asher turned just as Eli scrubbed a frustrated hand through his messy hair.

"Caroline had some issues, man, but she was working through them. Getting her out of Aaron's house was the first step. But she wanted Carly out, too. When everything fell apart, she was thirty days clean."

Eli wrung his hands in tight knots. Asher almost felt sorry for him. Eli's voice was quiet, resigned, when he finally continued. "Reed promised Caroline it would be their last trick–for both of them. But Caroline didn't make it–OD'd in the cab of some john and Reed tossed her out like day-old trash."

"Reed dumped her?"

Eli shrugged. "I guess. He wouldn't tell me. I would've told Carly where she was if I knew."

Asher listened to Eli's words, heard the pain in his voice. Proof the line between good and bad was wide and gray. Despite Eli's faults, it was clear he'd loved Caroline. It was never a healthy relationship, but Asher had no doubt it was the only kind Eli knew how to have.

Asher ran his hand over Carly's head. Raven hair matted with blood. To Asher she was a smart, sensitive, talented young woman. To Reed she was nothing but flesh and bone. A product. Disposable.

Bruises and gashes marred Carly's porcelain skin. Innocence taken. A whole life left scarred and broken. Asher wished he could start over. Wished he'd been man enough to turn Reed and Old Man Sutherland in when Emily died. He'd had enough evidence. Knew how the Sutherlands worked the business, where Reed's dad kept his stash, how he found his girls. But Asher had been too scared. Not for himself, but for his family.

Asher had grown up with constant threats to keep him in line. And he'd watched others pay the price of perceived betrayal. When the Sutherland's threats spilled over onto Ethan and their mom, Asher knew better than to ignore the consequences. Asher forced away the wave of regret and shook his head, anger and guilt bubbling inside.

Maybe if he'd met a cop like Moreno. Maybe he would've felt safe, seen. At the very least he could have gotten the

Sutherlands off the streets for a while, long enough to slow them down. Then maybe Reed never would have picked up where his father left off. Maybe Carly never would have been caught in his crosshairs. There were too many "what ifs."

Carly whimpered again and Asher stilled, speaking to her in soothing tones. He pulled her hand into his. But she jerked away with a ragged gasp. Her eyes flew open and she bolted upright, shoving at the blankets holding her prisoner with blood-stained hands.

Her eyes darted around the room and her chest heaved with panicked wheezes. She squinted, touching tender fingers against the side of her head. She drew her hand away, a fresh seep of blood tinting her fingertips. Asher could almost see her brain working to make sense of her surroundings.

"Phoebe," she managed. The word sounded thick and sticky. The syllables too round. Her tongue flicked over dry lips.

Carly shook her head, eyes wide, unreadable.

"No." A squeak more than a word.

Carly's hands went to her head. Palms pushed against both temples as her face scrunched into a grimace. She swiveled her head from side to side, slow at first, then gaining momentum. She pounded her fists against either side of her battered skull, numb to the gashes that reopened under the force of her blows.

"Stop, stop." Asher reached for her, circling her wrists in his hands. "Carly, just breathe. It's okay. Phoebe's okay. *You're* okay." He didn't care if it was a lie.

A single tear started down her cheek as her eyes locked on Asher's, widening as she breathed his name.

A bead of hope broke free in Asher's chest as she lurched forward, a sob echoing in her chest. She wrapped her arms around his neck, her skin like ice against the heat of his own. He pulled the blankets around her shoulders and leaned into her, his own breath pulsing back at him from the crook of her neck.

"You're gonna be okay," he breathed into her. His words halted by the creak of old floorboards overhead. Asher turned toward Eli, whose own eyes bulged like a rabbit ready to bolt from a predator.

"9-1-1," Asher glanced toward his phone, lying at the foot of the far kitchen cabinet. "It's your only way out."

"Just leave," Eli whispered.

Asher gathered Carly to his chest, blankets and all. Her muscles trembled against him with violent vibration. Moisture seeped from her clothes, cooling him. "It's okay," he whispered, nestling her head against his neck.

Eli lunged through the kitchen, snatching the phone from the floor and making short work of the space between the cabinets and the door. Asher noticed the shake of his hand, eyes flicking up the stairs and back again as he held the door open.

Reed's voice echoed from upstairs, calling for Eli as Asher slid silently into the backyard. He stepped in long strides to avoid the litter, slipping around the corner of the house and up the side toward the privacy gate that fenced the property in.

He could see his Jeep from here. Sunlight skimmed the top of the dark green hood. The heat of Carly's tears seeped onto his shoulder as he fiddled with the gate. *Reed and his locks. Damn it.*

She sobbed an apology.

He leaned against the side of the house, Carly's legs still wrapped around his midsection, and kicked with full force. Old wood splintered, and Carly screamed. He held her head to his chest to muffle the sound.

"We're almost there." His pulse echoed loud in his ears as he raced toward the car, girl in tow.

"If he follows us?" Carly managed through tears as Asher

turned the key and roared away from the curb. She'd seen what he'd seen—the angry man yelling obscenities from the porch of number 617.

"He will." Asher predicted. Jo was right. No one runs from their past without it eventually catching up with them.

The chatter of Carly's teeth pulled him out of his own head. Her eyes had closed, and she shivered on the passenger seat, blood seeping down the side of her face and into the blanket around her. She deserved better than this. Better than a cancer-ridden mother, an incompetent father, a drug addicted sister. She deserved better than to be caught in the crossfire between ghosts of a past she didn't understand.

⚼

WHEN ASHER PULLED into the emergency department drop off of County Memorial, Carly was out—dead asleep or unconscious, Asher couldn't tell. She was cold. Dehydrated. She'd lost a huge amount of blood if the puddle on the floor of Reed's basement and the growing saturation on the blanket was any indication. She needed help.

He carried her in, and the nurses swarmed. Before he knew what was happening, she was in a room and he was in a waiting area, peppered with questions he didn't know how to answer.

"What happened to her? Where did she get the injuries? Were you there when it happened? How long has she been exposed to the cold? How long has she been unconscious? How do you know her?"

Asher only nodded when the security guard stationed in the doorway of the waiting room told him, "We've called the police, we'll need you to stay."

He sat alone—blank walls, sterile scent. Only the magazines organized on the end tables showed any sign of use. He thumbed through the closest option, a *Parenting Today*. A ripped out reply card, filled in crossword, and ballpoint pen-colored eyes on the cover model were proof someone had come before him.

He checked his watch. *Shit.* He'd forgotten to call Ethan.

He bent forward, elbows on his knees. For the first time, he noticed the blood on his shirt and pants, the dark red flecks staining the skin on his hands. He rubbed. Friction heated his flesh. Lost in the action of obliterating remnants of the morning, now trapped in the crevices around his knuckles, he barely noticed when controlled chaos erupted from the ED across the hall.

First shouts and screams from behind closed doors. Heavy footfalls of the running security guards who disappeared behind the iron curtain of the double doors.

He stood–watching–as the opposite side of the hall erupted. A gurney rolled in from the sliding glass exterior doors. Uniformed medics pushed while a nurse sat astride the patient, holding white towels against an obvious chest wound. Her towels bloomed with an ever-expanding plume of red.

The doctors and nurses yelled at each other. Shorthand lingo Asher didn't understand. He stepped back into his white-walled cell. His hands shook, still stained by Carly's blood. He glanced up as the bed rolled by the open door. Blond hair peeked from the side of the gurney. Asher stumbled back onto the easy-clean couch, heart thundering in his chest, blood pulsing against his eardrums. *Eli.* One more life destroyed.

FORTY-EIGHT

CARLY

I was dressed in a gown—two, actually—one tied in the front and the other in the back, creating the illusion of an actual dress. The fabric was thin—white with light blue diamonds. The nurse who wheeled me up to this floor had promised pants and a proper shirt, like the other patients wore, but I hadn't seen her since she parked me in this office.

At least my ass was covered, but it sure didn't stop the draft. I lifted my wrists against the lined cuffs that kept them tethered to the wheelchair. I shivered. The cuffs clattered. I couldn't remember the last time I felt warm.

"Can I get you another blanket?" The doctor's voice was nice. Smooth. Caring. She reminded me of Miss Harrison.

"No, thank you." My throat felt lined with gravel. "I'd like to talk to Mr. Thompson, please."

I'd been on my best behavior since waking up three days ago—tied to a gurney with my head shaved, a row of Frankenstein staples up the back of my scalp—in what I only assumed was the psych ward. All pleases and thank yous, and no sirs and yes ma'ams for the better part of seventy-two hours. I needed out.

I didn't remember lunging at the triage nurse with a needle. But they said I did. Claimed I plunged it into my own neck when I couldn't reach her. None of it seemed right–real. But I had a fresh bandage on my neck, pain when I turned my head, and no memory of the event. Why would they make up a story like that?

"I understand you feel alone," the doctor said, all caramel-covered appeasement. "But until we can get more information about what happened–how you ended up in that basement covered with blood–I'm afraid no visitors are allowed."

"Is he a suspect?"

"Who? Mr. Thompson?" She shifted in her chair, pulled a notepad to her lap. He'd been the topic of most of our conversations so far. "Suspect for what?"

I glanced away from my wrist and up at her, not long enough to hold eye-contact. Black pencil skirt, burgundy blouse under a fitted black jacket. Her honey-blonde hair hung to her shoulders, smooth and styled in careful precision. She was everything I wasn't–calm, poised, confident–everything I would never be. She raised an eyebrow, coaxing me to answer.

"I just want to make sure you understand. He didn't hurt me."

"You've told me a lot about what *didn't* happen, Carly. But what I want to know is what *did*." Her eyes combed over me, a careful survey. "What happened in that basement?"

I'd already given her the backstory. My father's decline, Caroline's involvement with Eli and Reed, what it was like living with Aaron, the desperation to do whatever it took to break free. We'd covered the fact that I called Phoebe from New Dawn. Climbed into her car and forced her to drive to Reed's. I mentioned how I confronted him and how Eli and helped me escape. I'd even told her about going back when Reed cornered Phoebe in the alley.

The shrink, Dr. Blumenthal according to her shiny gold tag, shifted in her seat. "You know, Carly, you're here on a seventy-two hour hold. You attacked a nurse. Your best friend is still missing. By the end of the day, they'll expect me to make a recommendation for your course of treatment and I can't do my job if you don't tell me what you do remember."

I met her gaze. What she didn't understand was that I wasn't holding back on purpose. I legitimately had no memory of what happened in the dark of Reed's basement. Millisecond memories flitted through my brain like fireflies, lighting here and there, but impossible to capture.

I was now a hazard—probably considered suicidal, homicidal even. I'd caught a glimpse of my chart earlier when they strapped me into this chair and wheeled me from my room. The words, trauma-induced psychosis, now burned into my brain. After years of rape, abuse, inescapable damage at the hands of people I trusted, no one seemed shocked. They just checked my chart and looked at me with pity.

"I know all this is scary. But everyone here has one goal, to help you get better." She picked up a plastic cup of pills and held it toward me.

I nodded at her hand. "What is it?"

"Same as yesterday, Haldol and Xanax. There's nothing here that will hurt you."

I opened my mouth and she dumped the drugs in. I tipped my head back and swallowed, nearly gagging. The memory of the trucker's hands in the back of his cab, pushing pills down my throat, flooded back full-force. That was one thing I couldn't seem to control, the terrible memories that surged uninvited with even the slightest reminder. Why I couldn't trade those for the ones that mattered infuriated me.

I forced another gulp and the lump grated through my throat, clotting like a hardened clump in the center of my chest. Dr. Blumenthal offered a bottle of water, pouring a mouthful as she tipped my head back with practiced fingers. Three swallows later, the pain in my chest moved on.

In about thirty minutes, I'd be heavily medicated with a cocktail of anti-depressants and anti-psychotics that were likely to make my brain feel filled with fuzz. If I couldn't give voice to what happened now, there was no way I'd be able to conjure it up once those side effects set in. Not that it mattered. The bits I could remember from the basement, I hardly believed myself.

The doctor settled back in her chair, flipped open a green file folder and thumbed through a pile of rough-edged art paper.

"Where'd you get those?" A wave of anger, spawned by a sudden violation for reasons I couldn't name, rushed through me.

"You're very talented," she said in response. I had to give her credit, she was a pro at de-escalation. "Let me ask you something, Carly. Where do you see yourself in five years?"

Five years? I could hardly envision the next fifteen minutes. I shrugged.

"Do you enjoy art? Is it something you'd like to pursue?"

I blinked at her question. "If I'm stuck in here, what difference does it make?"

"Part of getting better, is creating a goal for ourselves, setting a new reality."

"I'd like to live in a house." I'm not sure where those words came from, but they escaped without effort, as if someone else had answered in my place.

Her eyes brightened. She liked that answer. "Describe it for me."

I picked at the peeling vinyl armrest beneath my

fingers, tried to conjure one up. A two-story, on a cul-de-sac, like Asher's. Maybe the childhood home where I'd grown up before Mom died. But no matter how hard I tried, how much imagination I used, Aaron's double wide, permeated with the stench of Reed's basement, was all I ever saw.

"What if I can't see it?"

She tilted her head, brows scrunching over her eyes. Scooting forward on her chair, she leaned in, so close I could smell the floral sweetness of her perfume, the same scent Miss Harrison wore. A lump took root in my throat. I missed Miss Harrison.

She stared at me, eyes locked on mine. "Forget five years, Carly. Let's start with right now. If you could be anywhere in this moment, where would you be?"

"At Mr. Thompson's. In bed."

She pulled away, scribbled something on her pad.

"No, not like that. He had this cover on the guest bed, a duvet, I guess. It was so soft, plush. Like sleeping under a cloud."

She was scribbling again, but I couldn't stop myself.

"His house was the only place I felt safe."

"Okay." I could tell by the way she said it I hadn't mastered the exercise. "And who would you want with you?"

"My sister, Caroline." That was too easy, not to mention impossible. "Mr. Thompson, Miss Harrison." An image of Phoebe, smiles and laughter, flirted with the edges of my memory before her lips morphed into a hateful smirk.

"What about friends, Carly."

"I don't have friends."

"Tell me about the last time you saw Phoebe Anderson."

"We were in the basement, at Reed's." I clenched my eyes closed, the sickening gurgle of her blood as it spilled onto the damp earth teased and tormented from the recesses of my mind. "Have they found her yet?"

"Should they have?"

I rolled my eyes. *Why can't you just answer the damn question?* I was tired of the circles. First in the emergency department and now here. I was tired of the one-sided expectations. No wonder the patients in this place were crazy. No one ever gave them straight answers.

The doctor sighed, setting her pad to the side. "They found her blood, Carly. In the basement. And on you. There must have been a fight. Did you hurt Phoebe?"

I shook my head. "You don't understand."

"Then help me understand, Carly. What happened in that basement?"

"She was wearing Caroline's necklace. Kept smashing my head against the floor. She was never my friend." The heat of a tear slid down my cheek.

"What was she, then?"

I shook my head, wiped what was left of a runaway tear on the shoulder of my gown. What do you call someone who takes all your darkest secrets and twists them until they're unrecognizable, even to yourself? "I don't know."

"Did you kill her?" Dr. Blumenthal asked in a tone that made it seem normal.

But it was the one piece of the puzzle I still hadn't worked out. Even now, after hours of nothing to do except process the past three days, I was no closer to the truth than I'd been on the earth in Reed's cold, dark basement. I'd failed everyone, put everyone I'd ever tried to help me in harm's way–Caroline, Mr. Thompson, Miss Harrison, Detective Moreno. In silent moments when I allowed myself to care, even Phoebe. After all, her actions were a direct result of mine.

I shook my head. Hot tears rising in the back of my throat.

"I had no choice." I whispered, for the shrink's sake or mine, I wasn't sure.

"We always have a choice."

"You're wrong." I waited for her to meet my stare. "Only the privileged have a choice. The rest of us have to settle for a chance."

FORTY-NINE

ASHER

Asher hesitated at the bottom of the steps, the cock-eyed 6-1-7 on the weathered porch pole taunting him. He wrapped one arm around Jo's midsection, silently enduring the vise lock she had around his other hand.

"I know this isn't easy," Moreno turned from his position on the top step. "For either of you. But I need you to walk me through what you remember."

Jo nodded, swallowed. Squeezed Asher's hand even tighter.

"It's okay, Jo. The cops are the only ones here. They cleaned the place out, remember?" Asher kept his voice low, rubbing her back as they climbed the stairs. He felt the rise and fall of her breath before she took the final step.

Moreno shot Asher a thankful look and continued on. "We've got some K9 units here today doing one last sweep, just making sure we find everything there is to find. Other than them, it's just us."

"I'm ready," Jo said, the waver in her voice shot straight to Asher's heart. It was his fault they were there. He was the one who'd gone back for Carly. If he hadn't, maybe Jo could've moved on, focused on healing instead of regurgitating the memory of a night he was sure she'd rather forget to cops from three different agencies.

Moreno took her hand from Asher and led her inside. "I'll go over Miss Harrison's statement first, then yours, if you don't mind. We'll keep everything straight that way."

Asher nodded, watched as Moreno disappeared down the hall with Jo. The air in the front room was still heavy, thick with the smell of weed and the unmistakable carbon stench of gunfire. The police had cut a square from the carpet, leaving exposed wood where Eli had fallen, bleeding out onto the living room rug.

Asher listened for the timber of Moreno's voice as he led Jo through the house. Heard the rise and fall of his gentle questions. "Did anything seem familiar—a smell, sound?" Anything that might help the detective identify this as the place where Jo's abductors had taken her.

The thought of Jo spending even one minute in this place made Asher's gut twist. The knowledge that she'd been in here, trapped, listening as Reed tangled with Carly, forced her into the basement, was too much to take.

Asher shoved his hands in his pockets and headed for the kitchen. He could hear Jo talking, Moreno following up with questions. It was clear Reed had abducted her, tossed her in the basement and gone about their business until Carly showed up. Reed had sent Eli to "get rid of" Jo. The phrase pounded in Asher's skull as he traipsed through the house. Three tiny words that made Reed's intention clear. If it wasn't for Eli's refusal to follow the command, his detour to the nearest emergency department, Jo would be dead right now.

They were lucky. Jo's bruises were fading. And Asher could be there for her, help her through the remaining fear. The same couldn't be said for Carly.

"Asher, Moreno is ready for you." Jo slid a hand down Asher's arm. Lifted up on her tip-toes to kiss his cheek.

Asher leaned into her warmth. If anything good had come from the events of the last several weeks, it was this. She'd let every suspicion go. Realized he wasn't the monster she once feared. He was a damaged bystander, just like her. And now that years of truth were trickling out, she understood why Carly had meant so much to him. He was an ally, not an enemy, and by the end of the year, he hoped to make her his wife.

Asher left Jo with Hastings, who nodded at him as they passed in the hall. The detective who'd once had it out for him had made a sudden and irrefutable change in direction since Eli's version of events—thanks to the hospital's trauma team and Eli's willingness to come clean—had made its way into public record. Anderson remained unconvinced, probably because his daughter was still yet to be found, but Moreno assured Asher that it was only a matter of time.

"Down here," Moreno called from the basement. Asher shrugged away the chill that shimmied down his spine. He'd never be comfortable here. Everything in this house was tainted, marred with memories he'd never forget.

Three large utility lights lit the once impenetrable space. The wooden ladder replaced with a heavy-duty metal unit. Two police dogs sniffed along the walls, checking for any para-phernalia that might have been missed during previous searches.

"What did you see when you opened the door, Asher?"

Asher relayed the memory. The beam of Eli's flashlight. The slice of light as the door first opened on Carly. The pool of blood. Her bashed skull. She'd been so still, too still.

"How'd you get her out?"

"The ladder was propped at the opening."

Asher thumbed toward the rickety contraption standing against the wall. For the first time, he noticed the spray of blood spatter along the rungs, against the roughened block walls. He swallowed and looked away.

"I carried her up to Eli and he took her to the couch." Asher pointed in the direction of the breakfast nook loveseat.

"Did either of you come back down here? After you got her out, I mean?"

"No. When we heard Reed upstairs, I carried Carly out the back and around the side to my car."

Moreno nodded. "Anyone else know about this basement?"

Asher shrugged. "Everyone Reed works with probably. I'm not sure it was ever a secret."

"What about keys?" Moreno tipped his chin in the direction of the door.

"Old Man Sutherland had a set when we were kids. Reed got a set when he turned fifteen."

Moreno stared at Asher for a beat before scribbling in his notebook. He bent to inspect dark footprints pressed into the earthen floor. A man's prints, Asher realized.

One of the dogs barked, whining when the handler tried to move him away from the spot of dirt on which he sat.

"Hey, Vic. Luna hit on something over here."

Moreno left Asher at the foot of the doorway. Cold seeped into Asher's skin. He hadn't dressed to stay down here long. But it was the memories more than the temperature that chilled his skin, caused his core to spasm.

"Bring the shovel." Moreno's voice as the dog went ballistic—whining, growling—at the far corner of the basement.

A forgotten memory—suppressed, likely—seeped into his brain with the cold. Jack Sutherland, hovering over him, shoving him into the wooden box, punishment for disobeying his demands. Asher could hear the crack of the belt as if the ghost of the man was still here, tormenting, assaulting, watching, smiling.

The methodic scratch of a shovel against earth shattered the stillness. The head coming in contact with hollow core wood.

The box–that's all they'd ever called it–was a makeshift coffin he and Reed had helped build. And today, it lay freshly buried, a couple inches at most, in the dirt in the far corner of the dungeon. He'd been forced inside once. And once was enough.

Wood cracked and splintered as the officers broke through the lock, ricocheted through Asher's eardrums. His knees weakened, and he grabbed the ladder's metal rung. Lines of tread pressed into his flesh. *Sutherland is gone. Pull yourself together, Thompson.* But the memory was there–vivid–drowning out the shouts from the group of cops twenty feet away.

"No." Asher's word was a whisper. "Please, no." He sunk to his knees, crawled forward on the stained earth. Watched from a distance as they slid back the lid. And waited for the Sutherland house to give up one last secret.

FIFTY

CARLY

They'd given me real clothes. That was a plus. Nothing fancy, just a sweatshirt and yoga pants–nothing with a string or a zipper. There'd been a lot of whispering in the past several hours. Odd glances as I sat in the lounge, coloring with crayons instead of charcoal or even a pencil. I'd asked, but there were regulations. Evidently Crayola had cornered the market at mental institutions.

"Carly?" One of the nurses–Nancy, according to her tag– approached from behind. I didn't do names. Refused to in this place, so I knew her as the young, tan one. Wavy blonde hair always gathered in a bouncy ponytail, she spoke to the patients as if we were toddlers.

I turned to look at her and she smiled. The corners of her lips curving up in a manufactured grin. I made her nervous. There was no reason to smile back. I couldn't remember the last time I'd actually forced a genuine grin. With Mr. T, maybe. Before New Dawn. I was a different person then. The world was a different place.

"You have visitors. Put the crayons away, hon. You'll need to come with me."

Hon, ugh. Who really talked like that? This was Ohio, not the deep South. I was *maybe* three years younger than her, if that.

I slipped the crayons back into the box and stood, leaving the drawings on the table where they lay. I noticed her glance at them, grimace. She was used to sunshine and rainbows. But I only drew what I knew, dark swaths of abandonment and betrayal.

The head nurse, a rotund woman with glasses perched on the end of her nose, produced my chair. I sat. Watched as she clipped my wrists and ankles into the cuffs, sucked in a breath as she wheeled me down the hall.

I hadn't had a visitor since I'd been here. Not that I'd expected any. The nurse stayed silent as she maneuvered me toward the row of visitation rooms at the other end of the floor. Glass-walled rooms lined the hall to my left as she slowed, veering my chair around a corner and turning me backward, before punching in a code on the panel by the door.

When she swung me around and into the room, Moreno was the first person I saw. His mouth opened. His gaze flicked from me to the nurse as he said, "Is this really necessary?" motioning to the shackles.

"Afraid it's protocol, Detective."

Moreno's whole body slumped, chocolate eyes stayed on mine as the nurse locked the wheels on my chair. He waited for her to exit before dragging a chair from the other side of the table, angling it close to mine. From the looks of it, the chairs were the only thing in the room not nailed down.

"I was going to ask how you've been, but ..." Guilt flashed in his eyes.

"I'm fine. I have my own room, so it's really not so bad," I lied.

I hated everything about this place, the white walls, the blue speckled floors, the nurses who treated me like a child, the shrink that asked the same questions over and over and didn't like my answers, the meds that made me sleepy, sometimes too fuzzy to remember why I was even here. I loathed every minute detail.

"Mr. Thompson and Miss Harrison are downstairs. They'd only allow one of us in at a time."

A spark bloomed in my chest. The first I'd felt since arriving in this white-washed version of hell.

"I thought you should know that we've made some progress in the case. Reed Sutherland has been arrested." He was waiting for me to look at him, waiting for a reaction. I swallowed. Unsure how much to reveal. "Phoebe Anderson is still missing. Her blood was found in the basement of the Sutherland house."

Silence stretched between us. I didn't know what he wanted me to say. I was sure Dr. Blumenthal had already told him my secrets. Maybe he just wanted to gauge my reaction.

"We found the gun you told Dr. Blumenthal about. Your blood was still on the grip. You're a lucky girl, Carly."

Lucky. "Lucky is relative, I suppose." I glanced around at the walls to make my point.

"True." Moreno sighed.

But even without Phoebe they'd been able to corroborate my story. They'd been able to uncover the truth of what happened in that basement. *Truth.* The word seeped into my psyche like smoke under a doorway. The way she'd fallen, her body heavy and limp on top of mine, I remembered. What I wasn't clear on, was how she'd disappeared. Gone by the time Asher pulled me out hours later.

"But thank you." I whispered. The urge to jump up and hug Detective Moreno, crawled over me. *Damn straps. Damn chair.*

Moreno leaned forward, clasped his meaty hand over my small cool one. Careful eyes bored into mine. He matched my whisper, "There's more." A pause so long I thought he might never speak again. "We found your sister, Carly."

The noise that erupted out of me was pure animal. A guttural, visceral wail, the response to a long-held release of pain. Pain that had been crammed down inside for far too long. Moreno wrapped his arms around me, gripping me in a hug I had no way to return.

"I'm so sorry."

And he was. I could feel it in his hug as he explained where she'd been, confined to a box twenty feet away as I fought for my life with Phoebe. I leaned against him as sobs wracked my torso. And for the first time I could remember, I didn't try to stop them. He cupped my healing head with his hand.

"We never could have gotten this far without you."

He was proud of me. I heard it in his voice. Felt it in his touch. Prouder than my own father had ever been.

Tears stung my cheeks. And I remembered where I was. I pulled out of Moreno's hug. Was this just another psychotic break? Was I really hunkered down in my cell on my cot, dreaming? Pounding my fists against my bruised skull in frustration?

I gripped at the sleeves of Moreno's jacket as he released me. No. He was here. He was real. I could feel him.

He nodded, as if he could read my thoughts. "It's over, Carly. I promise you." Moreno allowed me to finger the sleeve of his suit jacket.

"She was there, at Reed's, the whole time?"

Moreno nodded.

"Alive?" I asked. A whisper. I imagined my sister waking in the basement, cold, discarded, and alone.

"For a little while at least," Moreno admitted, his voice dipping under the weight of his own responsibility.

A tendril of guilt crept in before the surge of hate filtered through, brushing it away with the broad stroked of my own abandonment. She was the reason I was here. She chose this life, knew the risks, knew when she asked I'd say yes. She sucked me in and Phoebe had held me there.

I twisted my head to see the flock of nurses gathering outside the window. I bit against the reality that hit with brunt force. Moreno followed my gaze.

"I've been talking with your case manager, have another meeting with your psychiatrist this afternoon. Of course, there's a legal process here. But we've already got the judge involved. We're trying to work through the red tape. Asher and Jo have been in contact with some outpatient facilities that are willing to help. We'll do everything in our power to get you out of here, Carly, I promise."

FIFTY-ONE

ASHER

Asher pulled a glass from Jo's kitchen cabinet and wrapped it in newspaper before tucking it into the U-Haul box balanced on the counter. Jo slid up behind him, wrapped an arm around his waist and tipped up on her toes to reach his ear. She'd just scrawled, "Glassware," across the box in Sharpie and the scent of permanent marker hung thick in the tiny kitchen.

Asher closed his eyes, groaned, smiling at the pleasure of her lips against the sensitive flesh of his earlobe.

"I'm glad we're doing this," she whispered.

"Me, too," he said as she stepped back.

There wasn't a day that went by that Asher didn't think about what Carly had experienced. The before. The after. Both were bad, but he'd known the during, and those moments were the worst of all. He only hoped Carly could be stronger than him. Deal with the pain now, before it consumed her years down the road. And to do that, she needed support, support he hoped she'd get by spending the next few months with him and Jo.

"You're not sure, though. Are you?" Jo leaned against the refrigerator door, arms crossed across her chest.

Asher left the glassware and faced Jo, pulled her hands into his, letting his thumb graze the new diamond on her left ring finger. "I'm sure about us." He met Jo's gaze, ignoring the skepticism that twisted her lips. "But I worry about her," Asher admitted.

He turned to lift the box from the countertop and carried it toward the growing pile near the door.

"Are you afraid she'll do something? Become violent again?"

"No, I don't think so. But what happened to her runs deep, Jo. There's a lot of layers to dig through before she can heal from all that."

Jo threaded her arms through Asher's and pulled him close. "You managed."

One corner of Asher's lip twisted into a grin and he huffed a laugh. "I had a reason to heal. I have you."

Jo smiled and pulled away. "And she has us ... and Ethan," she added as the apartment door swung inward. Ethan popped in for the next load of boxes, his sandy blond hair grown out into a shaggy fringe.

"Who has me?" he asked, hefting the next two boxes for the trip downstairs to the U-Haul.

"Carly," Asher said to his brother.

"Sure," Ethan said good-naturedly. "Whatever she needs."

"She needs a friend," Jo added.

"Got it." Ethan readjusted the boxes in his arms. "Friend duty it is. I think I can manage that," he said, winking at Asher and ducking back through the door.

In the time since Caroline's body had been pulled from the Sutherland basement, the horrors—both his own and Carly's—had leaked out. Reed's trafficking operation had been dismantled, the girls sent home to dazed families or inpatient therapy. Moreno had arrested Reed and a couple others Asher didn't know. But he'd remained true to his promise, had kept the pieces of Asher and Carly's life out from under the microscope. His focus, in spite of Anderson's unfounded opinion, was clear. Reed was the target, the one perpetuating a life of abuse to line his own pockets. And he was the only one being held without bond.

Police continued to search for Phoebe, but the trail had grown cold. Her father's daily appeals to the media slowed to a trickle of once a week petitions. Asher watched every time he caught it on air, though. Like a car wreck, he couldn't force himself away.

The hope in the man's eyes diminished with each broadcast. Asher wondered how a father processed the accusations against his daughter. Was Phoebe still his "baby girl" even after being outed by Sutherland? According to Reed, Phoebe started as a mule, delivering drugs to upper crust kids at Millbrook. Then she volunteered to recruit, became his connection to higher quality girls, girls outside the neighborhood who were desperate, scarred, or unloved enough to be prime candidates for Reed's brand of abuse.

Asher was still trying to piece the timeline together. Caroline was the one who'd first pulled Carly in. But he looked forward to the day Phoebe would have to answer for her role in it all. Why she felt the need to watch from behind the scenes, conspire with Reed, pretend to be Carly's friend. All while pulling strings that forced Carly into the role of outcast.

"Carly's therapist is one of the best in the country." Jo went back to unloading cabinets, her voice yanking Asher from his daydream. She stacked dishes onto the countertop with concussive *shinks* as a shadow passed over her face. "Dr. Blumenthal will let us know if she sees any warning signs. If she does, we'll make sure Carly gets the help she needs."

Asher knew from his own past that it took remarkably little for a teenage girl to be coerced into selling herself if she thought it would buy drugs, money, fame, security, family. The list was as endless and varied as the girls Reed brought in. But it all came down to one underlying need on Maslow's hierarchy. What those girls craved most, what they couldn't get anywhere else, was love. It was the reason Asher never exposed Ethan to what happened at Reed's. Tried never to give him a reason to drift next door. He'd made his mistakes, but turning a blind eye when it came to his little brother wasn't one of them. He had a hard time understanding Caroline's motivation. And he likely never would.

Moreno may have taken one offender off the street. But there were more. An infinite string of them as far as Asher was concerned. And at this point, he wasn't sure who he could trust with Carly's future. Asher shook away the cloud of truth that hung over his head, watching Jo as she worked.

Jo had been pulled from the field and put on probation. Paper-pushing until she completed remedial coursework and proved both to the counseling board and her therapist that she was emotionally ready to go back into the field. But as far as Asher could tell, she wasn't in any hurry. Instead of enrolling in the classes, she'd spent her time helping him find a new job before what little savings they had ran out.

"Look at me," Jo prompted, catching him staring. "Carly will be fine. We'll be fine. In some ways I think we all need each other." Jo tilted onto her tiptoes, covering his lips with a warmth that drained insecurity away, pulling the plug like water in a sink.

"You're right. I'm sorry."

"I think this dinner tonight is a good idea." Jo's voice drew

Asher out of his own head. He wrapped a plate and stuck it in a box. "We can ease into this. I think you need to see her this way, without ..."

"Restraints," Asher finished what Jo couldn't. The image of Carly strapped to the wheelchair, her eyes less thunderstorm and more placid gray. He felt bad for only visiting once. But once was more than enough.

Jo rubbed her hand down his arm. "It's okay." She smiled at him. "It's over, Ash. A few more weeks and she gets to come home." Warm eyes, soft skin. Somehow, he'd made it. Faced his demons. Saved a girl. Renewed a relationship. He'd come out on the other side of hell a better man.

EPILOGUE

CARLY

After...

I stood on the curb outside the brick church, away from the rest of the crowd. A small girl with auburn braids skipped her way toward me, a basket of yellow, faux roses tucked in the crook of her arm.

"Did you get a flower yet?" she asked. Excitement gleamed in her eyes as she held the basket out toward me. "There's rice inside for you to toss at them when they come out." She giggled and picked a green stem from the basket and held the blossom toward me. "See?"

I smiled and plucked the cloth flower from her hand before she spun around like a ballerina and skipped away. The yellow satin sash of her gown floated like a tail behind her.

"Oh, I almost forgot," she called over her shoulder, spinning again, her dress puffing up around her in a perfect circle. "It's special rice so it won't hurt the birds."

I bit my lower lip to contain the chuckle that rose in my chest like a warm wave.

"Thanks," I called back, but she'd already disappeared into the crowd of happy wedding-goers.

A warm autumn breeze caught the hem of my dress, tangling it around my legs. I shuffled to free myself, pulling at the length of fabric as a yell rang out from the group flanking the front doors of the church.

I looked up just as the new Mr. And Mrs. Asher Thompson exited, holding hands and using their free arm to protect themselves against the barrage of heart-shaped puffed rice. I stepped to the side as they moved through. The crowd followed the couple like a wave down the steps of the church.

I swallowed the knot of emotion that crept into my throat like a silent thief as Asher helped Jo into the back seat of the classic Rolls Royce limousine, conspicuously out of place on the street behind me. Bridesmaids—an honor I turned down—stood huddled around Jo. Their pale yellow dresses matched the flower girl's sash and fluttered in the light breeze. I watched them fight to keep Jo's gown from dragging the pavement, stuffing extraneous fabric through the car door behind her as Asher stepped away. He eyed the crowd, making a quick detour to my spot on the pavement when he caught me watching.

"Carly," he smiled. "You came." His blue eyes sparkled, crunching at the corners like they did when he was truly happy. "How's the new apartment?"

"Great," I said. "You'll have to come for dinner when you get back from your honeymoon," I offered. I motioned toward the waiting limousine. "Congratulations. Tell Miss Harrison, too."

He stepped forward and took my hand. The heat of his skin on mine sucked the air from my lungs, ushering back the memory of a desperate choice I'd tried hard to forget. He leaned in and wrapped me in a hug, whispering, "Tell her yourself. You'll be at the reception, won't you?"

I nodded. The spicy scent of his cologne stuck in my throat, paralyzing my vocal cords.

"Good." He pulled away, trotting around the curvy front of the Rolls to the passenger door. He smiled at me once more before waving to the rest of the guests.

I sank back into the mob as the car pulled away, even joined in the cheer as the driver gave a celebratory honk, the couple making their way down Fourth Street toward the reception hall several miles away. A smile tugged at my lips, creeping onto my face as I followed the newlyweds with my eyes.

"Hey," I heard from the crowd behind me.

Faces flashed through my mind, nervousness creeping like a vine through my belly and into my chest. In a group of strangers, my past was a painful place to be.

"Are you a friend of the bride or the groom?" Ethan teased as I turned, clearing the Rolodex of dark memories. Tension from my old life had a way of creeping its way in. *How long would it take for that to go away?*

"Both, I guess," I managed and he smiled, a dimple materializing in his right cheek.

"I'm Ethan, by the way," he continued the ruse. "Asher's younger brother. We met a couple times, but you probably don't remember me."

I laughed. "Carly," I said, offering my hand and playing along. "And just because I left Brookside doesn't mean I've forgotten all of you."

"I know." His eyes bored into mine, and another memory, more solid this time, sparked at the edge of my consciousness, flickering like an old television set. "Asher said you're going to school this fall."

"That's right." I straightened up, pride radiating through my spine. "Columbus College of Art and Design. I got a scholarship. On my own this time." I felt my lips twist up into a sheepish grin.

"That's amazing, Carly, really well-deserved. But I never doubted you." He paused, his blue eyes fixed on mine. "I'll be expecting a signed original at some point."

Heat flooded my face, reminding me just how out of practice I was at accepting a compliment, or whatever this was.

"Are you coming to the reception?" he asked, pretending to ignore the flush in my cheeks.

"I don't think so." I caught sight of the Rolls as it turned the corner at the end of the street, out of view. Asher would understand.

"That's too bad." He seemed genuinely disappointed. "Well, I guess this is as good a time as any, then." He glanced up and down the block before reaching into the inner pocket of his tuxedo jacket. "I have something for you."

The box was small, covered in burgundy velvet. "What is this?"

He shrugged. "Think of it as a graduation gift." He laughed. A true chuckle. And I smiled.

"I've got to go. They're going to want me for pictures and you know how Jo gets if I'm late." His eyes held on mine and a ribbon of warmth bloomed in my core.

"Right," I answered, holding up the box. "Thanks."

He nodded, walked backward a few steps, still smiling before he turned and jogged a few steps toward the parking lot on the opposite side of the church. My heart fluttered in my chest. *Ethan*. I shook my head. Loneliness did funny things to a person.

"Ridiculous," I whispered under my breath, popping the box open with a creak.

The sun caught the stone inside, glinting back at me. I lost my grip and my knees buckled. The box dropped, tumbling across the sidewalk as the warm scuff of pavement sliced against my kneecaps. A muffled, involuntary yelp–my own–pierced the afternoon silence. My hand clutched against my lips–cool pressure rooting me.

I folded my legs under, firm against the heat of the side-walk. My fingers trembled as I reached forward for the box, teetering in teepee form on the cement. A warm wind kicked up, nature's breath of concern. Fingers of breeze tugged loose the hem of my dress, now tangled at my feet.

I brought the box closer. The opal winked up at me, shimmering fire in the summer sun. I fingered the necklace inside. *The* necklace. The custom designed original, an anniversary gift from my father to my mother, passed down to Caroline when Mom died. Cleaner than the last time I'd seen it. But everything about it was right, down to the aged blue fire of the stone.

A spark of memory unlocked in my skull–unfurling–a moment frozen in time. My vision opened up in slits, a shadow crawling from the ladder and toward me. Light filtering from the doorway above us. Phoebe's groans vibrating through me, stopping as blackness settled in. The next memory I have is her weight being lifted from me. My lungs finally able to function. His voice, a simple, *"I've got you, Carly."* I hadn't remembered it before. A surge of panic churned in my core. It wasn't. It couldn't be.

I stood, lurching forward. "Ethan?" I choked the syllables through the rasp in my voice. His name on my lips stopped him.

I blew out a shaky breath and started toward him on wobbly legs. The box bit into the scars on the palm of my hand, but I barely noticed the pain. Focused, instead, on the whisper playing on a loop through my mind, the memory of Ethan's voice a stark contrast to the tickle of a smile that threatened the corner of his lips now.

He spoke as soon as I was within earshot. "Do you remember?"

The shock on my face must have been painted on like the neon glow of the Truck-n-Go marquee.

I nodded, unable to form the words needed to engage in rational conversation.

"You took Phoebe." The words were quiet. But I was sure.

Ethan tucked a breeze blown curl behind my ear, my hair still in a barely-long-enough-to-do-diddly-squat stage I'd grown to hate.

"I was the little sibling once, too," he said, "watching as the one person I loved most in the world was destroyed." His lips twisted in almost regret. "I couldn't let that happen again. Besides–" He exhaled a puff of breath. "Did you know Reed was cutting her in? Phoebe got ten percent of everything."

Ten percent, the words swam in my head. Ten percent of my money. Ten percent of my safety. Ten percent of my sanity. Ten percent of my trust. Ten percent of my future. Ten percent of my innocence. Whole fractions of my life that I'd never get back.

"How do you know this?"

Ethan sucked in a breath, let it out slow. "You don't grow up on Presley Avenue and come out unscathed. After the night Asher brought you to my place, when Phoebe made those allegations against him, I knew she was working for Reed. Had to be. And when Jo disappeared ..." Ethan hesitated. "Well, ever since Ash cut ties, refused to recruit for Old Man Sutherland, Reed vowed to destroy him. And he almost succeeded when Emily died. Then, you came along–"

"And Reed tried again." I worked to process what Ethan was saying. "So I was what? Revenge?"

Ethan's eyes combed over me. "You were the perfect bait. The minute Reed saw you, he knew he could use you. Break open old wounds. Asher might like to think he kept what happened in the Sutherland house away from me. But I can keep secrets, too. And what happened on Presley spreads like disease, infects everyone who comes close."

"Even you?"

Ethan didn't answer, just reached for my hand. "I went to Moreno when I found out Phoebe was working with Reed. Didn't take long to figure out your best friend wasn't the innocent thing Stephen Anderson made her out to be."

"Moreno knows?" Breath hung tight in my chest.

Ethan nodded. "We all have ghosts, Carly."

I shook my head. Imagined Moreno's daughter at the hands of Jack Sutherland. A knot formed at the base of my throat.

One thing no one mentions to trauma survivors is the guilt that rears up, slashing with cloven hooves, as you try to process reality. Girls like Moreno's daughter, never able to go home to the families that loved them. Like Emily, mourned by a man who never truly knew her. And then there was me. Alive. Well. With a future ahead.

I swallowed against the next swell of memory. My knife in Phoebe's gut. The heat of her blood on my skin. I could feel it now, just as I'd felt it that night. *Survivor's guilt,* Dr. Blumenthal called it.

"I killed her," I whispered. Memory was a fickle beast, those moments in the basement coming in short snippets. But standing there, in front of Ethan, sunshine warming my shoulders, I was never more certain of anything in my life.

"You can't think of it like that," Ethan said. He gripped my shoulders and forced me to look him in the eyes. "Sometimes the line between right and wrong gets wide and gray, Carly. But when it does, we do the best we can."

"A person is dead because of me." I wanted confirmation. But the look in Ethan's eyes was all I needed.

"Maybe," he said softly. "But you survived."

His words were firm, matter-of-fact. And I liked the way they fell from his lips, free of judgment.

"Patterns like this, Carly," Ethan continued, "this emotional destruction that happened to you, Asher, Emily, even Moreno ... they'll keep repeating, tearing lives apart over and over again."

"Fractals," I whispered. Asher's voice slipped into memory, the ghost of his breath hot against my ear as he moved the next slide into position. "The same pattern, over and over again ... until someone stops them."

Ethan tilted his head, his brows pinching. "Yeah." He seemed surprised.

I smiled and the vise around my lungs loosened. "Someone like you."

"Like us," Ethan corrected.

A lone tear slid down my cheek, hanging on my chin for a moment before I pawed it away with the back of my hand.

"Are you okay?" Ethan's voice sounded far away. But I nodded.

I picked the opal from the box and handed the empty container to him.

"Let me." He unfastened the clasp and I turned around, glancing up the hill to a black sedan parked at the edge of the empty parking lot. One large man propped against the passenger side door, watching—Moreno. He nodded and I dipped my chin in return as Ethan secured the stone around my neck, my mother's memory falling into place over my heart.

"Perfect," I answered. I closed my eyes and sucked in a lungful of the sweet autumn air.

Ethan reached out a hand. "Can I give you a lift to the reception?"

I slipped my hand in his, the skin soft, warm, kind. "I'd like that."

I fingered the necklace as we walked, this token of choice, of risk, of sibling love, and now, a secret shared.

I pictured Asher's slide of happy tears, the fractals like branches reaching up and outward, taking up root and building a life for itself. I should have known from the beginning that my tears would never match those on Asher's microscope slides–even now.

Ethan squeezed my hand and I felt my lips tip up into a smile.

There would be tears. Life was full of them. But from this day forward, mine would be tears of survival.

DEAR READER

Fractals is a bit of a departure from the Blood Secrets series. And I've had more than one well-meaning friend warn me against writing such a dark tale. But sometimes, as a writer, a story takes hold and won't let go until it's on paper. Such was the life of Fractals.

And while this work of fiction may make some readers twitch, the issues it addresses are very real. Human Trafficking is, by definition, a form of modern slavery. As I researched, I learned that the latest statistics rank my home state of Ohio fifth in the nation for reported human trafficking. This data was the impetus for this story.

As of the date of publication, human trafficking continues to be among the most lucrative of illegal behaviors in the U.S. today, with traffickers pocketing more than $150 billion per year globally ([1]), and putting more than 200,000 American children at risk for trafficking into the sex industry each year ([2]).

This is no longer something that only happens to "other people." If you or someone you know needs help please contact the National Human Trafficking Hotline to connect with services and support for human trafficking survivors.

Call: 1-888-373-7888
Text: 233733
or Chat Online:
https://humantraffickinghotline.org/

Learn more about human trafficking and how you can help at DoSomething.org [3] or the Polaris Project. By shining a light on hard subjects, I know we can make a difference.

_____

1. "Human Trafficking by the Numbers." Human Rights First. Accessed July 31, 2019. https://www.humanrightsfirst.org/resource/human-trafficking-numbers.
2. U.S. Department of Justice. 2004. *Report to Congress from Attorney General John Ashcroft on U.S. Government Efforts to Combat Trafficking in Persons in Fiscal Year 2003*. Washington, D.C.: U.S. Department of Justice
3. https://www.dosomething.org/us/facts/11-facts-about-human-trafficking

ACKNOWLEDGEMENTS

Every book is a journey, and this one took longer than most. I first read a few snippets of what would eventually become Fractals to friends during an MFA residency in Greece. Little did I know then the twists and turns this book would take along the path to publication, but the fact remains, I would be nowhere without those friends and their resounding support, so I owe a big thank you to my Spalding MFA peeps. You know who you are.

To the students who continue to inspire me day in and day out, this book is for you. Although this is entirely a work of fiction, each of my students has a story to tell. Some are bright stories with unicorns and rainbows, and some are dark reflections of reality. But the world needs both kinds. If nothing else comes from my journey into authorhood, I hope I can inspire a few of my students to put pen to paper and tell their stories. No story is too bright or too dark to be told. Your stories matter.

Every author needs a tribe and I found mine in my Golden Heart® Persisters. This group of amazing ladies make this journey more fun. And Kandy, you may not be a Persister, but you are my writing sister. Thank you for your unwavering support and infallible advice. This book would never have made it this far without you.

Of course, I'd be remiss not to mention the wonderful editorial prowess of Holly Ingraham and Cameron Yeager, who both helped this novel find its legs. And to Emily Wittig, I can't thank you enough for listening to my disjointed ideas and putting them together to create the most amazing, gritty, darkly perfect cover I could have imagined. Thank you.

Continued gratitude goes to my parents for their constant support and encouragement. Without them who knows where I'd be. And finally, special thanks to my husband for his amazing ability to stand behind me every step of the way, even when I go off the rails, and to my daughter who makes every day brighter. I can't think of anyone I'd rather have with me on this journey. ♥ Thank you.

ABOUT THE
AUTHOR

Alicia Anthony's first novels were illegible scribbles on the back of her truck driver father's logbook trip tickets. Having graduated from scribbles to laptop, she now pens novels of psychological suspense in the quiet of the wee morning hours. A full-time elementary school Literacy Specialist, Alicia hopes to pass on her passion for books and writing to the students she teaches.

A two time Golden Heart® finalist and Silver Quill Award winner, Alicia finds her inspiration in exploring the dark, dusty corners of the human experience. Alicia is a graduate of Spalding University's School of Creative & Professional Writing (MFA), Ashland University (M.Ed.) and THE Ohio State University (BA). Go Bucks! She lives in rural south-central Ohio with her amazingly patient and supportive husband, incredibly understanding teenage daughter, two dogs, three horses, a plethora of both visiting and resident barn cats, and some feral raccoons who have worn out their welcome.

www.AliciaAnthonyBooks.com

facebook.com/AliciaAnthonyAuthor

twitter.com/AliciaAAnthony

instagram.com/AliciaAnthonyBooks